WHISKEY POINT

JONATHAN CULLEN

LIQUID MIND PUBLISHING

Liquid Mind Publishing

liquidmindpublishing.com

This is a work of fiction. Any resemblance to actual persons, living or dead, or actual events is purely coincidental.

ALSO BY JONATHAN CULLEN

The Days of War Series

The Last Happy Summer

Nighttime Passes, Morning Comes

Onward to Eden (Coming Soon!)

Shadows of Our Time

The Storm Beyond the Tides

Sunsets Never Wait

Bermuda Blue

Port of Boston Series

Whiskey Point

City of Small Kingdoms

The Polish Triangle

Love Ain't For Keeping

Sign up for Jonathan's newsletter for updates on deals and new releases!

https://liquidmind.media/j-cullen-newsletter-sign-up-2-jody/

ACKNOWLEDGMENTS

This book would not have been possible without the encouragement, support, and patience of some select friends and colleagues. First, I'd like to thank my wife Heidi, who continues to believe in me and my work. I would also like to thank Dr. Paul Edwards, Senior Fellow at the *Center for the Study of the Korean War* for his insights about the war and his suggestions about how to make my writing more accurate and realistic. I am grateful to Elliot Belin, whose staggering knowledge of the Boston Fire Department helped me to understand the workings of the city's emergency & rescue services during the 1960s. Finally, I'd like to thank Tom Kelley, friend and Vietnam War veteran, who answered my questions and graciously recounted his experiences in combat.

To Paul Steven Stone,
For Tending Our Soldier

"Only the dead have seen the end of war."
— George Santayana

CHAPTER 1

DECEMBER 8TH, 1941

THREE MILES south of downtown Boston, amid the rundown factories, old buildings, and three-decker homes of Roxbury, stands a small hill. At its center is a rocky peak which soars above the neighborhood and forms a sheer cliff on one side. Hidden by trees and bushes, you can't see it from the surrounding streets, yet from the top, there's a spectacular panorama of the city and harbor. Despite two centuries of development in the area around it, this site remains untouched. It's a slice of wilderness in a landscape of concrete and curbstone and is the only place in Roxbury with crickets. For as long as I can remember, people called it Whiskey Point.

When I was a child, every schoolboy was warned not to go there, but the mystique of Whiskey Point was a temptation few could resist. Because of its seclusion, it had a reputation as a haunt for vagrants, delinquents, and criminals. On the playgrounds of Roxbury, children whispered tales of murder and mayhem; of satanic séances and rituals of witchcraft conducted under darkness before blazing bonfires. Some believed that if you went there on a Christian holiday, you would be forever cursed. The rumors about Whiskey Point were as varied as they were absurd, but they fired the imagination of generations of youths.

Since third grade, Al Russo and I had talked about going. But each time we planned it we got cold feet at the last minute and agreed to go the next year. Many of the older kids at our school had already been, and the rest looked up to them as heroes or gods. For teenagers, going to Whiskey Point was almost a rite of passage, and no boy was considered a man until he had been.

Our chance came on the Monday after the attack on Pearl Harbor. That morning war was declared on Japan and school was dismissed early. With parents and teachers distracted by the calamity, something told me it was the perfect time to go. So I searched the hallways for Russo and found him at his locker.

"Whiskey Point," I whispered. "Let's go. You and me."

He looked up and down the corridor, worried someone might hear.

"You're nuts, Jody," was all he said.

"Are you chicken?"

He turned abruptly and our eyes locked. I had always been taller than him, but I noticed that he was catching up.

"I'm not chicken," he said.

"Then come with me."

He looked away thinking, his face strained by indecision.

"You know how to get there?" he said, finally.

"Does that mean you'll go?"

He repeated the question, emphasizing each word.

"Do…you…know…how…to…get…there?"

I nodded.

"I gotta be back by dinner."

We grabbed our coats and hats and flew out of the building, pushing through the crowds of exiting students and into the city streets. Whiskey Point was only five blocks away, but the journey seemed to take forever. When we made a wrong turn and had to backtrack, Russo started to worry.

"You sure this is the way?" he said.

"I'm sure."

I urged him onward and soon we came to a dead-end street lined with rundown three-deckers. The directions I had were from a classmate who had made it halfway up the cliff before a storm turned him back. He had told me to look for an opening in the fence behind the fire hydrant, and when I did, miraculously it was there.

"This is it," I said, glancing back at Russo.

I crawled into the gap, and he followed close behind, keeping one hand on my back as we trudged through the brush and searched for the cliff.

Soon we reached the foot of the hill, where the ground sloped gradually upwards, and the forest started to thin. It got steeper as we went, the soil and grass giving way to bare rock. Small shrubs and trees grew from the cracks in the surface, and we used them for support as we climbed.

"I can't make it," Russo said.

When I looked back, he was clutching the rock face, scared stiff.

"Don't stop," I said. "C'mon."

I reached down, holding out my hand until he finally took it. We continued to ascend, and soon I could see the top of the ledge. I pulled myself up, helped him over, and we landed on a clearing, sweating and out of breath.

While I dusted the leaves off my clothing, he tapped me on the shoulder and pointed. I turned around and saw the entire city spread out against miles and miles of coastline. The ocean stretched to the horizon, merging with the sky in a seamless sheet of gray and light. For two kids raised in the slums, the view was overwhelming, and we gazed out as if witnessing a miracle.

"We made it, Jody."

"Yes, we did," I said, smiling to myself. "We made it."

———

AL RUSSO WAS my best friend. We met on the first day of school in the 1st grade during a school year that happened to start on the 1st of September. He was a black-haired pipsqueak with thick eyebrows and bony arms. As a result of rickets, his legs were bowed and his back severely arched, and some of the older kids called him 'frogman.' Al was no wimp, but he came across as timid, and whenever he got nervous, he spoke in a high-pitched whine that made you think he had a whistle stuck in his throat.

His father was from Italy, a place I had only seen on maps, and his mother was born in Boston to Sicilian parents. They always treated me like a son, and whenever I visited, Al's mother would never let me leave hungry. One year when Mr. Russo got a pay raise, I stopped by Christmas Eve to find three presents for me, all mistakenly marked 'Joe Bray.' I got a balsa wood airship, wool socks, and a box of dime-store soldiers that Al and I played with all winter.

I realized only years later that their kindness was out of pity because I had no family. For as long as I could remember, I had lived at the Roxbury Home for Stray Boys, a sprawling brick orphanage across from Franklin Park. It was a hard place for a hard era, but the institution had housed, fed, and educated its charges through a world war and a depression. I never knew anything different, so I never felt deprived.

In a neighborhood of large and extended families, Russo and I were both only children, so we were drawn together by the peculiarity of our circumstances. We played stickball in the lots along Seaver Street and broke into the abandoned buildings near Dudley Square. We got into fistfights on the corners and chased girls down the alleyways of the tenement blocks. On the hardscrabble streets of Roxbury, we were an inseparable gang of two, and we looked after and protected each other like brothers.

"Who the hell are you?!"

Startled, we looked over and saw a boy on the other side of the clearing. He was well-dressed, with knickers and a blue wool coat, and he was holding a wooden sword and swinging it around in circles. He was bigger than us—and older too—and at our age, a couple of years was a lifetime of strength and ferocity. As he walked over, Russo and I stood up, but we didn't say a word.

"Know what this is for?" he said, running his hand along the blade. "For killing Japs! Ha, ha! Are you a Jap?"

He stepped up to Russo and stared into his eyes, his jaw sideways, teeth clenched.

"No," Russo mumbled. "I ain't no Jap."

"Then what are ya? An urchin, judging from that outfit. Ha, ha! A little beggar boy."

Russo glanced down at his shabby coat and trousers, shamefaced and humiliated.

"Leave him alone," I said.

The boy turned to me, raised his weapon.

"Got something to say, you little scamp? Dare to challenge Black-beard, eh? Answer me, beggar boy!"

Our eyes locked as he approached, and it was only when he got close that his expression went from scorn to ridicule.

"Ha! You must live at the Roxbury Home for Stray Dogs, am I right?"

"Stray *Boys*," I said.

"Know how I knew? Wanna guess? You all wear those same ridiculous boots."

The second I looked down—ugh!—he kicked me in the groin and I froze. My first instinct was to lean over and grab my balls, but instead, I stood up and went at him. I got him under the ribcage and charged across the clearing, thrusting him into the side of the rock, burying my knee in his chest. The boy's body went limp, but not for long, and he began to smash the back of my skull with the butt end of the sword.

"Ah, you little bastard," he shrieked. "Now I'm gonna murder you!"

I swung wildly, aiming for his face but sometimes missing altogether. When my knuckles made a direct hit, blood spurted from his nose. Being on top, I had the advantage, but the boy was much stronger, and I could feel him beginning to overpower me.

Finally, he let go of the sword, lunged forward, and instantly we were both standing. He grabbed me by the forearms and pushed me toward the cliff. I tried to resist, but my worn-out boots slid over the smooth rock. With blood streaming down his face, the boy seethed like a rabid dog, and I could see vengeance in his eyes. I glanced over to Russo in a panic.

"Al! Help!"

He couldn't speak. With arms at his side, he stood paralyzed by fear.

Although I couldn't see the cliff behind me, I somehow felt its approaching vastness. I was seconds from going over when, in a fit of rage, I shifted my weight and swung the boy around. Instantly, we swapped positions, and now I was shoving him toward the ledge. I would never have done it, and I only meant to scare him, but he slipped on some pebbles and, still clutching each other's arms, we crashed together to the ground. Next thing I knew the boy was on his stomach and sliding toward the cliff edge, and if I wasn't holding onto him, he would have fallen.

"Let him go, let him go," Russo said, suddenly emboldened. "Do it. Let him fall."

"Shut the hell up! Help me for Chrissakes!"

When he hesitated, I threatened him, and he quickly got on his hands and knees and crawled to my side. I looked down my arm and saw the boy's face, wide-eyed and shocked as he anticipated his fate. He may have been scared, but he didn't cry or beg, something I found strange even in all the chaos.

I dug my feet into a depression and pulled as hard as I could. At first, the boy didn't budge, but slowly he started to come forward. Russo took his other hand and in one final heave, we dragged him onto the flat surface of the rock. Then we all collapsed to the ground, relieved and exhausted, and minutes passed before anyone said anything.

"My family owns this land," the boy said.

When I looked over, he was perched on a rock, inspecting the scrapes on his chest and stomach.

"Good for you."

"You're lucky I didn't die—both of you." I looked over again and the boy was wiping dried blood off his nose. "Real lucky," he said. "You'd go to jail. My father owns a shoe factory—he's rich. He'd make sure. You better believe—"

"No!" Russo said. "*You* are lucky you didn't die! And we could've let you."

All at once, the tension returned. The boy laughed to himself, calmly stood up, and came toward us like he was happy for the chance to do it all over again. Right before he got to Russo, however, I ran over and got between them, one hand pointing in the boy's face, the other clenched and ready.

"Get the hell out of here or we'll both throw you off."

He stopped and took a step back, his eyes wavering between me and Russo.

"I see you here again," he said, "either of you, you're gonna get *walloped.*"

The boy spat on the ground and walked back to get his sword. He put it in his belt loop, sneered at us, and marched off into the woods.

Russo and I watched until his blue coat faded into the trees and he was gone. I felt something icy on my neck and looked up to see snowflakes—the first storm of the year. Russo picked up his school bag, and we went over to the shallow side of the rock, looking for the way we came up, hoping the descent would be easier than the climb.

And it was. We slid down the hill on our asses, using our feet for brakes, and when we reached the bottom, everything was covered by a thin layer of white. Squirrels and chipmunks scampered across the frozen ground, and every living thing seemed to run for shelter. Our adrenaline had long since worn off, and by the time we got to the road, our teeth were rattling from the cold.

It was almost dark, and the lights were on in all the homes. We walked without speaking, our shoes gliding over the wet snow. Russo must have known I was mad because he broke the stalemate of our silence with a stupid question.

"Jody, what does *walloped* mean?"

I stopped in the middle of the road.

"Never mind what walloped means. Why didn't you stand up to him?"

"I…I…I did," he stuttered. "You heard me, I stood up to him. I did."

"Not at first," I said. "Only after I tackled him. Only after he almost died. Only after he was out of breath and scraped up. Then you had guts!"

I took my hands out of my pockets and Russo flinched.

"You can't be afraid," I said, putting my finger in his chest. "You can't be afraid of bullies…"

He sniffled once or twice, but I couldn't tell if it was from the cold or because he was upset.

"…You gotta fight back."

As he stared down in shame, my anger turned to pity, and I lowered my voice.

"I won't always be there."

Russo nodded slowly but wouldn't look up. We started to walk again and, for the rest of the way back, he lingered a few yards behind me and said nothing. Streetlamps went on, the temperature dropped, and the night descended faster than we could go. We parted at a mailbox and went our separate ways, shaken by the incident but proud that we had finally gone to Whiskey Point and lived to tell about it.

CHAPTER 2

JULY 1966

THE CITY STANK IN SUMMER. Everything unpreserved seemed to rot in the heat. Dumpsters swarmed with flies, trashcans overflowed, rats scurried through alleyways for scraps. On the industrial back roads of South Boston, the stench of fisheries and meat-packing plants was blinding. I didn't know whether to hold my nose or hold my breath.

"You awake, Detective?"

When I glanced over to Harrigan, his black skin glistened with sweat.

"Just get me home," I said.

"You are home."

I tilted my head back and stared out the window.

"This town is filthy."

"Sweet dreams," he said with a grin.

And I was dreaming, although my eyes were open. Only two nights before I had returned from a trip to Ireland with Ruth, my first time out of the country since the Korean War a decade before. It was a magical week of long drives through endless and open terrain—bald hills and deep valleys, stone walls and white-washed villages. Having no itinerary, we got off the plane and flipped a coin to decide which way to go. Then we hopped in our rented Vauxhall Viva and drove north into the dusk.

It was there I fell in love with Ruth, I was sure of it. And I could remember the precise moment. We had traveled all day along the rocky coast of Connemara, making our way to the tiny harbor hamlet of Leenane. Halfway through the trip, we ran out of gas on some dusty gravel road between a pasture and a stream. We sat on the trunk, sipped coffee from a canister, and waited for someone to come along. When she noticed a foal in the distance, she hopped a fence and ran toward it. She had only gone a few yards before sinking into a pit of black mud that went up to her knees.

By the time I got to her, Ruth was frozen stuck and laughing hysterically. As I pulled her out of the muck, her legs and feet came loose but not her shoes. I threw her over my shoulder and carried her back to the road, where we rested against the car trunk to catch our breaths. The sun was beginning to set, and in the orange light of the late afternoon, I put my arm around her and knew she was the one. Not long afterward, a pickup truck approached. An old farmer gave us a ride to the nearest gas station, and we reached our destination just after dark.

"You know," I said, yawning, "I prevented a crime."

"Pardon?"

"In Ireland," I said, chuckling to myself. "Ruth and I were hiking. There was a cow with some calves, maybe three of them. She was herding them through a hole in a fence. The next thing I know, an old woman is screaming at the bottom of the hill. She's frantic. The cow was stealing the calves; ever hear of such a thing?"

I looked over to Harrigan, and he turned to me with a comic frown.

"I've heard of kidnapping, never cownapping," he said. "What did you do?"

"I ran at the cow, yelling God knows what, and scared it away."

"Crime has a nasty habit of finding you, Detective. That's for sure."

As he drove, I closed my eyes and thought about the incident, as amused now as I was when it happened.

Soon we entered residential Roxbury, where ugly factories were replaced by ugly apartment buildings and dilapidated homes. I was still exhausted from the vacation, but even at midnight, it was too hot to sleep. My back was sweaty, and I squirmed in the seat to get comfortable. But our shift was nearly over, and soon I would be home in bed. I put my head back and listened to the thump of potholes as we cruised through the empty streets. Under the fatigue of jetlag, the motion lulled me into a dreamy stupor.

"What've we got here?"

I opened my eyes and looked ahead to see an automobile smashed against a telephone pole. I was amazed the headlights were still on because the entire front was crushed in. Smoke rose from the hood, and there appeared to be flames coming from the undercarriage.

Harrigan immediately turned on the blues and pulled over.

"Call it in," I said.

As he reached for the two-way, I jumped out and went toward the wreck. The heat was so intense I could feel it from ten yards away and, as I got closer, I had to use my jacket to fend off the smoke. I made it to the driver's side door, where I looked in and saw a man slumped over the steering wheel. I couldn't see his face, but I was sure he was either unconscious or dead.

As I went for the door, I was blinded by a burst of black smoke. The front was burning up quickly, and the fire would soon be out of control. If the driver was alive, I thought, he wouldn't be for long unless help came soon.

I stepped back for air, and Harrigan hurried over.

"I thought July 4th was last week," I said, coughing into my fist.

For any street cop, cynicism and sarcasm were part of the job. But Harrigan was different, and he didn't see any humor in human tragedy.

"Was the door stuck?" he asked.

"No," I said, "too hot." I waved away the smoke with my hands. "We could try the passenger side."

Just as we went to circle the car, we heard sirens and two fire trucks came around the corner. We were both relieved at the sight, and I ran into the street to direct them. Their brakes screeched, and instantly men hopped out from all sides. Some went straight toward the crash, while others got the equipment. Two firefighters dragged a hose across the street and connected it to a hydrant.

"Anyone in there?" an officer yelled over.

I nodded.

"Just the driver—out cold."

When he held up his thumb, the men cranked a large wrench, and the hose began to swell. Soon the team was dousing the car, and the sizzle of the water over the scorching metal sent sparks flying in the air.

Harrigan went to our cruiser to turn off the sirens, and I retreated to the sidewalk, where I pulled out my last cigarette and tossed the box in the sewer. The second I lit a match, a dog growled from an alley between the houses. All I saw were his eyes and the faint outline of a jaw. When I didn't flinch or show any fear, the animal crept back into the shadows and was quiet.

Harrigan came back and stood beside me with his arms crossed, watching the event with a calm professionalism. Tired and distracted, I leaned against a fence and looked around the neighborhood. It was like any working-class section of Boston, a dense continuum of three-decker homes interrupted only by side streets with more of the same. Some of the buildings may have had flower boxes or lace curtains, but they were little more than tenements. The familiarity of the area somehow made up for its decay, and I suddenly realized we were a few blocks away from Whiskey Point. It loomed over Roxbury like a black mountain and was visible from just about anywhere.

"Evening, Detectives," a voice called.

I looked up to see a fire captain coming toward us. In his white shirt and service cap, he was the finest dressed but the least fit and his gut jiggled as he walked.

"Jody Brae," I said, flicking my cigarette. "This is Harrigan."

We all shook hands and the man asked, "You see what happened?"

"No. Came up right after. How's the driver?"

The captain glanced over toward the car.

"They're gettin' him out now," he said.

Despite the smoke, the fire was almost out, and three men were crouched in the door, working furiously to extract the victim. Tired residents, awoken by the commotion, watched from front porches and yards. There were fathers in undershirts and pants, elderly women in nightgowns, and even some children. Once or twice, someone tried to get close to the scene, but an officer ordered them back.

Finally, they got the driver out and everyone cheered. The timing couldn't have been better because an ambulance pulled up, and two men hopped out with first-aid gear.

I asked the captain, "What's your take?"

"Hard to say," he said, looking first to me then Harrigan. "Probably fell asleep. Could be drunk. Judging by the impact doesn't look like he tried to stop."

I heard a collective moan and turned to see the paramedics put a white sheet over the victim. He was dead. Horrified bystanders covered their mouths and a few women whimpered.

An officer ran over to us and said, "He's gone, sir."

"Any ID?" the captain asked, his voice dry with indifference.

The officer shook his head.

"Nothing. No wallet, no license."

"Good work. Tell the men the same."

The man turned to leave but stopped.

"Oh," he said. "There was this—on his coat."

He dropped something in the captain's hand then walked away. The captain held the item between his forefinger and thumb and rotated it under the streetlamp. It was a diamond-shaped pin with an orange "1" and the word "Korea" stamped vertically in gold lettering. I had never been much for military pageantry, but I recognized it immediately as a Marine Corps lapel pin.

"Some kind of war medal," the captain mused. He must have

noticed a change in my expression because he handed it to me and asked, "Were you in the service?"

"Korea," I said, staring at the piece. "It's a divisional pin. 1st Marines. My division." I looked up to the fire captain and said, "Mind if I hang on to this?"

"You're the detective."

I thanked him and turned to Harrigan.

"Whaddya say we call it a night? I'm beat."

"Ready when you are, Detective."

We waved to the other officers, but most were busy packing up the equipment. A tow truck had arrived, and the driver was trying to figure out how to haul away the wreck. As Harrigan and I walked over to the car, our shoes slapped against the wet ground, and I realized that my clothes reeked of smoke. It wasn't the sweet odor of a campfire, but an oily and chemical smell that reminded me of diesel trains. Now I was both exhausted and filthy. I got in the passenger seat and the hard vinyl felt like Egyptian silk to my aching body.

"What time is it?" I said.

"Twelve thirty-eight."

I sighed and put my head back against the headrest.

"I knew it was too quiet tonight. Always something right before the end of the shift. Always."

Harrigan turned the key and the engine rumbled to life.

"I believe they call that 'Murphy's Law,'" he said.

"The Irish get blamed for everything in this city."

In the dim glare of the streetlight, I could see him grin. He put the car in gear, looked over his shoulder, and pulled out. As we drove off, the emergency lights faded into the darkness behind us. I closed my eyes and dreamt of Ruth and of Ireland.

CHAPTER 3

"In the head?"

Jackson nodded once.

"A single bullet," he said.

"I'll be damned."

"You didn't see blood? No signs of injury?"

"I didn't see much," I said. "It was dark. He was slumped over."

The captain looked over at Harrigan.

"Same, sir. Impossible to see with all the smoke."

Sitting behind a walnut desk stacked with reports and affidavits, Captain Ernest Jackson looked like a midget on a trash heap. He was short and slight, with a full head of white hair and bushy eyebrows that flickered when he spoke. Although he may have sounded like a local, he was raised in Cornish, Maine, and first came to Boston to attend college. In the forty years he'd worked for the department, he only ever rented an apartment in Back Bay. He never married—never had children. The captain's real home was up north, in a cabin he built by hand just a few hundred yards from where he was born. Because his fierce leadership and hard character couldn't be attributed to an urban upbringing, they were said to be the result of frontier grit, and he was respected no less for being a hick.

Jackson spun in his chair and looked toward the window.

"This is gonna be a tough one. No witnesses. Dead of night. We'll be lucky to get the logistics right. Do we know when the coroner's report will be done?"

Harrigan raised his hand like we were kids in a classroom.

"I called this morning," he said. "Should be ready Friday."

"See if we can get it sooner."

Someone knocked at the door, and a pretty young secretary peeked in and held up a large envelope. The captain waved for her to enter, and she strutted across the floor in a tight black skirt that made us all look twice. She handed it to Jackson, he thanked her, and she walked back out with a wide smile. Once the door was closed, he opened the folder and took out a sheet of paper.

"From the Registry of Motor Vehicles," he said, pushing up his glasses.

As he scanned the document, I fanned my face with my hand. Even with the shades down, the room was only a few degrees cooler than the stifling heat outside. Cologne from a tough shave mixed with beads of sweat and rolled down my neck. I couldn't get comfortable, and I floundered in the chair like someone with a bad hangover, although I hadn't had a drink in years.

"Everything alright, Detective?" the captain said, glancing up.

"Sorry, Capt. It's the jet lag."

He looked across to both of us and began to read.

"Automobile registered to an *Alberto L. Russo, 9 Valentine Street, Roxbury...*"

I gasped. Everything he said after that was a blur, and I sat frozen in the chair with my mouth agape. He read another sentence or two before Harrigan noticed my reaction and said something.

"Now, what is it?" Jackson said, and he sounded annoyed. But when he saw my face, he dropped the document and leaned forward. I tried to reply but couldn't form the words, overcome by the strange sensation of choking without an obstruction. I had no doubt that I was in complete shock.

Harrigan reached over and put a hand on my shoulder.

"Detective, what's wrong?"

"My god," I said, "Al."

I shook my head back and forth, trying to understand how it could have been him. When they realized I was physically alright, the captain and Harrigan gave me a minute to collect my thoughts.

Finally, I looked up and said, "I know him. I know Al Russo. He's my best friend. *Was* my best friend. Years ago. When I was a kid. Then later—in the Service." As the memories flooded in, I spoke in short, scattered bursts. "We enlisted together, same day. Took a train to boot camp. Ended up in the same company too. We fought together...in Korea. And as kids, of course—fistfights. Combat was different, thought we were both gonna die, but we didn't, we lived, both of us." I was beginning not to make sense and I knew it. I put my hand on my forehead, took a deep breath, and said, "Man, I can't believe it's him."

It may have been the first time I ever spoke to Jackson about the war, and he listened with a gentle sincerity that was part respect and part admiration. He had been too young for the First World War and too old for the Second, and I often wondered if he felt cheated out of the honor so many of his peers possessed. But I knew he understood the bond between soldiers because he understood the bond between officers.

"I'm sorry," he said.

"My condolences," Harrigan added, and I thanked them both.

"This adds a personal aspect to the case," Jackson said. "I can put someone else on it—"

"No," I said. "Please. I promise."

"I need your word."

"You got it."

"Everything by the book. No vengeance. We're not judges and juries."

I glanced over to Harrigan first then said, "I understand, Capt."

Jackson leaned back and stared sullenly at the desk. For a moment, he seemed almost as distressed as me, which was a compliment to our colleagueship. Or maybe he had lost a good friend once too.

"Now," he continued. "Any reason someone would want him dead?"

I shook my head no, but the truth was that I really didn't know.

"Did he gamble? Own a business? Maybe it was a dispute over money?"

Harrigan said, "Perhaps it was random?"

"I haven't seen Al in ages," I said, a tinge of shame in my voice. "We lost touch."

"Well, then," Jackson said. "We'll see what Forensics comes back with. Let's talk to friends and family. They might be some help."

The three of us sat quietly as the noise of jackhammers, cranes, and other heavy equipment rumbled in the background. It was an awful clamor, but one we had gotten so used to that we sometimes mistook it for silence. The city had been under construction since the early Fifties and there was no sign of it ending. Structures that had been around since the Civil War were torn down to make way for glitzy apartments and office buildings. Streets were re-routed, blocks were leveled, and some neighborhoods were wiped off the map altogether.

Much had changed since the days Russo and I would hop a trolley downtown and roam the streets for hours. If we weren't stealing peanuts from the vendors in front of Filene's, we were getting chased out of the toy shops along Bromfield Street. We explored alleyways, climbed fire escapes, and crawled through open windows—we went any place we shouldn't have been. One time we took a half bottle of Crab Orchard bourbon from a sleeping hobo and stumbled five miles home to Roxbury in the freezing rain. Those faded but tender memories of my youth made it all the more difficult to accept that Russo was gone.

"Well, Gentlemen," Jackson said, and I was startled out of a daydream. "If there's nothing else, this meeting's adjourned." He stood up, put his hands on his hips, and looked directly at me. "Lieutenant, you take the rest of the day off. Harrigan will drive you home. That's an order."

I forced a smile and thanked him. Harrigan reached for his briefcase and started toward the door. When I got up, my shirt was stuck to the chair from sweat and my right foot was asleep. Just as I turned to leave, the captain stopped me. "And Lieutenant," he said, handing me the report across the desk. When I took it, he waited until he had my full attention before letting go. "I know this isn't easy. But remember, by the book. No vigilante justice."

"Of course."

"Whoever did this," he said, lowering his voice, "he's worth more to us alive. We can't convict a dead man."

Our eyes met in an unspoken agreement between men. Somewhere in the stacks of folders a phone rang. The captain picked it up and gave me a quick salute. I left the office to find Harrigan waiting by the water fountain, chomping an apple. With his dark suit and reserved expression, he looked like a butler eating a candy bar, and I had to say something.

"You bring that for the captain?"

The dig caught him off guard, but it meant that I was alright, and for that, he seemed relieved.

He took another bite and held it out.

"I brought it for you, Detective."

"You know I hate apples."

"That's why I brought it for you."

"Touché," I said, patting him on the back.

We walked down the corridor toward reception. As we passed by the main desk, someone called my name and I turned. A heavy-set woman with her hair in a bun waddled toward the counter with something in her hand.

"A message for you, Lieutenant."

She used my title, which was her first mistake because I still wasn't comfortable with the promotion. Despite my advancement over the years, I was never more than a street cop at heart. It was different in Korea, where rank was hard-earned, and respect meant life or death. But on the force, you could get promoted without ever having fired a gun, and more often than not it was a way of keeping an officer interested in his job.

I reached for the paper and stuffed it in my pocket.

"Thanks," I said, and she smiled.

Harrigan and I continued down the stairwell. We went out the front doors and into the thick and smoggy heat of summer. The sun was blinding, and I instantly reached for my sunglasses. We crossed the parking lot, got into the car, and drove into morning traffic.

As we navigated the narrow streets of downtown, I sat quietly and thought of Al Russo. Harrigan must have sensed my sorrow because he drove and didn't talk. He had more tact than anyone I knew, and he seemed always to know what to say and how to act.

Born in Saint Kitts in the West Indies, Trevor Harrigan came to America with his parents at age six. His father worked as a train porter in South Station and his mother washed floors at night. He spent most of his life in Roxbury and, like me, was an only child. If I was 5'10", Harrigan must have been 6'3" but he appeared even taller. He was built like a linebacker and should have played football when he had the chance. We both attended Roxbury Memorial High School, but because we were five grades apart, we never met. I always considered him a foreigner, maybe because he didn't have a Boston accent or because he used funny words like *poppycock, hullaballoo,* and *bamboozle.* Whenever he got angry—which wasn't often—traces of his Caribbean lilt slipped out and made you laugh at him when he was at his most serious.

Harrigan was different from most cops and not just because he was black. Those formative years in the islands had given him a refinement that stood out among the crude masses of working-class white officers. He seldom spoke without a 'sir' or 'madam' and, like anybody with class, he tended to listen rather than speak. Nevertheless, he could talk on any subject and had probably read more books than anyone else in the department. Although we were intellectual equals, he was cultured in all the ways I wasn't and had we been anywhere else but race-bound America, he would have been my boss and not the other way around.

I took a cigarette from my pocket and held it up.

"You mind?" I asked.

Harrigan glanced over.

"What if I said yes?"

"I'd light it anyway."

"Then no, I don't mind…"

I leaned toward the window and lit a match.

"…But I do hope someday you give up that addiction."

I took a deep drag.

"Addiction? I've been smoking every day for twenty years, my friend, and I'm not addicted yet."

He just shook his head.

We drove along the Boston Common, where afternoon shoppers and suited professionals crowded the sidewalks, wandered into the street without looking. Every few moments a cabbie or angry driver would hit his horn, but this was a part of town controlled by pedestrians and no one paid attention.

When we stopped short at a red light, ashes from my cigarette fell on my lap. I brushed them discreetly onto the floor and said, "Can we stop by the coroner…before you drop me off?"

"My orders are to take you home."

"It'll only be a few minutes."

"The autopsy won't be ready until—"

"It's not about the autopsy," I said, my voice cracking.

He turned and our eyes locked. Harrigan was never one to deviate from orders, but the death of a friend was something even he could make an exception for.

"As you wish, Detective."

THE MORGUE WAS in the basement of Boston City Hospital, at the end of a long corridor lined with supply rooms and utility closets. Whoever designed it must have had a spooky sense of humor because the location was as dank, dark, and remote as a tomb. The air tasted of mold, and there were cobwebs everywhere.

Although the hospital was old, the patient floors and laboratories had been updated with the change in building codes and political administrations. Yet the cellar was in its original state, with newspaper insulation, gas fixtures, and a coal repository that cast a fine layer of black silt over everything. Stock lists, supply ledgers, and nurses' rolls from the late 19th century were plastered along the beadboard like carnival posters, and they made for interesting reading as we walked. Medical devices that hadn't been in use for decades were stacked in boxes along the walls. There were ceramic sterilizing pots, glass drip bottles, chamberpots, and wheelchairs with wooden seats and wagon wheels. On top of a first-aid cabinet, I even saw a horse bridle, although it may have been an antique stethoscope.

We finally reached the entrance to the coroner's office and Harrigan knocked. We heard some shuffling inside followed by the slide of a deadbolt. The door then opened with a long creak.

"Morning, Detectives," a deep voice said.

"Mornin', Doctor."

For such a large hospital, it was unusual to have only one pathologist, but Doctor Ansell had worked there since the war and never had a complaint. With thick forearms, big jowls, and thinning hair, he wasn't much to look at, but he was one of the best in the field. Medical students lined up at his doorstep for internships, and coroners from Barnstable to Bangor would call him for advice.

Ansell wore pince-nez glasses yet still squinted. He talked from the side of his mouth like a Hollywood gangster, and his accent was gutter-Boston with a tinge of Yiddish. I heard rumors that he had once been a bruiser on the streets of Roxbury, and it wouldn't have surprised me because his hands were huge. On his right knuckle was a tattoo of the Chai symbol, faded but clear. The doctor called everyone 'kid'—as long as you were at least a day younger than him, and the only way you knew if he liked you was if he treated you like a peon.

Inside the room stank of smoke. If Ansell didn't have a fat cigar in hand, then he always had one smoldering nearby. Only someone with his status could get away with fouling up such a sterile environment, and no one dared suggest he smoke outside.

As he led us over to his desk, I saw that the back of his neck was damp. The coroner's office was constantly cold, but the doctor always seemed to be sweating.

"So, what can I do for you?" he asked.

"Did you get a body Friday night?"

"We get lots of bodies, kid," he said, "that's why I'm here."

"Alberto Russo," I said, ignoring the sarcasm, "an automobile accident."

He recognized the name immediately, and his eyes perked up.

"Quite an accident it was."

"So he was shot?" Harrigan asked.

Ansell stopped and turned around.

"One bullet," he said. "Right in the melon. Good shot too. Small caliber, definitely a handgun." He craned his neck and pointed to the back of his skull. "Right there, came out his neck...after bouncing around a bit."

Harrigan looked at me but spoke to the doctor.

"He's a friend of the Lieutenant's, sir," he said.

Ansell rubbed his hands together and his tone changed.

"I wasn't aware of that. I'm sorry, kid."

"Thanks. Can I see the body?"

"Of course."

He waved for us to follow, and we went over to a door with a small window and black lever. With two hands, he pulled the handle up and the lock released. We stepped into a long room lined with rows of gray steel doors. They were square and had shiny handles that reminded me of the front of iceboxes. At first, I was distracted enough not to notice the freezing temperature, but when I did, I started to shiver. Ansell led us over to a corpse compartment, where he verified the number and turned a latch.

Before he opened it, he looked up at me.

"Sure you want to do this?"

When I nodded, Harrigan whispered, "I'll wait in the other room, Detective," and walked out.

The doctor opened the compartment and carefully pulled out the bed. The corpse was under a white sheet, perhaps the same one they covered him with the night he died. Ansell looked at me as if asking permission to proceed, then he peeled the cloth back. And there, lying still with his arms crossed and eyes shut, was the body of Al Russo.

"I prettied him up a bit," the doctor said gently, "I always do. Didn't take much, was a clean hit."

With blue skin and a lifeless expression, Russo was nothing more than a wax figure, a plastic likeness of the man I once knew and loved. His soul was somewhere else. I glanced down and examined him with a cold detachment, looking for some scar or blemish that I remembered, something to prove it was him.

"We should all look so good," I mumbled, but Ansell was in the corner pretending to be busy.

"Sorry, kid, what?"

"I just said, he looks good. For someone who hit a pole, I mean."

The doctor came over and looked down at the body.

"He didn't die from the impact; I can promise you that. If you wanna know the truth, your friend was stone drunk."

I looked at him surprised.

"That's right," he continued, "smelled like a ginmill when they brought him in. But it might've saved his life…if he hadn't been shot, that is."

"How do you mean?"

"Well," he explained, "it's a strange phenomenon. Alcohol relaxes the body, calms the nerves. When drunks get in an accident, they don't tense up. They withstand the shock better. It's like trying to snap a ragdoll—can't be done. It ain't a myth, I seen it hundreds of times—" As he walked away, he shook his head and said, "Now how's that for science?"

The chill was starting to get to me, and I suddenly realized I was in a room full of corpses. With no more questions and nothing left to do, I took one last look at Russo and said a silent prayer. Then I pulled the sheet back over him, turned to Ansell, and called over, "Thanks, Doc. That's all."

HARRIGAN and I didn't talk for the whole ride home. I smoked one cigarette after another, and he didn't complain. It was a somber silence, something of a vigil for my dead friend, and I just stared out the window in thought. It was strange to lose someone you had forgotten about, and in a way, they die twice—once in memory and again in real life. Russo and I had been apart for so long that vast periods of our friendship had vanished from my mind. But every few minutes something new would emerge and the scale of his loss became more and more real. We had survived a brutal childhood and a brutal war, only to have him assassinated on a dark city street. By the time we reached my apartment, I was choked up.

Harrigan pulled up to the curb and I got out.

"Detective," he called out, and I realized I had left the door open. As I reached for the handle, he said, "If you need anything, call."

I looked at him with a trance-like wonder and shut the door. As I lumbered up the front steps, I knew he was watching.

I lived at the top of Mission Hill, in a three-floor wood monstrosity that was as square as an airplane hangar and just as plain. It was no different than all the other homes on the street and had been built to house the immigrant factory workers of the area's breweries. The neighborhood had a working-class pride, and although the buildings may have been tenements, they always had tidy yards and fresh paint.

My landlord was an Irishman who had been in the country for over a half-century but sounded as if he just stepped off the turf of County Galway. Jeremiah may have been ninety—he could have been over a hundred—and when I jokingly asked if he remembered the Potato Famine, he laughed but didn't say no. We got along well, and he enjoyed my company, often reminding me that even if Brae wasn't an Irish surname, it was an Irish noun, which was enough of a blood link for him. Like any old immigrant, he was eccentric, and he kept two scarecrows in the backyard to protect a tiny vegetable garden. According to an elderly neighbor, he once kept a horse there too until the city forced him to remove it.

"Brae," I heard, and I turned to see Jerry standing at the end of the hallway. "I gotta move a slop sink in the basement."

Because of his age, he had trouble maintaining the house and was always asking for help with things.

"Not now, Jerry," I said, "Maybe later, I gotta rest. Still tired from the trip."

I was halfway up the stairs when he peered up and said, "I want to hear all about it. Did you get to Connemara? Please say you did. I was born in Letterfrack. Of course, we moved to Kylemore when I was three. My mother didn't want to, but my father did. His sister lived in Bunowen, but my mother fancied her a bitch so..."

He was still talking when I reached the top landing. I found my keys, went inside, and collapsed on the couch. In the solitude of my apartment, the significance of my friend's death hit me like a sudden flu, and I was sick with grief.

Al Russo and I had been blood brothers, reared in the rough-and-tumble heap of Depression-era Boston. We harbored a natural resentment toward everyone and everything that was more than just an attitude—it was a core ingredient of our souls. We had gotten hit by the same punches, leveled with the same disappointments, and smacked down time and again by the gutter expectations of a world that was half-kind at best. Our whole lives we had wanted nothing more than to get the hell out of Roxbury, and we did but only for a time.

The day Russo and I walked in the snow to South Station to enlist in the Marines was the day we became men. I was nervous, but he was scared, and after we signed the paperwork, he even considered reneging, which would have made him AWOL. Still, we kept our pledge and, after drinking all afternoon in a Southie bar, we took a midnight train to Parris Island. There we roomed in the same barracks, ate at the same mess, and survived thirteen weeks of basic training. Fate must have been with us because we even ended up assigned to the same company.

It was a bittersweet privilege to fight alongside a friend, and every time there was gunfire, I worried that he would become a casualty. During those lonely nights on the line, I often played out the scenario in my mind, wondering how I would explain it to his mother. Yet Russo's presence in my unit had also given me a reason to fight and a reason to live, and I watched over him like a little brother. In the end, we both survived, unscathed and unscarred, which was a miracle considering the statistics. And although we hadn't been wounded, we discovered later that we were injured in other ways.

CHAPTER 4

TRAFFIC WAS THICK AS I DROVE TO RUTH'S APARTMENT IN BEACON Hill. At rush hour everyone seemed to be going in the same direction —trying to get to the same place. Car horns blared, engines revved, and occasionally an annoyed driver would shout out profanities. But all the chaos disappeared once I turned into the neighborhood and began to ascend its narrow cobblestone lanes.

With gas lamps, brick sidewalks, and wrought-iron grillwork, Beacon Hill was something out of a Dickens novel, without the poverty. It was the oldest part of the city, built for Boston's 18th-century merchants, and the streets were lined with bow-fronted Victorian brownstones that were like small castles.

The area may have been quaint, but it was impossible to navigate, and the curbs were crammed with parked cars. When I couldn't find a legal spot, I pulled in front of a hydrant, knowing that if I got a ticket, I could fix it in the morning. There I waited until six o'clock when Ruth would appear at the front door to wave me in.

Ruth was a firecracker. I met her two years before when she worked as an intern at headquarters. The first night we went out, she got so drunk she almost fought the bartender. On our second date, she didn't drink but she ended up tearing off the side-view mirror of a taxi after the driver overlooked us for a better fare. Both times I had to show my badge to settle the confrontation, and now I just made sure to take my .38 on every date.

Ruth may have been spirited, but she was a whole lot more. She was a blue-eyed beauty from San Diego, an opposite in every way from my hardened Yankee cynicism. She came to Boston on a bet, left everything behind, and was hired after her first interview. Having minored in forensics in college, she was fascinated by crime and may have watched one too many episodes of Dragnet. Her high hopes were dashed when she discovered that she was little more than a glorified secretary. She worked at the front desk answering phones, and the closest she got to the evidence was typing classified letters. As a result, she left that job at headquarters, a decision that was better for both of us. She pursued her other passion, which was nursing, and received a certificate after attending night school for eighteen months.

The front door opened, and I watched Ruth peek out. She looked around until she saw my car then waved. I got out, crossed the street, and walked quickly up the pathway to the door. She kept looking back into the foyer, making sure no one was around, and when I reached the threshold, she moved aside so I could get up the staircase.

"Hurry, hurry, hurry," she whispered.

For all her pluck and pizazz, it was ironic that Ruth had been raised a Mormon. And although she had abandoned the faith, she still used it to her advantage. She lived in a Mormon rooming house that rented only to fellow Mormons, one of a nationwide network of 'safe houses' for members who were working, attending school, or fulfilling their two-year missionary service.

The house matron, Sylvia, was a stout woman in her mid-sixties who ruled over her boarders with the pious severity of a nun. Her policies were taken straight from the Book of Mormon—no drinking, no smoking, no coffee, and no pre-marital relations. The young and unwedded were forbidden from having visitors of the opposite sex, and the place had a feeling of cloistered austerity. Ruth broke every rule, and she argued with Sylvia so ferociously that I was amazed she hadn't been expelled yet. Luckily for us both, Sylvia was half-deaf and almost blind, and she seldom left her first-floor chamber.

When we got inside the apartment, Ruth closed the door and locked it. She came up to me, slid her hands behind my back, and we kissed. She pulled me toward her, and I felt her warm breasts against my stomach.

"I missed you," she said, looking up.

Her eyelashes fluttered, and the scent of her perfume got me aroused. I went to put my hand on her chest, but she backed away. "Want something to drink?"

"I don't drink," I joked.

"Funny. How about some tea?"

"Water's fine."

As I sat on the couch, she walked over to the kitchenette and got a glass.

"How was work?"

"Same," I said. "Actually, I was at the morgue."

"You were at the hospital and didn't stop in to see me?" she said, glancing back with a frown.

"I was only there a few minutes. It wasn't planned."

She walked over, handed me the water, and sat down. She curled her legs on the couch and said, "Since when do you do anything unplanned?"

I gave an awkward smile and took a sip.

"Actually, an old friend died last night. He was murdered."

"My God, Jody, I'm so sorry!" she said, putting her hands up to her mouth.

I looked down at the glass thinking.

"I haven't seen him in years. We grew up together. We were in the war together."

She nudged closer to me.

"Was he from the orphanage?"

"No," I said, with a nervous smile. "He lived down the street. We met in first grade. Al Russo—a feisty little guy. We did everything together."

I grinned when I remembered the time Russo and I were smashing ceiling tiles with sticks in a boarded-up building that was a former soap factory. When one of them broke, there were three or four rat skeletons above it, and they came down on his head. He shrieked like a girl and ran all the way home.

"He was a rascal—we all were then. But he had a good heart." I turned to Ruth and said, "A big heart."

She reached over and took my hand.

"I know he did. I'm so sorry." She paused then asked, "Do you know who did it?"

I shook my head.

"No idea. He was driving. Alone. Someone shot him and he hit a pole. Harrigan and I found the accident. I saw a man slumped over the wheel. I didn't see a face. I didn't know it was Russo 'til this morning."

We sat in silence for a minute or two, our hands locked and gazing down at the rug in empty reflection. The sound of her slow breathing soothed my nerves and calmed my soul.

Finally, she looked up and asked, "Are you okay?"

"I don't know what I am."

I felt her grip tighten.

"I know what you are."

"I'm a heel."

"What do you mean?"

I turned to her and said, "After the war. I abandoned him. I let him go. My best friend."

"People grow apart. There must've been a reason."

I hesitated and said, "There were lots."

She reached for a matchbook on the coffee table and said, "Get the light."

I flicked the wall switch behind me and the room went dark. She leaned forward and lit two magenta candles, which cast a soft glow across the furniture and walls. I didn't know the remedy for sorrow, but I was willing to let her show me. She snuggled beside me, and I could feel the warmth of her body everywhere. She craned her neck and found my lips, and, in an instant, we were embraced in a kiss. The hunger pains from twelve hours without food disappeared, and I yearned for only one thing. I reached under, put my hands up her back, and drew her close to me. As I did, she began to rub my thigh and I groaned. I unbuttoned her blouse and unsnapped her bra, and her breasts poured onto my chest. Our breaths and movements grew equally erratic, impassioned by the agony of anticipation, and soon the couch creaked under the weight of our writhing bodies.

It was well past midnight when I awoke staring at the ceiling from a damp mattress. Ruth was sound asleep and tangled in a sheet with one arm flopped over her face. As I lay naked and uncovered, I listened to the sounds of automobiles on Beacon Street, the occasional footsteps of late-night pedestrians. My body was calm but inside I was stewing, and I couldn't stop thinking of Al Russo. Memories of our years together raced through my mind like an out-of-control film-strip, sometimes in color and sometimes black and white. I saw him as a boy, as a teenager, as a soldier, and at every age in between. Our friendship had spanned twenty-five years and two continents but was erased in an instant.

A car horn beeped and Ruth woke up. She twisted her neck and yawned, her head on the pillow as she gazed at me.

"You're thinking about him," she said.

"Can't help it."

"It's okay."

"He's in a better place."

"You know he is."

I leaned over, kissed her on the forehead.

"Go to sleep."

Once she did, I got out of bed, put on some underwear, and crept into the kitchen, where the flicker of the last candle gave just enough light for me to find the kettle and fill it with water. I stepped over to the couch and fished into my pants for a match. My hand came out of the pocket with a matchbook and the crumpled note the secretary at headquarters had given me. I lit the burner and unraveled the message:

. . .

JODY,

IT'S BEEN A LONG TIME. *I am in town for the veterans reunion at the Lenox Hotel this weekend and would very much like to see you. Hopefully, time has healed some wounds.*

YOURS,

TRAVIS KEMP, *Staff Sergeant, 1ˢᵗ Division, 3ʳᵈ Battalion, USMC.*

I REREAD THE NOTE, over and over again, but it made no sense. Visions of the war appeared against my will, and for the first time in years, I felt the terror of battle. It was a flashback from hell, more intense than anything I had ever experienced, and I fell back to the couch. When the kettle whistled, I didn't hear it, and when Ruth came out of the bedroom, I didn't notice. She turned off the stove and ran over to me.

"Jody, what's wrong? You're trembling," she said, putting her arm around me, feeling my forehead.

"I couldn't sleep."

"You look like you've just seen a ghost."

The note fell from my hand, and I turned to her.

"I may have."

CHAPTER 5

THE SECOND TIME AL RUSSO AND I WENT TO WHISKEY POINT WAS ON A blustery Wednesday in March. It had been a tough winter, with one cruel storm after another, and clinging to everything was a permanent frost that made you forget what the world looked like without it. Enormous icicles hung from the eaves of the old houses, and gutters split from the weight of the snow. Automobiles were buried, sidewalks vanished, and anything lost didn't turn up until spring, if it did at all. Even children were grumbling about the weather.

The most recent squall had left the streets impenetrable, and school was closed for the day. Russo and I were out wandering the streets, dressed in wool coats and trapper hats, when the idea came to visit Whiskey Point. I could never remember who first suggested it, but once the notion was planted, we couldn't avoid going.

As we left the familiarity of our neighborhood, I began to feel that addictive thrill of mischief. We continued down side streets and zigzagged our way toward the cliff in the muffled silence of the afternoon. Plow trucks passed by, and a few people were out shoveling, but for the most part, the roads were barren. We walked down the median line because it was the clearest, dragging our boots over the frozen slush like artic adventurers.

Soon we reached the dead-end street and dug through a snowdrift to find the opening in the fence. I took one look at Russo, counted to three, and in we dove. The forest was a wonderland of whiteness, with crystalline branches and sparkling brush, and the glare hurt my eyes. There were no sounds—nothing moved. We searched for the way, but winter had turned the ground into a featureless expanse of snow and ice, and the path we had taken in December was nowhere to be found.

In the distance, we could see the start of the hill, but each time we went in that direction we encountered an obstacle. First, Russo fell into a depression and began screaming that his leg was broken. Then I tripped on a fallen bough and tumbled head-over. In a fit of frustration or maybe panic, we began to run and almost immediately got caught in a thicket. We thrashed and we flailed, kicking up a cloud of snow dust that made it impossible to see. By the time it settled, we were out of the trap and standing at the edge of a small clearing. And there before us was a towering wall of gray shale, so high we couldn't see the top. Somehow, we had ended up at the base of Whiskey Point.

Our arms went limp, our mouths hung open, and we gazed up at the mountain with amazing wonder. I thought of the boy with the sword and realized how close we had come to death.

"What's that?"

Russo pointed at something ahead, and when I looked, I saw a dark mass near the foot of the cliff, its color and shape unnatural against the wild terrain. We walked over with a slow curiosity, one step at a time, and Russo started to get nervous.

"Is it a bear or something, Jody," he asked, averting his eyes. "Maybe a deer? Huh? Tell me—"

"Will you shut up?!"

As we came up to the object, my stomach went into a knot.

"My God," I muttered.

Below me was the body of a man, frozen stiff and lying on one side. He had a heap of brown hair, tangled and dirty, and his face was bruised. When I knelt to look into his eyes, two black circles stared back. He wore a long overcoat, the collar upturned, and old workmen's boots with flattened heels. From the sleeves, his fat hands stuck out like gnarled stumps, his fingertips cracked and bloody.

"Holy Christ!" Russo stuttered. "Is it? Don't say it. I don't wanna know. Let's go, let's go now."

"Shh," I said, gazing at the corpse.

I tilted my head back and looked up to the cliff, to the edges of gray rock that protruded like razors along the entire face. I knew then that the man had fallen to his death.

"We gotta go, we gotta go now. C'mon," Russo said in a high-pitched whisper. When he tapped me on the back, I stood up and smacked his hand and his mitten went flying. "We can't just leave, you idiot. We gotta tell somebody!"

He backed away.

"We can't, no. They'll think we did it, they'll think we pushed him. We'd go to jail—"

Suddenly, he stopped talking. Our eyes met in a silent struggle that was the choice between doing what was right and doing what was easy.

"I'm going," he said, finally.

He picked up his mitten, and as he started back across the clearing, I took one last look at the man. It was a tragic sight, but a dead stranger was not worth losing a living friend, and I knew I had to go.

"Wait," I called out.

Russo stopped but didn't turn around. I ran over to him, and we crawled into the woods, following our earlier footsteps out to the street. Once back in civilization, I put the incident behind me, and we never spoke of it again. But I always regretted not reporting the body, and I remembered that day as the first time I ever truly experienced the feeling of shame.

CHAPTER 6

WHEN THE CALL CAME OVER THE TWO-WAY, HARRIGAN AND I WERE parked and having ham sandwiches. Because I hadn't eaten since the day before, I was tempted to ignore it and finish my lunch. But the dispatcher repeated himself twice, calling for any available detectives, and Harrigan gave me an urgent look. So I leaned forward, adjusted the frequency, and we listened.

"West 4th Street Bridge," Harrigan said.

"Let's go."

I tossed my food out the window, he hit the sirens, and we made a U-turn and sped down Harrison Avenue. We reached the West 4th Street Bridge in less than five minutes and saw three cruisers and an ambulance parked by the guardrail. A patrolman stood in the middle of the road to direct cars, but the route was seldom used so his job was easy. Other officers gathered at the edge of the bridge, looking over and pointing. When Harrigan and I parked and got out, a rookie came toward us.

"It's a body," he said eagerly, but I walked right by.

"Sully," I called out, and an officer looked over with a big grin.

"Brae," Sergeant Suliman said, "I mean, Lieutenant...sorry. No disrespect." As I approached, he held out his arms in jest. "Let me polish your badge. Or maybe it's your shoes need polishing."

I looked up at his bald head and said, "Why don't you polish that crown?"

Two younger cops, amused by the remark, started to laugh until Sully turned around and they both went straight-faced.

"Still bartending?"

"With what BPD pays, I have to," Sully said, squinting in the sun.

"Weren't you the third-highest in overtime last year?"

He shrugged his shoulders.

"It all goes to the ex-wife. I do it for her."

"You're a regular Robin Hood."

Sergeant Michael Suliman had been on the force for over twenty years and was fazed by nothing. He had fought in the Pacific during the Second World War on a destroyer that survived four separate kamikaze attacks. He might have been wider than he was tall, and he waddled around like a constipated duck. He had a permanent tan that was more than easy work details and golf weekends could produce. Every other word out of his mouth was a wisecrack, and the only thing he seemed to take seriously was horse racing. Because his nickname was "Sully," people assumed the sergeant was just another Irish cop, yet his parents were Lebanese Christians. He was the only man I knew who wore gold jewelry on his wrists, and he used more cologne than an Italian.

Harrigan and I followed him over to the guardrail.

"What's the story?" I asked.

"Someone's takin' a long nap."

"In this weather? They should be at the beach."

I watched Harrigan smile as I leaned over the fence. Below the bridge was a dozen pairs of train tracks that ran straight into downtown. Some were for the commuter line, others for freight, and they were all rusty from years of overuse. Puddles of polluted water filled the crevices and depressions of the ground, and there was trash everywhere—milk bottles and doormats, old tires and tissue boxes, plastic bags and pillow covers. I even saw a child's baby carriage, wheels upright and half-submerged in the muck. I just winced and looked away.

"What a dump."

"Ha, literally," Sully said. "A little squeamish since the promotion?"

I ignored the taunt and said, "Is it a hit?"

"Whadda I look like, Philip Marlowe? That's for you guys to figure out." He moved closer to me and pointed below. "Look down there, between the pilings." At first, I saw only beams, crossbars, pigeon nests, and road debris. But as my eyes adjusted, I could see the body of a man lying flat on the dirt.

"Suicide?"

Sully nodded.

"Probably. Maybe a drifter. We'll know soon."

We heard sirens, and I turned to see two fire trucks rolling up. The ground shook from their weight, and a flurry of seagulls burst from under the bridge and into the sky. Firemen got out carrying helmets and other equipment, and a moment later the Fire Chief headed over.

"Mornin' Gentlemen," he said, tipping his hat. "…and Sully."

Everyone chuckled.

"What've we got?"

"A body," Sully said. "Behind that middle piling."

"Where's the ME?"

One of the cops shouted over, "On his way."

No one could touch or move the corpse until it was cleared by the medical examiner. The firemen were prepared and waiting, but the suspense was over, and many of them just stood around smoking, making small talk. I asked Harrigan to come, and we walked to the start of the bridge, where a grassy embankment led down to the tracks. We hopped a railing and began to descend, stepping over litter and rubble. Large sections of dirt crumbled under my feet, sliding down the hill like the sheets of an avalanche. I was so focused on not falling that when I got to the bottom, I didn't notice that a freight train was going by.

With half a mile of boxcars, it took almost five minutes to pass and when it did, I was so anxious to move that I didn't look where I was stepping.

"Dammit!" I said as my shoe sank in a pool of oily water.

By the time I pulled it out and shook off the mud, Harrigan was at the scene. I walked over and he was holding a handkerchief over his nose. The corpse was lying face-up, dressed in a dark suit, with hundreds of flies swirling around it. The face was swollen beyond recognition and covered with nicks, cuts, and dried blood. The smell could have killed a small dog.

"Christ," I said, "So much for lunch. I won't eat for a week."

We heard a familiar voice and turned to see Dr. Ansell crossing the tracks with a leather case in one hand, a cigar in the other. He must have been having an argument with himself because he twitched, and his lips were moving.

"Doctor," I said, "fancy meeting you down here."

Ansell kept his eyes on his feet as he made his way through the debris.

"Can't anyone die in accessible places anymore? Two weeks ago, I had to walk a quarter-mile down a goddamn tunnel 'cuz someone kissed the front of a subway train. Rats everywhere..." He walked by without acknowledging us. "...I ain't afraid of rats," he grumbled, "I just don't like to see 'em. Was pitch black. Gave me the heebie-jeebies. In the war, we slept three nights in a catacomb waiting for supplies. Krauts everywhere. But this was worse. I'd have faced a Kraut any day rather than listen to those little bastards crawling—"

"Fire is waiting," I said. "When can they get him?"

Ansell dropped his case and crouched down next to the body.

"When I'm finished, kid. That's when." He took out his instruments and got to work. "We need a body bag. We don't want to lose any parts. I'm not coming back to this cesspit to look for an arm or a leg."

Harrigan and I searched the area for clues but couldn't find any. When the doctor completed his inspection, we climbed back to the top and waited by the guardrail. Ansell put up a thumb to give his consent, and the fire department began the evacuation. Two men carried a stretcher down the embankment and under the bridge. They put the victim in a body bag, loaded him on the stretcher, and secured the straps. The rescue was over in less than ten minutes, and once the deceased was placed inside the medical examiner's van, the fire-fighters unstrapped their helmets and packed up. The truck engines roared, and plumes of diesel exhaust shot into the air. While the traffic cop directed, they reversed into the street and were gone.

Harrigan and I went over to Ansell, who knelt beside his van cleaning some implements. With the cigar gritted between his teeth, I couldn't tell whether he was breathing in his mouth and out his nose or vice versa.

"Any foul play?" I asked.

He shook his head and sweat fell off his brow.

"Don't know. The cranium is pretty bad, even for a train. I gotta get him under the light, make some cuts, take him apart a bit. Look around."

"Identification?"

"Not in the conventional sense," he said, standing up and dusting off his hands "No keys, no wallet, no watch—nothing." The doctor put his gear in the back of the van and slammed the door. Then he spun around and gave me a sharp look. "I rolled up a sleeve, to pull blood. I saw something I didn't like, kid. Right here."

He slapped the side of his shoulder and said, "A tattoo. Marines. An eagle and a globe, with an anchor. Black and smudged. Real amateur stuff. Probably got it in some opium den in Osaka. But that don't matter. What I mean is, it's a shame. Because he's one of us. And we don't like our kind dying, right?"

"Right."

Always in a rush, Ansell hurried to the front of the vehicle, and I followed, stopping him before he opened the door.

"So, it's obviously a suicide?"

He took a puff of the cigar and glared at me.

"Nuttin' in this world's obvious, kid. Except for lies and maybe loose ladies." He opened the door and got in. "Like I told you," he said, leaning out the window, "let me get him under the light. It looks like he walked into a train, but I don't know."

He seemed like he had no more time for questions, so I gave him a salute and walked away.

"Lieutenant," he said, and I spun around. "I'm sorry about your friend Russo. I really am."

The comment caught me off guard—I got suddenly choked up.

"He was a good guy."

"He *is*," Ansell said, revving the engine. "No *was*. He *is*. And don't forget it."

With that, he let out the clutch and sped off.

CHAPTER 7

On Tuesday evenings Sylvia hosted Mormon friends for cribbage and crumpets. She stayed up later than usual and sometimes left the apartment door open, both of which made it impossible to sneak in the front. Instead, I would duck into the alley next to her building and go to the back. There I'd knock on a drainpipe and wait for Ruth to come down. If she didn't hear me the first time, I would usually sit beside the dumpster and have a cigarette then try again in a few minutes. Some men might have balked, but I spent so much of my career in secrecy that doing it for a woman was a relief.

Finally, the rear door opened, and Ruth waved me in.

"About time," I said.

"Not used to strange men knocking at my back door."

The stairwell was dark, and every step creaked as we tiptoed to the top floor. Her apartment door was open, and when we entered, I realized she was dressed for an evening out. She had on a black shirtwaist dress with pearl buttons and a belt-tie waist. The thin cotton hugged her body as if the garment had been made first and she was born into it. Her hair was set in ruffled curls that bounced with each step or turn of the neck, and she smelled like a field of lavender.

"Hope you're hungry," she said, bending over to blow out a candle.

"Actually, I am but—"

"Because I'm taking you to dinner. There's a new French restaurant on Beacon Street."

I looked down at my outfit and said, "I don't have a change of clothes." When she saw my muddy feet, she cried, "Oh, you're tracking dirt." She grabbed my arm and moved me onto the doormat. "Stay there, don't move. I just need to get my bag."

"You sure?" I said. "I wore this suit yesterday."

"It's only a bistro. It's casual. You look fine. Who cares?"

She got her pocketbook, kissed me on the cheek, and then pushed me out the door. As we went down the front stairs our stealth was blown when my knee hit a banister.

"Ruth?" I heard. "Who's there with you?"

I peered over the railing to see Sylvia hovering in the foyer.

"I'm alone mum. You're hearing things again," Ruth said, trying not to giggle. I crouched at the landing while she continued down to the front hall. When she got to the last step, Sylvia got in her way and wouldn't let her pass.

"Who's with you?" she said haughtily.

Ruth attempted to get around her, but Sylvia was so fat she covered the width of the staircase.

"Get out of my way."

"Don't tell me what to do, this is my house," Sylvia barked, and I could feel the tension rising. It wasn't the first time I heard them bicker, but each time was worse than the previous, and I always worried Ruth would jeopardize her stay.

"This place is owned by the Church," Ruth said. "You're lucky to have a room. Now move!"

She tried to get by again, but Sylvia sidled and blocked her.

"Listen, you old witch," she said, and I cringed. "Let me out before I call my boyfriend who's a detective. He'll make you move if it takes a crane."

With that, she turned aside, and Ruth stepped onto the floor of the foyer. Sylvia stood with her arms crossed while Ruth pretended to fix her hair and lipstick in the mirror. Finally, Ruth turned to her and said, "What? You're gonna stand there all night?"

"I'm waiting for you to leave."

"Fine. I'm leaving."

When Ruth went for the door, I got nervous. She put her purse over her shoulder, snickered at Sylvia, and marched out. I held my breath and retreated into the shadow of the landing, listening for Sylvia and planning how I was going to get out.

A minute later, I heard movement below and glanced down to see Sylvia opening the door to her apartment. Inside I could hear the crotchety laughter of a half-dozen spinsters who sat around a cribbage board sipping tea and nibbling crackers. When she closed the door behind her, I ran down the stairs and out into the night.

I didn't see Ruth until I got to the sidewalk, where she was hunched over, laughing hysterically.

"You trying to get me killed?" I exclaimed.

"That old crab, she couldn't harm a fly."

I started to walk, but she didn't move. She took me by the waist and gave me a long kiss and I knew she was trying to taunt Sylvia. If she had had a few drinks, it might have been even racier. Ruth had a loving soul but a rebel heart, and she was the only person I knew more hotheaded than me.

"C'mon," I said, "let's not look for trouble now."

She gave me a seductive smile.

"Does that mean we can look for trouble later?"

We continued up Mount Vernon Street and along the crest of Beacon Hill. The overhanging trees were dense with leaves, and they entwined to create a lush tunnel. Flowers blossomed with petals of deep purples, pinks, and the whitest whites, and birds fluttered in the branches. The whole world seemed alive and thumping and for those few moments, I was truly happy.

We walked along the Boston Common and past the Statehouse, where Beacon Street became a narrow, single lane. She stopped and pointed to a restaurant on the ground floor of a ten-story building.

"There it is. Isn't it cute?" she said, her eyes beaming.

"If *cute* means fancy."

"You'll be fine. Let's cross."

As we came near, I could read the print on the burgundy awning: Café Absinthe. Out front were two tables, empty and unset as if there for decoration only. The door was wide open, and we could hear the good cheer inside.

We entered and were met by a grinning maître d' who scribbled something in a reservations book and instructed us to follow. He led us over to a table by the wall, and before I could sit, Ruth said, "No. Near the window. Please."

The man paused, as considering the request.

"As you wish, Madam. Please come."

We went over to a corner table that overlooked the street, and he pulled out a chair. Ruth curtsied with a smile and sat down.

The restaurant may have been small, but it was elegant, with mahogany paneling, and Tiffany lamps. The tables were set with plumb-colored cloth, silk napkins, and real silverware, stamped 'Schofield, Baltimore.' On the back wall was a tapestry of fields and streams in some faraway land, probably rural France. The chatter was lively but restrained. Sinatra was playing.

As I looked around, some people had on casual suits, but most were dressed in evening attire, and I wouldn't have felt more out-of-place at the court of Versailles.

"Lovely, isn't it?" Ruth said with a sigh.

She reached for her bag and started to fix her lipstick. A waiter came up with menus and seemed appalled by her lack of etiquette. As he handed one to her, she looked up and pursed her lips.

"How's this Monsieur? Any smudges? Too dark?"

The man stiffened up and didn't know what to say, but when she winked, he couldn't help but grin. With a bow, he left to give us time to look at the menus. The entrées were in both French and English, but I didn't recognize a single dish and decided to get whatever Ruth ordered. My years in the service and on the force made me adaptable, and I would eat cold soup and Swanson TV dinners with the same enthusiasm as Lobster Newburg or Coq au Vin.

The waiter returned shortly with an order pad and pen. He held them out in front of his face and glanced down at us.

"Je voudrais le boeuf Crêpe Maison," Ruth said, and he raised his eyebrows as a compliment to her French.

"Et à boire?"

"Une bouteille de Bordeaux."

The man then turned to me.

"And to eat, sir?"

"The same."

"To drink?"

"Water, please."

"Merci," he said.

He scooped up the menus, forced a smile, and marched back to the kitchen.

"You never told me you spoke French," I said.

"You never asked."

"Do you speak French?"

Ruth leaned back in the chair with a sexy smirk.

"Sometimes."

I looked down and laughed. A minute later, another waiter came by with a bottle of wine. He yanked out the cork and put a little in her glass to taste. She smelled it, drank a little, and said, "Perfect, thank you." He poured half a glass and stopped, but Ruth said, "To the top, please." The man glanced at me as if seeking my permission to proceed then filled it to the rim. It was only after he left that I realized he hadn't uttered a single word.

She took a few sips and looked at me across the table.

"You're distracted."

"I don't mean to be."

She tilted her head and a wisp of hair fell over her eyes.

"You're thinking about him, aren't you?"

"I don't know," I said, looking away. "Maybe. It brings up a lot. Stuff I forgot about. Stuff I wanted to forget."

"I don't want you to take this the wrong way but—" She started to speak and stumbled. "Was he...was he involved with bad people? I mean, did he get into trouble?"

I reached for the ashtray and lit a cigarette, taking a long drag before replying.

"I don't know, it's been years. After the war, when we got back, I didn't see much of him."

"Was there a falling out?"

I shook my head, fidgeted with the silverware.

"Not really. More of a slow drift, I guess." I looked up to her and said, "To be honest, I let him go. Cut him loose. I wanted to put everything behind me, the war, childhood, the booze..."

She glanced down uncomfortably at her glass.

"...Unfortunately, our friendship was a casualty in all that. He was a good guy, but he never got over the war."

"Did you?"

I laughed to myself.

"Don't know. Maybe I didn't get over it, but I definitely went around it."

By now, Ruth's eyelids were low, and her face was flush from the wine. She was starting to get tipsy.

"Who would want to?—"

"I don't know!" I said, and she flinched. I quickly softened my tone. "I'm sorry. I have no idea. Don't know if we'll ever know. I'm going to see his mother tomorrow. She might know something."

She held her glass by the stem, gave me a hesitant smile.

"Listen," I said. "Let's forget that, for now. Let's talk about us."

Bang! A corked popped, glasses clinked, and somewhere behind us, someone made a toast. Ruth looked over, and I turned to see a tiny elderly couple surrounded by family and friends. If they were celebrating a wedding anniversary, it could have been ruby or golden or diamond. They sipped wine like newlyweds, grinning bashfully while the whole restaurant looked on. As I turned back, something caught my attention, broke my train of thought. It would have been too obvious to look again, so I faced Ruth and waited for another chance.

The waiter came back with two glasses of ice water, and I reached for one and took a big gulp. When I saw that my hand was shaking, I put down the glass before Ruth noticed. Clang! Another toast. I looked over and saw two lovers hunched forward, staring at each other over a centerpiece candle. They held their wine glasses together like a long embrace and slowly pulled them apart. As they did, the figure of a man appeared in the background, his eyes focused on me with an unwavering glare. Although I turned away, I noted every detail.

"Are you okay?" Ruth said, stopping mid-sentence. "You keep looking over there."

"Sorry. Yes. I'm listening. Is it hot in here?"

She shook her head.

"No. I mean…I'm not hot."

The man was big, with wide shoulders and the crooked posture of someone who suffers back or hip pain. He had receding hair and a thick mustache, and although his features were hard to see through the smoke, I noticed something familiar in his eyes. Worried he was someone I had arrested or put behind bars, I scanned my mental police lineup of former criminals, and nothing matched up. When I looked a third time and he was gone, I thought I might have imagined him.

"You did it again," Ruth said, and I blushed.

"Did what? I—"

"You keep looking over there. You sure you're alright?"

Before I could reply, she made an awkward cough, and the stranger was standing right beside me. I threw my shoulders back as if ready for a fight, but when I looked up, I knew he was no threat. The man smiled at Ruth, then turned to me and held out a trembling hand.

"Jody. It's me. It's Travis."

FOR YEARS I thought Travis Kemp was dead. The last time I saw him he was being whisked away in a chopper after a mortar attack killed a dozen men. It was only November but in the Korean mountains, it was so cold that batteries wouldn't work, and urine froze before it hit the ground. A snowstorm had blocked the only route to the depot that week, and when fresh supplies finally arrived, we had a make-shift celebration at rear division. Any officer not on duty—and even some who were—showed up, and so many lieutenants were in one place that someone joked the line was being commanded by corporals.

That night my shift ended at nine o'clock, and I walked a quarter-mile alone to the base. Those moments of peace I savored, and I even took the longer path, which brought me by the northern ridge that overlooked the entire valley. Below the Han River meandered through miles of frozen flatlands, past peasant villages and dormant rice paddies. It must have been close to zero because my feet were numb, and I hurried to keep my blood moving. When I reached rear division, I heard activity in a squad tent and went in to find men from several companies huddled around tables drinking San Miguel beer. Some were playing cards, and there were enough crumpled US Dollars and Korean Wons to buy us all tickets home. A radio in the corner was tuned into the AFKN and playing Walkin' to Missouri.

The party went on for hours, and although we drank as if the war was over, it had only just begun. By midnight, the crowd dwindled as soldiers went to bed or returned to their posts. Something from the mess didn't agree with me, and I was sick from the combination of booze and bad food. I folded my poker hand and stumbled out of the tent, where I puked behind a stack of empty munitions boxes. The radio announced that the U.S. 17th had reached the Yalu River, and cheers erupted across base.

That was when the first mortar hit.

I was knocked to the ground, and everything went blank. When I awoke, men were running in every direction. I heard a second explosion, then a third. Soon we started to fire back, pounding the North Koreans with M101 Howitzers and M1 mortars. There was small arms fire too, but the enemy was too far for even the fifty calibers. I knew it was a hit-and-run because the shelling stopped as quickly as it started, and an eerie silence resumed.

I ran back toward the line with a couple of privates, past bomb craters and damaged equipment, a jeep upturned and in flames. We came to a clearing and injured men were everywhere. Some had been thrown by the force of the explosions and suffered minor cuts and bruises, but many were worse. To my right, four soldiers were crouched around one of the wounded, applying first aid. When a medic jammed a morphine syrette in the man's shoulder, someone shone a flashlight, and I realized it was Travis Kemp. I ran toward him just as two Sikorsky's descended from the darkness, and their down-wash forced me back. Everyone moved out of the way and the choppers landed, idling at full speed because the pilots were worried about more enemy fire.

Soldiers rushed over with the wounded, sliding the stretchers into the cabin one by one. It was almost full, and I began to panic that Kemp wouldn't be evacuated. When one of the choppers started to lift, I looked through the cockpit glass and the pilot pointed at his watch. They couldn't wait. I shouted at the medic, even threatening him, and finally, they brought Kemp. I ran over and helped with the stretcher, and I felt a cold hand on my wrist. I looked down and Kemp's dry lips were trying to speak, but he only made a gurgling sound. His face was white, and his fatigues were singed black. As I leaned over to inspect his wounds, he groaned, and his eyes rolled back into his head. I turned to the medic, who wiped blood off his chin and shook his head.

The copilot yelled that they were leaving. I put one hand on Kemp's shoulder and whispered good-luck and good-bye. As we placed him in the chopper, I watched until his face faded into the shadow of the cabin. The door slammed shut, I fell back, and the helicopter pulled up and vanished into the night sky. That was the last time I ever saw Travis Kemp.

RUTH ASKED the waiter to bring a chair and Kemp squeezed in between us. I took a good look at him and was amazed. His hair was gray, and he was twenty pounds heavier, yet the essence of him was there unchanged. What struck me most was how his body had aged, but his voice was the same, and I wondered if people said the same about me.

For those first few minutes, I couldn't speak, and Kemp was no less dumbstruck, staring at me with a subtle grin. Finally, Ruth broke the awkward silence with a question.

"So, you're here for a veterans conference?"

Kemp nodded, smiled nervously.

"At the Lenox Hotel."

"You keep in touch with K Company?" I said, surprised. "I mean, you go to reunions?"

When he turned to me, his arm hit my glass and knocked it over.

"Oh my gosh," he said. "I'm all thumbs."

He took a napkin and started to wipe it up, and Ruth helped.

"I go to the reunions when I can," he continued. "Just drove in yesterday."

"From Cleveland?"

"What a memory," he said, looking at Ruth. "This guy was the smartest in the company. Should've been a colonel."

"Why didn't you fly?" I asked.

He looked down bashfully.

"Never was too fond of flying. Terrifies me, to be honest."

"It was a chopper flight that saved your life."

"More like the MASH surgeons. But I'll give the choppers some credit."

"Quite an effort to get here. At the Lenox, you say?"

"The Lenox Hotel. Friday and Saturday night. Come down and see some of the guys."

Another waiter came up with two plates of food, and Kemp got uneasy.

"I should go," he said, and I stopped him.

"No. You're my guest. Did you eat?"

"I did."

"Then you don't mind—"

"Of course not," he said, turning to Ruth. "If this lovely young lady doesn't."

She put her hand on his arm.

"Are you kidding? Please stay."

"Thank you," Kemp said. "I'm gonna order another drink. Can I get either of you anything?"

I shook my head no and Ruth simply pointed to her wine bottle.

"A reunion, eh?" I said, cutting into my dinner. "I didn't hear about it."

Kemp looked first to Ruth and then to me.

"You've been MIA, Jody."

I put down my fork and stopped chewing. The memories of a past life I had long ignored were too much to bear, and I fought to resist them. He was right. Since returning from the war, I had made few efforts to stay in touch with the men from my unit. There were bulletins, conventions, reunions, and all the clubhouse activities of an alumni association. I never opened those letters but kept them stacked in the bottom drawer of my dresser. Someday, I told myself, I would tear them open and learn the fates of those many men I had served with.

In the years following the war, I wanted nothing more than to forget—to forget my childhood, to forget Korea, to draw a line in the sand and start anew. But there always lurked within me a deep and nagging uncertainty that kept me awake at night and made me restless most days. My life seemed to move forward but not advance, and I felt disconnected from the world. I always assumed it was the result of job stress, and I never thought it was anything more. But the moment I saw Kemp, the burden of a thousand unanswered questions melted away like a fluke snow in springtime, and I experienced a terrifying relief.

I shook my head and looked at him.

"More like AWOL."

CHAPTER 8

AFTER DINNER, KEMP ASKED ME TO CATCH UP OVER DRINKS, AND I SAID
yes only because Ruth kicked me under the table. It was Tuesday and
she had to work early, so I put her in a cab then Kemp and I walked
around the corner to Diamond Jim's Lounge. Across from the Boston
Common, it was a late-night haunt for well-dressed drunks and girls
who might be prostitutes but only at the right price. Diamond Jim's
was somewhere between a dive and the Ritz, depending on the hour.
The paneled walls, crystal lamps, and oil paintings gave it an air of
respectability that attracted theatergoers looking for a cordial after
the show. But the later it got, the more desperate the clientele, and by
midnight the bar was filled with stragglers, single ladies with too
much lipstick, and the occasional queen.

"Sure I can't get you a real drink?" Kemp asked, pointing to my
glass.

"Water's fine."

"When did you give it up?"

"Not soon enough."

"A good thing. We both drank too much over there. You ever
miss it?"

I thought for a moment.

"Let's put it this way," I said, "if I didn't have a problem with alcohol, I'd drink every single day."

Kemp just grinned, shook his head. Seated in dark leather chairs, we faced each other over a round glass-top table. Each time he put down his drink, I worried it would crack, and if it did, I told myself, I wouldn't let him pay for it. Over three hours I nursed a single soda water while he put back five bourbons. The room that was full when we arrived at ten o'clock was now almost empty.

"Two goddamn years?" I said, trying to hide a yawn.

"Twenty-five months, three days and…I don't know. Who counts hours anyway? Maybe inmates."

"Must've been hell."

I leaned over and put out a cigarette in a bronze ashtray that was overflowing.

"Didn't feel much pain. Morphine is a wonder drug."

"I watched the medic inject you," I said. "You went like this."

I rolled my eyes and stuck out my tongue like I was choking.

We both laughed.

"Don't remember a thing. Heard it was raining mortars."

"It was fast, but it was effective. Gooks were lucky that night."

"They owed us one," he said, leaning back in the chair. Something in the tone of his voice changed, and he looked off dreamily. "That was payback, I'm sure it was."

I gave him a curious look.

"Payback? How do you mean?—"

"Excuse me, Gentlemen," a soft voice said, and we both looked up to see a blonde waitress. "We're closing now."

"Now or soon?" I asked.

She made a cute frown.

"Ten minutes ago."

"Leave us the keys, we'll lock up," Kemp grumbled, and he might have been serious.

"Here," I said, handing her a twenty-dollar bill. "Keep it."

"Thanks, Mister."

When I looked over to Kemp, his eyes were half-shut, and he even started to snore. For all those years, I thought he had died that night and yet there he was, a little fatter, a little more somber but alive nonetheless. It was almost comical. I let him doze for a few minutes while I reminisced and thought about what he had told me.

The mortar must have landed only yards from him because the shrapnel shredded his organs and broke most of his bones. When the chopper landed at the MASH, he was ten pounds lighter from blood loss, and his vitals were flat. But some young medic found a pulse, then a heartbeat, and finally, a breath. The surgeons worked into the morning, cleaning, stitching, and transfusing blood until he was stable enough to be airlifted to a hospital ship. If there was ever such a thing as a miracle, Kemp was it.

"C'mon big buddy," I said, shaking him to. When he woke up, he started to cough, so I handed him my water. "Forget where you are?"

He yawned and looked around the room.

"Thought I was dreaming."

"I know what you mean," I said warmly. "We gotta go."

Over at the bar, the bartender was tabulating the evening's sales, and the waitress was putting on her coat to go home. The lights were on, the jukebox music was off, and a young barback was getting ready to mop.

Kemp tried to rise but couldn't, so I took him by the shoulder and helped him up. He was disoriented and wobbly, probably as much from his war wounds as from drunkenness, and I stayed close to him as he hobbled toward the door. I waved thanks to the waitstaff and went out into the muggy night.

"Where's your car?" I said. "I'll walk with you."

"Thanks. I left it at the hotel. I'll get a cab."

"How 'bout some coffee to sober you up?"

I nodded to a diner a few doors away, but he just shook his head.

"No thanks, Jody. I gotta get back. I'm exhausted."

I hailed a passing taxi, and it made a U-turn and pulled up to the curb. I leaned into the passenger window, showed the cabbie my badge, and told him to get Kemp home safely. When I went to shake Kemp's hand, he grabbed me in a bear hug and wouldn't let go.

"I missed you, brother," he said, slurring.

"Missed you too, Trav."

"Please. Come to the reunion."

"I'll try."

"I'll be waiting."

He crawled into the cab and lay flat along the backseat. A drunk his size was like a big, lumbering animal, and the driver and I had to push his legs inside so the door would close. As the taxi drove away, Kemp raised his thumb in the rear window. Once the car vanished around the bend, I began to wonder if I had imagined the whole encounter. It was that incredible.

I stood on the sidewalk for a few minutes and listened to the sounds of the city. Somewhere in the distance, a brass band was playing mambo and across the street, I saw a young man strumming a guitar. I flicked my last cigarette and started back up Beacon Street, where I passed the Café Absinthe. The lights were dim, and inside I saw waiters wiping down tables, cleaning the floors. The streets of Beacon Hill were dead quiet, and as I made my way back to Ruth's place, I thought about the war.

CHAPTER 9

A BLADE OF SUN BROKE THROUGH THE WINDOW SHADE AND LANDED ON
my face. When I rolled over to hug Ruth, I felt only the wrinkled
emptiness of cotton sheets and knew she had left for work. The room
smelled of lavender and hairspray, and as I lay on my back, I savored
the fading embers of her presence. I looked at the clock on the dresser
and realized I had overslept. I was late for a meeting with the captain.

I ran into the bathroom, washed my face, and brushed my teeth
with Ruth's toothbrush. I put on yesterday's outfit, reached into the
nightstand drawer for my wallet and gun, and crept down the rear
stairwell.

The route to headquarters took me through the narrow lanes of
Beacon Hill, past glistening maples and terrace flower gardens. A
group of young mothers stood talking at the corner with their baby
carriages. In front of a grand brownstone, an elderly matron was
trimming her lawn with scissors. It was a perfect summer day.

When I opened the office door, Jackson looked up with a smile.

"Lieutenant, how're you feeling today? Better, I hope."

"Sorry I'm late."

"Please, sit," he said, and I did.

The captain was freshly shaven, and Harrigan had on a summer gray suit which made him look even younger than he was. I felt almost as underdressed as I had in the restaurant the evening before.

"You get some sleep?"

"Not enough. Never enough. Ran into an old friend last night. Went to Diamond Jim's—"

Jackson raised his eyebrows.

"That's enough," he said, looking over to Harrigan, "I think I can fill in the rest." He paused then continued, "Now let us move on to business, shall we?" He pushed his glasses up his nose until they were firm. "If I didn't know any better, I'd say Doctor Ansell is a friend of yours."

Harrigan said, "The autopsy from that body at the West 9th Street bridge came in this morning."

"I don't understand," I said. "Why'd he send it to homicide?"

"Because that's just what it is."

The captain reached for a folder on the desk and began to thumb through the documents. He scanned the first pages, looked across to both of us, and began to read.

"*Caucasian Male, approximately 38 years old. 5'10", medium build, brown hair, and blue eyes. Massive systemic trauma, suspected to be the result of getting hit by a train...*"

He skipped some details and went straight to the bottom. "In addition," he said, peering up before continuing, "*entry wound from a bullet below posterior rib cage. Exit wound at the left armpit. Severe internal lacerations as a result.*"

He dropped the document, clasped his hands, and stared at us. Two homicides in as many days wasn't a record, but it was a pattern, or at least the beginnings of one.

"You have something to say, Brae? You look troubled."

"I'm not sure," I said, and Jackson looked confused. "I mean...I do, but I'm not sure if it's relevant." I glanced over to Harrigan but spoke to the captain. "Doctor Ansell noticed something on the victim's shoulder. A tattoo, a Marines tattoo."

Jackson tapped his fingers together, squinted in thought.

"Is that so? And you're sure?"

"I didn't see it, the tattoo, but the doctor knows. He was in the service."

"He was bothered by it," Harrigan said. "And rightly so."

"No one likes to see a veteran die," I said, "especially another vet."

The captain reached for a pen and scribbled something on a notepad.

"Another dead serviceman," he mused. "Not only a tragedy, but a coincidence too. A troubling one at that."

He got up, stretched his back, and began to pace the room. Harrigan and I craned our necks to follow him, but by the time Jackson reached the file cabinet in the corner, I had given up.

"Do we have any idea who he is?" I wondered.

"Not unless you're clairvoyant."

Harrigan turned in the chair, "Anyone reported missing?"

The captain made a full circle and sat at the edge of his desk. From my angle, he appeared tall, and it was one of the few times I actually looked up to him.

"People are always reported missing," he said, tapping a pile of folders. "This is the missing persons stack," he said. "Goes back to '45. It should be in the cabinet, but I keep it here. It reminds me that our work is never done. Or if it is, there're always the unsolved cases. The past is a bitch, Gentlemen."

He may not have meant much by the remark, but it was profound enough to make us all pause and reflect. The past *was* a bitch. It was something I had been trying to forget for most of my adult life, and I had even been successful for years at a time. But life was like a tread-wheel, and the things that were farthest behind were also the closest in front. What could be more distant than death, I thought, and yet Kemp had come back from the ether. His appearance had changed my understanding of time and consequences, and maybe Jackson was right when he said I looked troubled.

"I'll submit this for an artist rendering," he said, picking up the report. "Should have something in a few days."

"Good luck," I said.

"That man was unrecognizable," Harrigan said, leaning forward. "Completely disfigured. Beyond description."

"Well," the captain said. "I don't care if the rendering looks like the Elephant Man. We need to identify him. Or at least try." He put his hand on the top of the missing persons stack and said, "One more and this thing will topple. It's like investigative Mahjong. It falls and we lose."

He smiled at his own cleverness then went over to the window to raise the shade. When the sunlight came into the room, Harrigan and I squinted. The noise of construction, which had been there all along, was suddenly more apparent. Sensing that the meeting was over, I got up to stretch my legs and Harrigan did the same. The captain gave us a curt salute and said, "Now go out there and make history, Gentlemen."

Harrigan and I left and went down the hallway, nodding to colleagues and strangers alike as we headed to the exit. Headquarters was busiest at noon, and everyone from senior officials to clerks was moving about, going to lunch or just out for a stroll.

I passed the front desk and a feminine voice called out, "Officers?" We both looked over, but only I walked to the counter. It wasn't the same woman from Monday, but they all looked the same—middle-aged, short, and dowdy—and I avoided their names because I would forget anyway.

"If it's a note, you can keep it," I said.

The lady smiled and held up a piece of paper. "The address you requested." She put it on the counter and ran her finger along the handwritten lines, "Natalia Russo, 9 Valentine Street, Roxbury."

"Nice to know some things don't change," I muttered to myself.

"I'm sorry?"

"Oh, nothing. This is perfect. Thank you."

I stuffed it in my pocket and went over to the stairwell, where Harrigan was waiting.

When we came outside through the double doors, four secretaries were lounging on the front steps smoking. They were pretty and young—a deadly combination—and I had to struggle to keep from gawking. The moment they saw us, they shuffled a bit, and one woman adjusted her skirt.

"Ladies," I said, and they smiled in unison.

We continued across the lot and Harrigan said, "Two days for an autopsy. Sounds like a record."

"Three if you count Monday."

Before he got in, he looked across the car roof.

"I guess Dr. Ansell's not the cantankerous curmudgeon we all thought," he said, and I just frowned.

"I don't know what you mean…but I know what you're sayin'."

"Was that a favor?"

"Was what a favor?"

"The autopsy. So quick. Everyone knows there's a backlog."

"Ansell is a veteran," I said. "Maybe it was personal."

"You know, sometimes I envy your comradeship."

"Our camaraderie?"

"You always watch out for each other, protect each other."

I thought of Russo and said, "I wish that were true."

WE DROVE through the South End and crossed Massachusetts Avenue into Roxbury. In the distance, I saw the brick factories I once explored as a child, their faded names still visible on the crumbling façades. The area may have gone from white to black, but the poverty was constant, and everywhere were the signs of a deep neglect. The buildings leading up to Dudley Square were boarded-up, and the billboards were covered in graffiti. Side streets that had once bustled with immigrant children were now deserted, and many of them had more abandoned lots than houses. Whether it was from too much cement or not enough trees, Roxbury always felt a few degrees hotter than the rest of the city.

On a corner by a bus stop, a dozen shirtless men sat on upturned shopping carts, passing around a jug of Wild Irish Rose. They stared us down as we went by and not because they knew we were cops.

Everyone in Roxbury looked intimidating, and even the elderly walked around like they were ready for a fight. In a place with little hope and lots of rage, respect and fear were one and the same.

At the next intersection, I reached over Harrigan and pointed.

"Pull over there, please," I said.

He cut across traffic and parked in front of a small flower shop. The owner was a quiet Portuguese woman who had owned the place since I was a child. She was probably close to seventy yet still wore the long dark braids she had when I was young, although now her hair was more gray than black.

When I got out, she was watering some lavender out front, and she may have recognized me because she looked twice and smiled. I walked inside and searched among the pots and baskets until I found some lilies. I went over to the counter, handed her a five-dollar bill, and she said something in broken English.

I came out and Harrigan was leaning against the car, his arms crossed, staring at the sun through his sunglasses. Although he would never admit it, he felt more comfortable in parts of town that weren't all white. He got along well with everybody, but it wasn't easy being one of the only black detectives. In a city where everyone hated everyone, Boston's racism was oddly egalitarian, but it was still a place where the phrase 'he's a nice nigger' was viewed as a compliment.

"C'mon," I said, "let's hit it. You look too relaxed. Makes me think you wanna be at the beach."

"I was born at the beach."

"Always one for metaphors."

"No," he said, as we got in the car. "Literally. I was born on a beach. My parents were at a beach festival for Emancipation Day. My mother went into labor. I was delivered by a Pentecostal minister, who was also the parish physician."

"That explains a lot," I said. "I learn something new about you every day."

We went south along Washington Street, past several liquor stores, an elementary school, and a garage that repaired city buses. Harrigan turned right at Valentine Street, and we drove up a shallow hill. The homes looked smaller than I remembered, and the front lawns were all overgrown with weeds. When I saw the white mailbox with the number eleven, I grabbed Harrigan's forearm.

"Stop. This is it."

He pulled over and shut off the car.

"Do you want me to come?"

"Mind waiting?"

"I'd prefer to, actually," he said. "This is more than business."

"Thanks."

"Good luck."

I took the flowers and got out. I walked over to the sidewalk, stood in front of the house, and started to reminisce. It was a small but ornamented colonial, with cedar shingles and a slate roof. In the narrow yard to the left was the peach tree Al had fallen from and broken his wrist. The front stair railing was painted over, but I could still see the spot where we had carved our initials into the wood. In those few seconds, my entire childhood flashed across my mind.

I stepped up to the porch and banged the knocker twice. As I stood waiting, a part of me hoped she wasn't home so I could turn around and go. But inside I heard footsteps then a lock, and the door swung open. And there stood Mrs. Russo, twenty-five years older but with the same gentle smile. She was a petite woman, with long brown hair and a small mouth that reminded me of the Mona Lisa.

"Yes?" she said, peering up. "May I help you?"

"Mrs. Russo, it's Joseph Brae."

Her expression went from disbelief to joy, and her eyes got teary. Before she could respond, I held out the lilies and said, "I'm so sorry about Al."

Instead of taking the flowers, she leaned forward and hugged me like a mother would her son.

"My God, Jody," she said, finally letting go. "You look so old...I mean, mature."

We both laughed.

"I know what you meant."

"Please, come in."

I always thought she had an Italian accent like her husband, but when she spoke, I realized she did not. I stepped into the darkness of the parlor, and she closed the door and locked it. Inside the ceilings were low and the walls were covered with floral wallpaper that had been out of style for decades. The furniture was shabby but clean, and I noticed the walnut credenza Mr. Russo had built by hand when we were kids. On the mantel was a photograph of Al and his parents at Niagara Falls. With his father's arm around him, he smiled at the camera with a toothy grin.

When Mrs. Russo saw me looking, she put the flowers down and took the picture in both hands.

"Those were better times," she said. "The three of us. Now it's just me."

"And Mr. Russo?"

"Alberto Senior died five years ago. Heart attack, they think. He just didn't wake up one morning. Went to bed, never woke up."

"I'm sorry."

"Thank you. Al found him. I was up early. Didn't even notice. Can you believe it? It was a Sunday morning. My husband always slept late Sundays. He went to Mass on Saturday."

She wiped off the photograph and put it back. As we continued down a short hallway, she turned and said, "Al took it really hard—thought it was his fault."

"Why would he think that?"

"He never made much of himself, Jody. Thought he broke his father's heart."

She led the way to the kitchen and invited me to sit. She turned on the kettle, then reached under the sink for a ceramic vase. She clipped the ends of the lilies and arranged them neatly before placing them on the windowsill. As I watched, I was amazed by how beautiful she still was after all these years. Her skin was clear, her hair shone, and she had the figure of a woman half her age. Mrs. Russo may have lost her entire family, but she didn't let the grief destroy her.

"Are you hungry?" she asked.

"No. Thank you."

"Tea?"

"That'd be fine."

When the water boiled, she poured two cups and took a seat.

"This isn't just about condolences," she said hesitantly.

"I wish it were, but...no. I'm on the investigation."

She looked down, stirred her tea.

"I knew you were a police officer. Al told me. A long time ago. How long have you been?—"

"Thirteen years," I said. "I'm a detective now. A lieutenant."

She looked up with a sad smile.

"He was proud of you, you know."

"He was a good friend."

"When was the last time?—"

"I don't know," I said, and I knew I was nervous because I kept cutting her off. "It's been years. Maybe '54 or '55. Sometime after the war anyway."

"Ah, the war," she said.

Outside birds were singing in the bushes, and I could hear children playing in a nearby yard.

"Al never got over that," she went on. "It was hard on him. It was hard on all you boys. And that's what you were—boys."

I had the urge to respond, but instead, I sipped my tea and listened.

"After the war," she said, gazing toward the window, "Al went back to the fishery, but he got fired for drinking. Then he drove a cab, but he lost that job too. He ended up living on the streets, which broke both our hearts..."

She closed her eyes, shuddered at the memory.

"...Some adjusted better than others, I suppose. You've adjusted, Jody. You look well."

"A lot of time has passed," I said, feeling a pit in my stomach. "When was he on the streets?"

"Sometime in the mid-Fifties. He slept at Dover Street, South Station, the Boston Common. It was awful, but there was nothing we could do. Al Senior used to drive around looking for him at night, taking him food, a few dollars. This went on for years. He eventually convinced Al to move home, thank God."

"When was that?"

She looked up, thinking.

"When was that plane crash, where those rock and roll stars died?"

I smiled and said, "You mean Buddy Holly?"

"Holly? Yes, that's him."

"'59, I think."

"Al moved back home that week. He couldn't stop talking about it. He loved music, even rock and roll."

"He loved a lot of things."

"He loved alcohol more, unfortunately. That was his crutch. If only he could've given it up. His father never drank. I never cared for it either. Maybe a highball at New Years. It makes me dizzy."

"Mrs. Russo," I said, shifting in the chair.

"Please, Natalie. Call me Natalie. Makes me feel younger."

"Natalie. Anyone he didn't get along with? Anyone he might have had a dispute with?"

"I knew this question was coming. I've thought about the answer. None. Al hadn't an enemy in the world. Except for maybe a million North Koreans."

When I laughed out loud, she seemed pleased.

"Al was quiet," she continued. "He worked nights at the liquor store in Dudley Square. He collected stamps—I know it sounds silly. He helped around the house. Sometimes went to hear Jazz at Wally's Café. Of course, he drank. He always drank. Mostly in his room or when he was working in the garden. He didn't socialize much—kept to himself. He was a loner, for the most part."

"Was he associating with anyone new lately?"

"No," she said. "I mean…" She stopped and put her hand under her chin. "Well, maybe. He did get a phone call."

My face lit up.

"When?"

"Last week. He gets calls sometimes, usually old friends or work. I answered it. They talked a few minutes and that was it."

"Did he say who it was?"

"No, he didn't. But it must have been someone from the military, which is odd."

"And why's that?"

"Because it was about a reunion," she said, and our eyes met. "But Al hasn't talked with anybody from the war in years."

CHAPTER 10

The next time Al Russo and I went to Whiskey Point was on his fourteenth birthday. We both had jobs bagging groceries at Flanagan's Market on Washington Street, and on Friday nights we worked until closing. When the workers heard about Russo's birthday, they hid some beers for him in the trash, a small gift for an employee who was well-liked. At six o'clock we punched out and went to the dumpster, where we looked in it to find a bag of Pabst Blue Ribbon bottles. Because it was his birthday, I offered to carry it and he didn't argue. We walked down the back alley, crossed over the train tracks, and headed to the cliff.

Russo and I had talked about getting drunk for months. Now that we were teenagers, our curfews were later, and we didn't worry as much about the consequences. He had to be home by eleven, which to me seemed like the freedom of an adult. The *Home*, however, was not so generous, and any child under sixteen who was not in by nine o'clock would be punished with a week of housekeeping duty.

We crawled through the fence hole into the woods, and Russo immediately opened a beer. They must have gotten shaken up from the journey because when he twisted off the top, white foam exploded over his face and jacket. He ran in circles like a dog on fire, trying to catch the beer in his mouth and making a mess of it. When the liquid had settled, he handed me the bottle and I drank too. We had a second then a third, and soon we were overcome by the warm tingle of intoxication. We stumbled up the hill, zigzagging over the steep ground so we wouldn't lose our balance. By the time we got to the top, we had finished a six-pack and were stone drunk.

Somehow, we made it over the crest and onto the clearing.

"I gotta piss," he said.

While he went into the woods, I walked to the ledge and put down the beers. By now it was dark, and the city glowed in the distance like those futuristic places in pulp magazines. I was mesmerized. The night sky was clear, with more stars than I had ever seen. Because we had been studying astronomy, I searched for Orion but couldn't find it.

Russo was only gone a few minutes when I heard voices. I crept to the tree line and looked over to see him standing in a gully, surrounded by three older boys. What at first I thought were fireflies were actually matches that they were flicking at him. He ducked and sidestepped, trying desperately to avoid the tiny flames. When one landed on his head, a piece of hair caught fire and he shrieked, "Ahhhh!"

Without thinking, I ran toward him. One of the boys saw me and said, "Who's this? A friend coming to save you? Looks like a pansy. Maybe it's your girlfriend?"

As the others laughed, he walked over and grabbed me by the throat. His fingernails tore into my skin, and I started to gag. I was too drunk to fight back, but it wouldn't have mattered because the boy was much stronger.

"Hold on, Bonzo," one of the others ordered, and I assumed he was the leader. He came over, held a lighter to my face, and instantly I recognized the boy we had encountered on the cliff two years before.

"I remember you," he said, waving the flame back and forth. "The little gutter boy who broke my ribs." The boy lifted his shirt and pointed. "These ones, three of 'em. I was spittin' blood for weeks."

"I don't know what you're talkin' about."

"Shut up!" he yelled. "Don't speak until spoken to. Where do you live?"

"Oz."

Smack! He backhanded me across the face and I felt my cheek swell up. But it didn't hurt because I was drunk and the most it did was make me dizzy. He then gripped the collar of my jacket, pulled me toward him, and said, "I'm gonna ask you one more time. WHERE DO YOU LIVE?!"

Now more angry than intimidated, I stared into his bloodshot eyes and said, "the Roxbury Home for Stray Boys."

"Aha, now I remember. It *was* you." He looked over to his cohorts and said, "Hey boys, we got Oliver Twist here."

They both laughed and he snapped the lighter shut.

"So, what do we do with these rats? Throw them over the ledge? Isn't that what we do with rats?"

The others nodded with drunken grins.

"Bonzo, Cronk, you take him," the leader said, looking at Russo. "Let's go."

They dragged us to the clearing and marched us toward the cliff. I had always heard that booze gave you courage, but I learned that night that it only made you useless. Woozy from the alcohol, I fell and my kneecaps hit the rock. "Ow!" I shouted and the boy whacked me on the back of the head. "Shut up, you little dog. Get up!" He kicked me in the ass and I continued to walk.

I looked back once to see Russo being prodded by the other two. When they had us near the edge, the leader tripped over something and I heard a clink. It was the beers.

"Oh," he said, and he let go of my collar. "We struck gold, fellas. You boys bring us some tribute? That what this is?" He turned to his friends and said, "Well, we accept."

He leaned over to grab the bag and I looked at Russo. When our eyes met, I knew he was thinking what I was thinking. With the three boys busy inspecting their plunder, I winked at him and shouted, "Now!"

I booted the leader in the thigh and he fell over. Then I spun around and shoved one of the others, giving Russo a chance to run. Together we sprinted toward the woods and didn't look back. Branches scraped my face, and my ankles buckled in the uneven terrain. I heard Russo panting behind me and every few seconds I turned to make sure he was still there. The other boys must have been drunker than we were because they didn't chase us or if they did, we had easily outrun them.

Once we were a safe distance away, we sat behind an elm tree with our backs to the trunk and rested.

"What's that?" Russo asked.

"Shhh," I said. "Lower your voice. What's what?"

"That sound."

I closed my eyes and listened.

"Crickets. Those're crickets, you blockhead. Little bugs, little insects."

"I've never heard them before."

"They live in the woods."

"That's why I never heard them before."

We stayed there for over an hour. By the time we got up, the alcohol had worn off, and I was left with a raging headache. The scratches on my neck itched and my throat was dry. We were afraid to go back to the cliff, so instead, we went straight, hoping to eventually reach one of the surrounding streets. We had only gone a few yards when I noticed lights in the distance. They were too close to be from the neighborhood, and we went toward them out of curiosity.

We came over a shallow embankment and looked across a clearing to see a large house. It had white clapboard, black shutters, and three chimneys—one at each end and one in the middle. On the roofline was a weathervane with the angel Gabriel blowing his trumpet. The home was ancient and sprawling and reminded me of those New England farmhouses from books about the Revolution. Situated remotely at the top of the hill, it was like a hidden castle.

"Wow, who lives there?"

"Shush! Keep your head down."

We heard a noise in the distance, the crunch of leaves. As I peered through the weeds, I watched the leader of the gang come out of the woods. I turned to Russo and covered his mouth before he could say anything. The boy walked across the lawn with something under his arm, and I was sure it was the beers he had stolen from us. Suddenly, the porch light went on, the door opened, and a tall man stepped out.

"Son? Is that you?" he called out.

I couldn't see his face, but he had the stern voice of a schoolmaster. With nowhere to hide, the boy stood in the openness of the yard and didn't move.

"Son? I'm talking to you!" his father said, this time louder.

He walked casually over with his arms out, and I thought he was going to hug the boy. But the moment he got close, he swung and punched him in the face, so hard it sounded like a branch breaking. The bottles fell, the boy stumbled backward. Russo and I froze in terror.

"Tell me how you got out?!" the man barked.

Before his son could reply, he lunged and shoved him to the ground, kicking him in the back, chest, and head, over and over again. The boy grunted a few times, but he didn't scream or cry for help.

"Holy shit, Jody!" Russo said in a panicked whisper. "He's gonna kill him!"

"Keep it down or we'll be next."

The episode lasted only twenty seconds, but it was something we would remember the rest of our lives. When the beating was over, the man smoothed out his shirt, dusted off his hands, and went back into the house.

"We gotta go! C'mon!" Russo said.

"That ain't right. We gotta tell somebody."

"I'm not telling anybody. That guy's nuts."

As he got up to leave, I looked over and saw the faint outline of the boy, lying in the shadow of the lawn, perfectly still. We stepped away from the clearing and headed back into the forest. With Whiskey Point as our only reference point, we had to return there to find the path down the hill. But eventually, we did, and we scrambled to the bottom, where we burst through the fence and ran for no reason.

At the end of the street, we slowed to an easy pace, and Russo said, "You think he killed him?"

"Probably not."

"Think he'll have black eyes."

"I bet he will."

"How'd you like to have a father like that?"

I didn't answer. After another block, I stopped and leaned against a streetlamp. I felt dizzy and couldn't stop swallowing—something was wrong.

"I'm gonna—"

Before I could finish, I opened my mouth and a stream of yellow vomit poured out. Bent over the gutter, I held my gut and retched for several minutes. When I was finally empty, I stood up and was out of breath. I had puke on my collar, but most of my clothing was spared.

"You okay?" Russo asked.

"Must've been something I ate."

"I didn't mean to say that."

I spit out a few chunks and looked at him.

"Say what?"

"Aw, never mind."

CHAPTER 11

I TOSSED IN MY BED AND MY MIND RACED AS I THOUGHT ABOUT THE war. The memories flashed by in hazy half-approximations that had no coherence or chronology. I saw soldiers I hadn't thought about in years; buck-eyed privates and grizzled sergeants, corporals who hated everybody and medics who were tattooed with the blood of the ones they couldn't save. I remembered names without faces and faces without names, and the dead blended with the living in a camp show pageant that seemed to parody the madness of combat. By 4:00 a.m., I surrendered and walked out to the kitchen to make tea.

The next morning, I got to headquarters so early the captain wasn't there, and the night staff was still on duty. I walked to the cafeteria in the basement, got a coffee and donut, then sat in the corner and read yesterday's Record American that someone had left behind. When I was done, I threw out my trash, and as I was leaving, Officer Suliman was coming in and stopped me.

"Mister Lieutenant," he said. "You look like crap."

"Thanks, Sully. Nice to see you too."

He came up close, lowered his voice.

"Heard they identified that stiff under the bridge."

My eyes widened.

"You serious?"

"Dickson was dispatching yesterday. He took the call. Jackson has the info. Go see him."

"I was about to…" I said, and Sully walked away. He only got a few feet before turning around and saying, "Hey, I'm sorry about your buddy. Really, I am."

I waved thanks and continued out to the stairwell. As I looked down the corridor, the captain's door was shut, which meant he was there. I knocked then walked in to find him and Harrigan discussing something.

"Morning, Lieutenant," he said. "Early for you?"

"Couldn't sleep."

"That's understandable. Please, sit."

I took a seat and nodded to Harrigan.

"We may have a lead on that body found under the West 9th Street bridge."

"I know," I said. "Just heard."

Jackson raised his eyebrows.

"So much for confidentiality."

Neither of us laughed because he wasn't being sarcastic. The captain detested the casual gossip of police bravado, which he viewed as a threat to the integrity of the department. If he asked who informed me, I would have had to tell him. But when he reached for a document on the desk, I knew the matter was over.

"This isn't going to be easy," he said, adjusting his glasses. "We got a call from a supervisor at the St. Francis House in Providence. It's a homeless shelter—for veterans."

I glanced at Harrigan, but he seemed to avoid making eye contact.

"One of their residents came to Boston last weekend. He was supposed to call his counselor. The last they heard of him was Sunday."

"He could be anywhere," I said. "What makes you think the body was him?"

"He was staying at a veterans shelter on Albany Street. I confirmed that he arrived Sunday morning. He went out that night and didn't come back."

I looked at Harrigan again and he was still avoiding me, so I turned to the captain.

"There're hundreds of vagrants. What's the connection?"

"He was in the 1st Division, US Marines," he said, and I started to get anxious. "His name was William Minerva, thirty-eight years old, dark hair—"

"Stop," I said, and Jackson did.

I sat stone-faced and numb, absorbing the news with a bitter dread and trying to make sense of it all. I didn't even consider it could have been someone with the same name because I knew it was true—another member of K Company was dead.

Billy Minerva was a lanky Italian from Providence, Rhode Island. He was technically 6' 3" but would have been taller if he didn't hunch over. With his black hair, Roman nose, and deep voice, he was debonair before his time, and women probably went gaga until they realized he was just a bricklayer from Federal Hill. We met on the first day of our deployment. When the company commander kept mispronouncing his name, we took to calling him 'minnow,' and he seemed to like it. Minerva took orders easy and never complained, and his only downfall was that he drank too much and didn't eat enough. He was a good soul and a competent soldier, and the fact that he ended up homeless told me that the war had never really ended for him.

"Detective?"

I looked up and Jackson and Harrigan were staring at me.

"I know Billy Minerva," I said, and the words sounded funny. "He was in my company. In my platoon. We served fifteen months together."

"I'm sorry. You didn't recognize him?"

"Recognize him? I guess I didn't. I didn't look hard. The body was ravaged. Stank to high heavens."

"It was pretty bad, sir," Harrigan said.

The captain turned back to me.

"Did he have any enemies?"

"No," I said as if offended by the question. "I mean, I don't know. I haven't seen him since the war."

"Were you two close?"

"Close? As close as any soldiers, I guess. He was solid, pretty quiet. We used to joke around. He liked his beers and I liked mine. Never got to know much about his life back home, if that's what you mean."

"From what I've been told," the captain said, "he didn't have one." He peered down at the report and read, "Parents deceased, never married, no surviving relatives in Rhode Island." He squinted to see the details. "A sister in Hawaii and a brother serving in the Peace Corps in Nigeria—"

Jackson mentioned a few more facts, but I didn't listen because I already knew what he wanted to ask me. To make it easy for him, I interrupted and said, "Do we need someone to identify the body?"

His expression didn't change, but I could sense that he was relieved.

"Is that something you can do?" he asked, speaking with a gentle compassion. "Something you are willing to do, I mean?"

When I looked over to Harrigan, he finally looked back.

"I've already been to the morgue for one friend this week."

CHAPTER 12

I HAD NEVER GONE TO A VETERANS REUNION. WHEN I RETURNED FROM the war, I wanted nothing more than to move on with my life. I entered the police academy that summer and got my badge and gun twenty weeks later. Many of the rookies were veterans, and we all seemed to practice a collective amnesia which made forgetting the war not only easy but acceptable too. We were young, alive, and forward-thinking. We had lived through hell and wanted to experience a little heaven, which we did in spades.

When I got home on Friday night, I found a letter under my door. I scooped it up, sat on the couch, and tore it open. Inside were five color photographs and a note from Ruth in that flowing cursive only a woman's hand could produce:

JODY,

ENJOY YOUR TIME at the reunion. I thought you might like these.

· · ·

Love, *Ruth*

I FLIPPED through the pictures of our vacation to Ireland, and it made me smile. We were only back a week, but the trip seemed years in the past, and I viewed them with warm nostalgia. The first one was taken beneath the awning of a pharmacy during a sun shower in a tiny Connemara village. The next was of us leaning against our rental car at a crossroads in Mayo, surrounded by hills and white stone walls. We had asked a farmer to take our picture, and he held the Voigtlander 35mm with the delicacy of a horse's bridle, as amazed as he was to see a camera. The last three were of Ruth lying on a beach during low tide along the shore of Achill Island. She wore a blouse and skirt that were whiter than the bleached pebbles and shells around her. I ran my finger along the edge of the photo and then to the center, from her hair to her bare feet and everywhere in between. I was captivated by the majesty of that day, and I yearned to get it all back.

I took a quick shower, changed my clothes, and headed out. By the time I reached the Lenox, it was nine o'clock and the bars and restaurants along Boylston Street were crowded. As I pulled up to the hotel, a black Fleetwood Sixty Special was leaving, and I slid into a spot that was better than good.

The moment I walked through the doors, I felt a rush of cool air and heard the soft notes of piano music from a tuxedoed player beside the lobby fountain.

The Lenox was in the heart of patrician Boston and, with its marble walls and gilded ceilings, smacked of old money elegance. A half-century ago, a blue-collar cop from Mission Hill wouldn't have been there except for business. The social barriers between the WASP establishment and immigrant ethnics had once been as rigid as a lobster's tail. But times had changed, and things had moved beyond the class-bound pettiness of the city's ancient rivalries.

"May I help you, sir?"

A brunette concierge in a black skirt and white blouse came over to me.

"Is there a reunion here?"

"Yes," she said with a smile. "Please, come this way."

I followed her past a lounge and down the main hallway to a banquet room across from an elevator bank. Above the door was a hand-carved sign which read 'Whitcomb Hall,' another indication of the hotel's genteel past. The woman opened the double doors, and the music and noise shattered the quiet of the corridor. She gestured for me to enter, and I walked in and stood timidly by the wall. There were hundreds of men, and the room had the masculine energy of an over-booked stag party. The smoke was thick, the laughter loud, and in the back, a band pounded out the rhythms of the be-bop standards that were popular during the war. Draped above the stage was a banner with the insignia of the 3rd Battalion 1st Marines—the Thundering Third—an angry Bull with flames shooting out of its nostrils.

"Brae? Jody Brae?"

I turned to see a man pushing through the crowd, and when he got closer, I realized who it was.

"Paul Munch?" I muttered. "Holy shit."

He ran up and threw his arms around me, squeezing until my spine cracked.

"Brother!" he said. "You're as ugly as ever!"

"Still a wisenheimer, Paul?"

He kept his arm around my shoulder, and I could smell hard booze on his breath—either Vodka or Gin. I tried to pull away, but he wouldn't let me go.

"I can't believe it's you, man. Where've you been? Don't tell me, you're a stockbroker? Or a scientist? Working for the NSA? You were the smartest little fuck in K Company." I blushed, and he said, "Or should I say, Sergeant Fuck? We gotta respect rank, right?" He finally let go. "Man, I missed you."

"Likewise," I said.

Private Munch was the white version of Harrigan, a half-Scandinavian giant from Moorhead, Minnesota whose main passions in life were ice fishing and hockey. He was a foot taller than me, with large hands and a square jaw, and he looked like Frankenstein with blonde hair. Munch had been one of the most athletic men in my unit, but now his shoulders were hunched and his arms flabby. With a plaid dinner jacket, wool pants, and white socks, he looked like he had been outfitted by the Salvation Army.

Yet Munch still had some strength left, and when he grabbed me by the arm and dragged me to meet some friends, I couldn't resist.

"Gentlemen," he said. "Remember Staff Sergeant Brae?"

I looked across the table and a dozen hands waved in unison. Some of the men were familiar, but most were strangers. Our battalion had over a thousand soldiers, so it was impossible to know everybody. During the war, the composition of units was in constant flux as soldiers died or were wounded and new recruits arrived. The men I was closest to were those in my platoon, or more specifically, my squad.

After Munch and I made our rounds, we walked over to an open section of the bar, and he yelled for the bartender.

"Double scotch, your highness. No, make it a triple."

"You got it, pal," the bartender said, then he looked over to me.

Munch turned also and said, "Jody, it's on me. Anything."

"Just water."

"Water? Water it is. Get this man some water. He must be on fire."

Munch laughed and tried to pat me on the back, but he stumbled and knocked over an ashtray. His eyes were yellow and his teeth green, and I wanted to tell him he looked terrific, but it would have been a lie.

"So?" he said. "What've you been up to all these Goddamn years?"

"I'm a detective with the Boston Police."

When he smiled, his forehead wrinkled, and he looked old.

"Not surprised. You'll be captain someday. I've no doubt about that." He softened his voice and said, "You look great, Jody, I'm proud of you. We gotta stay in touch."

"How 'bout you? Where's life brought you?"

He leaned against the bar for support and looked off.

"Phew," he said. "Where hasn't it?"

He shook his head and went to speak, but the bartender interrupted him by handing us our drinks.

"Thanks," he said, then he turned back to me. "You want the long version or the short one?" Before I could answer, he continued, "Actually, either will do. I can give it to you in one sentence. Two words, no less." He held up his drink with a dramatic flair and shouted, "FUCKED UP."

Two men at the bar frowned, and even the bartender rolled his eyes at the melodrama.

"Can't be that bad," I said.

"Oh, Jody, you have no idea. Let's sit. I'm a little wobbly. It's the injuries."

I smirked and said, "You weren't injured."

"Must be battle fatigue. I hear ringing, see things. It makes me dizzy."

He did an impression of a zombie walking and I just chuckled.

We found a table in the corner that by some miracle was empty and sat against the wall. Scattered about were plates of half-eaten prime rib and vegetables from the earlier meal. Some of the cups still had coffee in them and others had been used as ashtrays. I sipped my water and looked out to the crowd.

Everywhere veterans joked and drank and smoked like it was the eve before an offensive. The only woman in the room was a blonde waitress with big breasts and a purple skirt that bunched up at the hips. She had square features and perfect posture, and above her head, she balanced a tray with more drinks than she could handle. When she walked by us, Munch grumbled, "How'd you like to tame that heifer?" and she turned around and sneered at both of us. He let out a loud belch and then reached for a half-smoked cigar someone had left behind.

"Got a light?" he asked.

I laughed for the first time since entering the room. I sparked a match, and he inhaled deeply and started to cough. He reached for someone's leftover drink, and I couldn't tell if it was bourbon or ginger ale. When he was done, he wiped his mouth with a used napkin and turned to me.

"I've made a mess of my life, Jody. I won't deny it."

"I wouldn't say—"

"No!" he said. "There's nothing you can say. It's okay. I'm a fuckin' loser. But it's alright. I served. I fought. I'll always have that. No one can take that away. I was there. You were there." He smiled and I smiled back. "When Rosa left me," he went on, "must be five years now. Yeah, five years." His speech was now slurred, and I had trouble following the starts and stops of the conversation. "She said I was a bum 'cause I drank too much."

"Did you?"

He looked down at his glass, shook it a little.

"Of course. Who wouldn't after the shit we saw?" Hunched over the table, he looked at me from a side angle and said, "This world ain't fair."

Suddenly, a man came through the front door and went over to the bar, where he was greeted by some friends. He wore a military dress uniform, one of only a handful in the room, and had the nervous air of someone who had overslept or gotten lost. Somebody handed him a drink and he looked in the mirror behind the bar to fix his hair. With his blue coat, epaulets, and white gloves, he cut a dashing image, and a civilian might have guessed he was a general. But I recognized him immediately as our old lieutenant.

"Look at that rat," Munch snickered. "Dressed like a fuckin' prince. Bet he thought we were all holding our breaths for him to arrive."

Thomas Goddard took over the platoon in September of '50 after our commander was hurt in a jeep accident. He was a wiry, blonde-haired lieutenant with a bad temper and a mean streak. His eyes were so blue they seemed to glow, and he had a permanent grimace that made you think his underwear was too tight. We had grown up together in Roxbury, although he went to private schools. When I was in fifth grade, we were on the same baseball team, but he was kicked off for throwing a bat at the pitcher. It was rumored that his family had money, but he still played in the streets and got into trouble with all the other neighborhood kids. He used his size to his advantage and would harass anyone smaller than him. But after an early growth spurt, he seemed to stay the same, and by the time we were teenagers, I had four inches and ten pounds over him.

Goddard must have fancied himself a gentleman soldier because he smoked Pall Malls and shaved daily. Not everyone disliked him, but few respected him, and he couldn't even order the men to fall in without someone mocking him or making a farting sound. On the march, he was always at the rear, and on more than one occasion he ordered us in the wrong direction then blamed the point man. He was edgy to the point of paranoia, and he sometimes heard the KPA in the dark, even when we were miles from the line. The NCOs would laugh, and the privates would just bite their tongues. If Goddard had been anything above a lieutenant there might have been a mutiny, but we tolerated his arrogance because we had to.

"Looks like the war's treated him well," I said.

"He should be dead."

I lit a cigarette and said, "Wasn't my first choice for a leader. But sergeants don't decide."

Munch's face was pink, and he started to wheeze from the smoke.

"That rank was bought—you and I know it. There's more to being an officer than having a college degree."

"Let dead dogs lie," I said, and he laughed.

"Dogs is right. Anytime the gooks hit us he was under his sleeping bag whimpering like one."

"You can't blame the war on one man."

Munch stamped out the last of the cigar and looked at me. The music paused between numbers, and he waited for it to resume before speaking.

"Jody," he said, his eyes intense. "That man's a criminal. Don't be fooled by those pretty blue eyes. He's a fuckin' tyrant. I know a lotta time has passed, but that don't change facts."

We stared at each other until we could stare no longer, and I knew that, despite his drunkenness, he was never given to exaggeration.

"I took his orders for a year and a half," I said, "and I'm alive."

I tried to laugh it off, but he didn't see the humor.

"You grew up with Goddard. You must know. What was he like? He pull the wings off flies? Poke cats' eyes out with sticks?"

"He was a bully," I said. "I won't deny it. And a spoiled one. His folks were rich."

Munch looked over at Goddard with a snarl.

"Little bitch is what he is. If he wasn't a lieutenant, I would've ripped his balls out."

Goddard must have noticed us watching because he looked over and raised his glass. He made a halfhearted smile that was more of a frown, and I could see two rows of gleaming white teeth. The war had destroyed many men, but Goddard had aged with grace, and he looked like the youngest guy in the room. With his GI glasses and pressed uniform, he could have been mistaken for a professor from a military college.

Munch shook his head and blinked.

"Listen," he said, lowering his voice. "I'm talkin' foolishness. Pay me no mind."

"I wasn't."

He laughed.

"So, what brought you here?"

"Kemp, actually. Travis Kemp."

"Sergeant Kemp?"

"I saw him at a restaurant the other night. He told me about this. To be honest, I always thought he was dead."

"Might as well be," Munch said, and he burped. I looked at him with surprise and he added, "Because he hasn't been in touch with anyone from K Company in years."

"You sure about that?"

"Sure as shit. I'm one of the coordinators of this fine event. Been involved with all the reunions. Never seen Kemp, never heard from him."

A chill went up my back. The noise of the room seemed to fade into the backdrop, and I felt alone among three hundred men. Either Kemp had lied to me or Munch was wrong, but it couldn't have been both. As I went to ask him, a voice called out, "Paul? Paul Munch?" Two men came over to the table and he got up to receive them. He could barely stand but hugged them anyway, and they immediately fell into conversation. Someone tapped my shoulder and I turned around to see the concierge.

"Call at the front desk, sir," she said.

I held up my finger for her to wait then tried to get Munch's attention, but he was too busy talking. So I followed her to the lobby, where she reached over the counter and handed me the phone.

"Lieutenant Brae," I said.

"Detective, it's Harrigan."

"Harrigan?"

"Jackson told me to find you. We've got another homicide."

"How'd you know I was here?"

"Travis Kemp."

"Kemp? How do you know Kemp?"

He paused before answering.

"He's at the station. He was arrested an hour ago."

CHAPTER 13

THE HOTEL HOLLOWAY WAS A DILAPIDATED SIX-STORY BUILDING wedged between a strip joint and a peepshow parlor in the heart of the Combat Zone. It was so obscure that it didn't even have a sign, and you had to ring a buzzer to get in. Rooms were rented by the day or by the hour, and most floors had a shared bathroom. The only reason it was registered as a hotel was so it couldn't be called a flop-house. Like most establishments in the area, it had a seedy reputation and experienced its share of dead hookers, assaults, and drug busts. The rumors ranged from wild orgies to sadomasochism, and it had the eerie mystique of a haunted house.

By the time I arrived, the police and ambulances were out front, and people were watching from the sidewalk. Emergency sirens clashed with the flashing signs of sex shops, and the street was lit up like a carnival gone mad. I turned down a narrow lane and parked by a strip club. When I got out, I could hear rats scuttle in the shadows, and in an alleyway, a sailor was mauling an overweight prostitute. I walked back to the street and saw Harrigan talking to some cops in the doorway of the hotel.

"Detective," he said, as I came up.

"What the hell happened to Kemp?"

"A car accident."

"Car accident? Since when are we privy to auto accidents?"

"It was more than that. He was drunk—belligerent too." He turned away from the officers and whispered, "They found a gun in the car. They've got him at the jail."

"Jesus Christ," I said. I stepped back and looked up at the building. "Where's the stiff?"

Harrigan nodded to the open door, where a crooked stairwell led up into the darkness. When I walked in, I immediately smelled puke, and the corkboard beside the front counter was covered with leaflets advertising sordid services for all tastes. The stairs were so steep I could reach out and touch the next step, and the wall had holes where chunks of plaster had fallen off.

"Why hasn't this place been condemned?" I wondered.

"They pay their taxes."

"It's a cesspool."

"It's certainly not the Lenox, Detective."

We turned on the landing and heard two-way radio chatter coming from a room on the right. As I went toward it, I also heard giggling and peered up to see three girls looking down from the third floor. One wore a negligee, another a pink halter-top, and they all had too much makeup. They smiled and waved kisses, and I smiled back with a polite grin.

Harrigan and I walked in, and two paramedics were standing over a body covered in a white sheet. The room was smaller than most foyers, and the only furniture was a single bed and a wooden dresser with black knobs. The walls were gray and cracked, with a massive water stain in one corner. It reminded me of a prison cell, except the window had no bars. When I stepped over the body and looked outside, I saw that the crowd was growing.

"Tough night's sleep?" I said to one of the paramedics.

The young man ignored the joke and proceeded to describe the victim's condition. "He was shot. There's an entry wound over the left eye. Powder burns suggest—"

"Are you with BCI?" I blurted.

"Pardon?"

"Bureau of Criminal Investigations. Are you here to assess the crime scene?"

"No, sir. I'm not."

"Then just give me the facts."

I looked back to Harrigan with a smirk. The paramedic's partner stood formally by the bed and didn't say a word. Their attitudes suggested they were either new to the job or that they took it far too seriously.

"Entry wound above the eye," the man continued. "No visible exit wound."

"Any other signs of injury? Contusions? Abrasions? Fractures?"

"No, sir. Not that I could detect."

"Who reported this?"

"The desk clerk."

Just then a young man in a white t-shirt appeared in the doorway and said, "I found him, Officer." He had a mop of red hair that fell over his forehead, and I could only see his pupils. "I came in to change the sheets. He was lying there. I didn't touch him."

I looked around the dingy room.

"Change the sheets? You change sheets at night?"

"Here we do," he said with a sour smile.

"Any ID?"

The paramedic pointed to a wallet beside some keys on the night-stand. I opened it and found a few dollar bills, a receipt for a six-pack, and a photograph of a young girl in a white communion dress. I felt something stiff and when I looked between the fold, it was a California license. I took it out, and the moment I saw the image, the hair on the back of my neck stood up. But I kept a straight face and looked over to the employee.

"You see anyone suspicious tonight?" I asked him.

"No, sir. I mean, uh, people come in and out all the time."

"I bet they do," I said. "There's a buzzer, right? You buzz people in?"

"It...it...it doesn't work. It's broke."

I looked at Harrigan, who was leaning against the wall, as calm as a funeral director. Then I turned to the paramedics, who were still but hardly calm.

"You two scram," I said, and when one of them hesitated, I shouted, "Now!"

They quickly got their bags and went into the hallway. I knelt beside the body and bowed my head, thinking of everything and nothing at the same time. When Harrigan walked over and put his hand on my shoulder, I startled.

"You know him, don't you?" he said.

I nodded.

"From the war?"

I nodded again.

"Don't do this to yourself," he said. "You already know. It serves no purpose."

I appreciated his advice, but I wasn't going to heed it. With my back to him, I raised my hand and said, "Please."

"What should I tell the officers?"

"Tell them to interview everyone staying here. Nothing's to be touched until the ME arrives. After that, they can dust, seal the room off, whatever the hell else they do..."

Harrigan stepped away so quietly I didn't hear him, and when I glanced behind, he was gone. I took a deep breath and gently pulled back the sheet. And there, as plain as the day, was the body of Private Rodrigues.

Douglas Rodrigues was a starry-eyed country boy from Yuba City, California. He grew up on a peach farm his great-grandfather built and, until he went to boot camp, had never gone farther than Sacramento. With his jet-black hair and olive skin, he could have been mistaken for Mexican. But his family had been in the country for generations, descendants of rancheros who had arrived before the Mexican-American War. With the help of his parents, Rodrigues enlisted at seventeen, and he joined K Company halfway through my tour with a group of replacements from Pusan. He was the youngest in our platoon—possibly the youngest in the battalion—and everyone treated him like a kid brother. Because he never spoke but giggled constantly, the men took to calling him 'Chuckles.'

When I looked at his face, I saw a black dot above his left eye, a small hole that looked no more threatening than a mole. A trickle of blood ran down his forehead, pooling on the floor. He looked exactly as I remembered him, a little older and with some grays, but with the same boyish innocence. His eyelids were not completely closed, but enough that I couldn't see his eyes, and he looked peaceful despite the injury. I thought of the picture in the wallet, wondering if the girl in the white dress was his daughter.

"Detective," Harrigan called out softly. "Medical examiner is here. Everything's under control."

I put the sheet back, stood up, and gazed around the cramped room. The walls were peeling, and the wooden floor was covered in stains from beer or worse. I was repulsed by it all.

"Let's get outta here. This place makes me sick."

As Harrigan and I were leaving, two men from Ansell's office were coming up the stairs. Outside news vehicles were double-parked on the street, and a dozen reporters stood waiting for a scoop. Some were talking to the patrolmen and others were interviewing bystanders. When a newsman saw us come out, the whole throng turned and rushed at us.

"Quick!" I said to Harrigan. "Let's go."

We darted across the street and headed for his cruiser, which was parked a block away in front of a Chinese restaurant. The reporters must have been afraid to leave the crime scene because they didn't bother chasing us any further. Even so, we jumped into the car, Harrigan started it, and we peeled out into traffic.

"Now I know how the bad guys feel," I said.

"At least they were cameras, not guns."

The Combat Zone was bustling with midnight stragglers, and everywhere I looked I saw drunks, prostitutes, and perverts. None of the establishments in this area made the tourist brochures, but everyone seemed to know how to find them. At the next intersection, I saw a middle-aged man with a wedding ring standing alone on the curb. With his nervous eyes and peculiar grin, he was either lost or had sneaked out for some debauchery after the kids went to bed. Across the street, a show must have gotten out at the Shubert because ladies in fur coats and men in black suits stood waiting for valets. Boston was a city of savage contradictions. It was a blue-collar seaport and a financial mecca—an enlightened university town and a provincial backwater. It was where the movement to end slavery began yet was as segregated as Selma, Alabama. Only in such a place would the theater district be next to the red-light district.

"Kemp has got a lot of explaining to do," I said. "How'd you hear about him?"

"A call came over the radio telling me to phone the jail. The captain on duty wanted to know what to do with him. Kemp dropped your name, said you were at the Lenox. Then the call came in about the homicide."

"He should've been at the hotel. He was probably on his way."

I lit a cigarette and leaned toward the window.

"What's your take on things?" I said.

"I think I should be asking you."

"Don't give me that—"

Harrigan jerked the wheel and pulled over. He turned to me, looked me straight in the eye.

"Detective, you know these men. You served with them. Not me, not the captain. You're the only one that can make the connection."

"I don't know. I'm telling you," I said, loosening my tie, sinking back into the seat. "I haven't seen any of these guys in years. God knows what they've been up to. Life goes on after war."

There was a short pause.

"Is that true?"

"What?" I said, turning to him, "Whaddya mean?"

"I mean, has life gone on…since the war?"

"Don't be dramatic," I scoffed. "For me it has."

"We're not talking about you."

I ran my hand through my hair and looked over to the Statler Building. A hooker in a ginger skirt and top hopped out of a cab and I was momentarily distracted. As we sat idling, I felt a strange tension building. I tapped my fingers on the side of the door, trying to buy some time, but I knew I couldn't dodge his questions much longer.

"Did anything happen in the war?" he asked.

"Everything happened in the war."

"Think back—"

"I don't want to think back!" I snapped. "Korea was a fucking nightmare! Ever hold a friend in your arms and watch him drown in his own blood?" When Harrigan shook his head no, I punched the dash. "Ever watch a twenty-year-old cry for his mother..." I hit it again, this time harder. "...seven-thousand goddamn miles from home?!" On the third punch, the glove compartment dropped open and things fell out. "Ever? Huh?"

"No," he murmured. "You know I haven't."

Harrigan was still and quiet, maintaining a respectful restraint that I probably didn't deserve. Something had burst within me that I didn't have the power to control, and the memories of war bowled me over like a tsunami wave. "That gurgling sound," I continued, shaky and out of breath, "I still hear it, man. I still hear it when I sleep. It's still there. It never goes away. Ever."

Harrigan said nothing. With the exception of Ruth, never before had I admitted to another person the effect the war had on me. When I walked off the gangplank in San Francisco on a spring morning in 1951, I was determined not to be a victim. But as time passed, I struggled under the guilt of having survived where so many others perished. Most people wouldn't have noticed, and those who did might have attributed it to the workaday cynicism of police machismo. Harrigan was the first colleague ever to see me crack up, and I wasn't embarrassed. It was he above all whom I trusted, and even if the entire force disbanded or vanished tomorrow, our friendship would endure.

"Jody," Harrigan said, and it may have been the first time he ever used my given name. "These men don't deserve to die."

"They all have one foot in the grave," I said. "They've destroyed their lives. Russo, Minerva, Munch—"

"Who's Munch?"

"I met him at the reunion tonight. He was a mess. A complete train wreck."

"Everyone has their demons."

I sighed and said, "It's more than demons. These guys are like the living dead—drunks, divorced, bitter, angry, paranoid. I just hope that's not me."

Harrigan grinned.

"You don't drink," he said.

"You're a bastard."

"I learn from you, Detective."

"Can you spare a quarter?" I heard, and we both turned to see a homeless man in the window. He had long, ratty hair, and a big smile and most of his teeth were missing. Harrigan looked at him with polite surprise and I just laughed.

"A quarter?" I said. "What happened to 'brother, can you spare a dime'?"

The man thought for a moment, shrugged his shoulders.

"Inflation, I guess."

I dug in my pocket and grabbed a handful of change.

"What if I told you we're cops?"

"I'd ask for a dollar."

This time we both laughed. As I reached across Harrigan, the man cupped his hands, and I gave him everything I had—the quarter he wanted and the rest for the entertainment. He tipped his hat then disappeared into the shadows.

"See? I'm not such a bad guy now, am I?" I said.

"Never said you were."

CHAPTER 14

WHEN THE OFFICER OPENED THE CELL DOOR, THE FIRST THING I smelled was piss. I ducked my head and went in and there on a soiled mattress was Travis Kemp. Leaning to one side, his gut bulged over his belt. His mouth was dry, his eyelids encrusted, and a string of drool dangled from his bottom lip. Torn between pity and disgust, the latter won out, and I would have let him rot in jail had I not gone so far to help him.

"This it?" I asked the officer.

"His belongings are in the safe box. I'll get 'em."

"Something to drink too, if you could," I said.

"You got it."

Once the officer walked away, I leaned over the bed and shook Kemp until he awoke. His body shuddered, his eyes popped open, and he had the same dazed expression of someone coming out of a long coma. He tried to get up but fell back to the mattress and mumbled, "Jody."

The jailor returned with some water and a canvas bag containing Kemp's things. I held Kemp's head up and fed him the water, which he guzzled. The fluids worked magic on a body that was wracked by alcohol dehydration, and soon he was well enough to move. I grabbed his bag then crouched so he could put his arm over my shoulder. We hobbled down the corridor toward the lobby, past a dozen cells and a small waiting room. He struggled with each step, and the limp from his war injury seemed worse than before. As we passed the front desk, I glanced over at the officer.

"Thanks again."

"Any time, Lieutenant," he replied with a mock salute.

We turned the corner, descended a stairwell, and went out into the night. As we made our way across the lot, Kemp tried to apologize, but I wouldn't listen. I lowered him onto the seat, slammed the door, and we left.

The streets were calm in the early hours, and except for taxis and police cars, no one was on the road. As we cruised down Boylston Street, the bars and nightclubs were all closed, and the crowds were gone. Here and there I saw a drunken couple swaying arm in arm along the sidewalk. At the corner of Massachusetts Avenue, an old vagrant in a straw hat was singing the National Anthem at the top of his lungs. When I looked over and laughed, I noticed that Kemp was out cold.

We got to my apartment at 4:00 a.m., and I parked as quietly as I could. Through the front window, I saw Jerry sitting on his rocker in the parlor, a smoldering cob pipe in his mouth. Even with his eyes closed, he was never truly asleep, and he would nap on and off all day.

I helped Kemp out of the car, and he was able to get up the stairs on his own. Once inside, I ordered him to sit while I went to the kitchen.

"Coffee or tea?" I said.

"Jody, first I wanna—"

"Coffee or tea?!"

His head dropped and he said, "Tea's fine, thank you."

I turned on the kettle and leaned against the counter, staring at him with a look of disgust. His eyes were bloodshot, his armpits stained, and I could smell his sour breath from ten feet away. Despite the suit, he looked like every garden variety drunk.

I cleared my throat and spoke firmly.

"I'm gonna ask you some questions. You're gonna answer."

He nodded in agreement.

"This ain't a joke. You'd be looking at a felony if it wasn't for me. You need a license to carry a pistol in Boston. You know that?"

"I wasn't—"

"Do you?!"

"Jody," he said, looking up. "It was a field issue. I've had it since the war. I leave it in the glove compartment. Cleveland's a dangerous place. What can I say?"

I walked over to the couch and sat at the far end.

"Why weren't you at the reunion? I was there. Why weren't you?"

When he chuckled, I could tell it was from nervousness.

"I got pinched. I was on my way. I swear."

"You got picked up at 10:00," I said, lighting a cigarette. "You missed the dinner. When were you gonna arrive, midnight?"

He shrugged his shoulders and hacked.

"I fucked up. *I'm* fucked up. I had a few drinks."

"A few? They said you were legless."

"No," he said, shaking his head. "It's not like that. Truth is I've been taking Benzo's."

"Benzodiazepine? For your drinking?"

"For lots of stuff. But yeah, drinking too. You see, it makes me nuts."

"It's supposed to do the opposite."

"It doesn't mix with booze. I know it. But I thought a couple of drinks would be fine."

I took a drag and handed him the cigarette.

"Thanks," he said humbly.

I let him smoke for a few minutes while I just observed. Kemp was beaten down, a broken man, with tired eyes and a furrowed forehead. Even in the dim light, I could see tiny scars from the shrapnel that had riddled his entire body. They were worst around his lip and nose, but his thick mustache covered it well.

"You remember Private Russo?" I asked.

"Of course. Al Rust we called him. Skin was the color of rust. Little Italian. Good kid. Good soldier."

"He's dead."

His face dropped.

"What? How?"

"He was shot last Friday night. Driving. He hit a pole. I was at the scene."

"My Lord," he said, rubbing his cheeks with both hands. "You two were buddies. Jody, I'm sorry."

"Remember Billy Minerva?"

"Minnow?" he said, and I nodded.

"He's dead too."

He handed me back the cigarette and I smoked it down to the filter.

"I got a call tonight—"

"The cops asked me where you were," he interrupted. "I told them. I hope you don't mind."

"It's okay. I'm glad you did. They found a body in a motel. I showed up at the scene, went to the room." His eyes beamed with a conflicted suspense, like he wanted to know but didn't. "It was Rodrigues. Shot in the face, right here." I put my finger above my left eye.

Kemp stared across the room with a stunned gaze, his red face now white. Learning that three former comrades had been murdered brought up more than just questions. It put the war once again at the forefront of our lives, a war we had spent years trying to forget. I wasn't mad at him any longer—I couldn't be. As the first sounds of the morning came through the window, we sat on the couch in a drowsy semi-haze and reflected on everything.

"Who would want this?" I asked him.

"I don't know."

"Would you tell me if you did?"

He hissed as if I had insulted him.

"Jody, we're brothers. I'd tell you anything. Think I'd let this happen?"

I didn't answer. I got up, walked over to the kitchen, and put my cup in the sink. I went into the bedroom to look for a pillow and blanket for him. I searched under a pile of laundry in the closet and found an old wool military blanket I had brought back from the service and never used. I didn't have an extra pillow, so I took a pillowcase and stuffed it with clean towels. When I came out of the bedroom, Kemp was lying on his side and fast asleep.

———

I DREAMT that night of Whiskey Point. I must have been sixteen years old because I was with my first girlfriend Margaret. We had met in the school cafeteria when I was a sophomore and she was a freshman. She had strawberry blonde hair that hung to her waist in ringlet curls. Her eyes were as big as her mouth was wide, and she had a dimple on her chin. She was the closest thing to perfect that I could have imagined at that age, and I asked her to marry me on the third date. She laughed but didn't decline, and for the rest of that summer, we spent every day together. We took the trolley to Carson Beach in South Boston—we walked hand in hand through Franklin Park. We had our first kiss behind the rectory at St. Joseph's—we skinny-dipped in Fort Point Channel.

In line with the coincidences that marked our friendship and lives together, Russo fell in love that summer too. She was a tall Greek girl, gangly but feminine, who always wore blue dresses and patent-leather shoes. She had long, straight hair and black eyes, blacker than I had ever seen. Her voice had a nasal drawl that sounded like she was talking through her nose. Her father owned a bakery on Blue Hill Avenue, and she worked after school behind the counter. Anyone else would have gotten fat off the donuts and cupcakes she brought him, but Russo still couldn't gain a pound.

By August, he and I decided we had both put in enough time to warrant more intimacy, and he suggested we get some liquor and take our girlfriends to Whiskey Point. In normal times, I would have thought it pointless because no girl that age was willing to lose her virginity on a rock. But that summer was different. With the German surrender in May and the Japs falling fast, a wonderful optimism was in the air and everything seemed possible. People smiled as if for the first time, and strangers said hello as they passed by on the streets. After four years and a half million dead, the Second World War was finally coming to an end.

Adults may have been anticipating the peace, but Al and I were looking forward to getting laid. It was a sunny Wednesday morning when we met the girls at the schoolyard and told them we were going on a picnic. Although it was eighty-five degrees out, Russo wore a long coat, and when I asked about the booze, he patted his sides and grinned. By the time we reached the dead-end street, he had already finished two bottles and was singing 'Ain't Nobody Here but Us Chickens.'

We helped the girls through the fence opening and the four of us started toward the cliff. Russo and I had been so many times by then that we knew the quickest route up, and we got there in ten minutes. Once on the clearing, he took out the beers and passed them around. The girls had never had alcohol before, and they were tipsy after the first one. Drunk and horny, we separated into couples and went to opposite sides of the rock. Margaret and I found a secluded spot behind a tree, where we cuddled clumsily on a bed of moss. Somewhere behind us Russo and the Greek were having an argument and he wasn't winning.

As Margaret sat admiring the view, I leaned forward and kissed her. Because she was receptive, I reached under her blouse and began to rub her breasts. She sat back with a groan, and I went to undo her skirt. Bang! A sharp crack sounded in the distance and echoed over the cliff. We both froze and she looked at me, drunk and disheveled, her blouse pulled up to her bra.

"What was that?" she said.

I heard footsteps and Russo came through the bushes.

"Jody, you hear that? Holy Christ. That's a gunshot. I know it. My dad's got a gun. I've heard it before."

As I got up, I could feel that I still had an erection.

"Calm down. It's a bottle rocket."

We heard a second crack and looked at one another nervously.

"Oh, man," he said, and he started to twitch. "That was definitely a gun. I'm telling you."

Margaret fixed her blouse and stood beside me, calm but concerned. The Greek came through the weeds with lipstick smeared across her mouth and burrs in her hair. We listened quietly, but the only sounds were the insects and the hot wind whooshing through the trees. I took Margaret's hand and told the others to follow, and we headed back to the path. The girls were too drunk to make it down the steep side, so we had to find a different way. With me in the lead, we trudged single file through the brush and eventually came to a gully. We went down it and up the other side, stopping to catch our breaths. When I pushed aside some ferns and looked ahead, I saw the old house we had stumbled upon two years before.

"I remember this place."

"Lovely house," Margaret said, and the Greek agreed.

"Brae, we gotta go," Russo said. "C'mon man, we gotta go. C'mon."

We heard the sound of breaking wood, but I couldn't tell where it was coming from. Margaret pointed and we saw someone squeezing out a narrow window on the third floor. Clutching the sill, he dropped his legs and hung suspended against the side of the house. When he turned his head, I recognized the boy who had tried to throw us off the cliff twice before.

"He's gonna get killed," the Greek said.

"Shhh."

"What the hell's he doing?" Russo wondered.

The boy looked side to side with panic in his eyes. The strain must have been too much because he started to flail. Without warning, he let go of the window and dropped twenty-five feet to the ground. His body hit like a sack of flour and I thought I felt the earth shake. The girls gasped—Russo's eyes popped open. But just when we thought we had witnessed a suicide, the boy stood up dazed. He crept to the corner of the house and glanced around to the front. Then he stepped back and hobbled toward an old shed a few yards away. He went behind it and disappeared.

"Quick, we gotta go," I said.

After what we had just witnessed, no one was ready to disagree. We walked back through the woods and fear must have sobered us up because we easily found our way to the street. When we got to the schoolyard, we kissed our girls goodbye and whispered small promises in their ears. For me and Russo, the fact that we didn't get lucky was overshadowed by the incident, and we talked about it for the rest of the way home.

The next day the second atomic bomb was dropped on Nagasaki, Japan. On the front pages of the Herald and Record American—below the broadsheet coverage of the catastrophic destruction—was an article about a double-murder in Roxbury. If it wasn't for the bombing, I wouldn't have read the newspaper, but I did, and when I saw the photograph of the house, I couldn't believe it. The report said that robbers had broken in and shot a mother and father to death, leaving their only son alive. Jewelry was taken, as well as other valuables and family heirlooms. According to police, the assailants had been camping out on the property, on a cliff that was a known hangout for drifters, criminals, and people of 'low moral character.'

If the event didn't traumatize the neighborhood, it was at least a source of intrigue. Old women gossiped about it on the sidewalks; in the barrooms, men speculated about who did it. A fundraiser was held for the boy; at mass, the priests said a prayer for the family, even though they were Protestants.

But in the end, it seemed that more outrage was directed at the cliff than at the murderers. There was talk of cutting back the trees so it couldn't be used as a hideout. A local politician even suggested sealing it off with barbed wire. For all those who ever despised the place, it was the perfect time to let it be known. So while the rest of the country was waiting for the war to end, residents of Roxbury were talking about Whiskey Point.

WHEN I WOKE up in the morning, Kemp was lying on his back and snoring like a grampus. Each time he breathed in, his top lip would vibrate and he exhaled with a boom. I made some tea, poured a bowl of cereal, and sat by the kitchen counter flipping through Life Magazine. The room was already starting to get hot, and I would have turned on the fan but didn't want to wake him. Suddenly, the phone rang, and I ran to the wall to get it.

"Hello," I said quietly.

"Detective, the captain needs to see us this morning."

Kemp grunted and I heard the couch creak. I pulled the phone cord into the bedroom and shut the door.

"What's up?"

"Not sure, but I'm leaving now. Want me to get you?"

"No. I gotta pick up Ruth tonight. I'll be there in a half."

I hung up and quickly got dressed. Before I left, I put a clean towel on the coffee table along with a five-dollar bill. On a napkin I had taken from the Lenox, I wrote that I could be reached at headquarters and left the number. Then I stood over Kemp, shook my head, and said goodbye, knowing that he probably wasn't listening.

The streets were calm for a Saturday morning, and I assumed most people had had enough of the city heat and were at the beach. When I got to headquarters, I found a spot by the front entrance. Inside the corridors were empty, the offices were locked, and most of the lights were off. A black janitor was running an electric polisher over the floor, and when I waved, he smiled. As I passed the evidence room, a patrolman came out carrying a box. I reached the end of the hallway and knocked on Jackson's door.

"Lieutenant, good morning."

The captain stood up when I entered, something he never did, and I could tell he was uneasy. Harrigan's expression was even more serious than it normally was, and it was the first time I had ever seen him without a suit jacket. Already I knew something was wrong and the meeting hadn't even begun.

"Please, sit," Jackson said, and I did. "Things have taken a turn." He held up a copy of the Record American and there on the front page were the words, SOLDIER KILLER. It wasn't the main article, but it was prominent, and the entire city would be demanding to know what the police department was doing about it.

"Have you said anything to the press?"

"No, nothing," I replied. "They were at the Hotel Holloway last night. Harrigan and I walked right by."

Jackson's white hair was a mess, and he paced back and forth behind the desk, rubbing his chin and forehead. He rarely sweated, but he was now, and the room temperature was nowhere near its afternoon high. He was so distressed he was making me anxious.

"Lieutenant," he said. "What happened to your friend Kemp last night?"

I looked first to Harrigan then said, "He...he had an accident."

The captain put his hands on his hips and looked straight at me.

"That's not all. Tell me what else."

"Uh, I don't know. He was drunk?"

"He had a gun, for Godsakes!" he said. "Don't beat around the bush!"

I look down in embarrassment.

"Yes, he did, sir. He had a service pistol in the car. He admitted as much."

"He told you that?"

"This morning."

Jackson glanced over to Harrigan.

"What do you mean this morning? He's in custody."

I planted my feet on the ground and braced for a lashing.

"Actually, I...I...I picked him up last night."

"You picked him up? Where is he? Where is he right now?!"

"At my house."

The captain turned to Harrigan and yelled, "Call the Chief! Tell him we need support. Three cars, at least. Go, now!" Harrigan got up, grabbed his briefcase, and left the room. I was so mixed up I didn't know whether to apologize, shut up, or jump out the window.

"Captain, I'm—"

"You shouldn't have done that," he said, pointing in my face. "You shouldn't have gotten him out. That's a gun charge; it's not just drunk driving. I'm sorry—you're out of line."

He went back behind the desk and sat down, shaking his head in exasperation. In all the years I'd worked for him, I had never seen him so angry.

"Lieutenant," he said. "You've gotta know you made a big mistake. Real big."

"I don't understand."

He finally steadied himself and looked across to me.

"Kemp was staying at the Hotel Holloway, in the room where they found Rodrigues."

CHAPTER 15

WE RACED TO MISSION HILL WITH ONE CRUISER AHEAD OF US AND TWO behind. Harrigan drove while I sat dumbfounded and staring out the window. I couldn't believe it—I couldn't accept that Kemp was involved. It was a situation every cop dreaded but few would encounter, when the personal and professional collide, and everyone was left reassessing their allegiances. As far as old friends went the only thing worse than finding one dead was arresting one for murder. My body swayed to the bumps and potholes of the road, and I must have looked bad because Harrigan said, "Detective, have a cigarette, please."

Chatter on the two-way called for any available officers in Roxbury to report to 121 Calumet Street for an apprehension. The suspect was possibly armed, the voice said, and might be dangerous, both of which I knew were untrue.

When we got to the top of the hill, the cruisers spread out and blocked off the street at both ends. Harrigan pulled over, slammed the shifter into park, and turned to me.

"You want to try to talk to him?"

I looked out to my building, up to the small top windows of my humble third-floor apartment. Then I looked back to him and said, "About what?"

He didn't ask a second time. He quickly jumped out and I did the same. Most of the officers were standing beside their patrol cars, waiting for instructions from either us or headquarters. As a matter of procedure, two men went down the side yard to cover the back door and fence.

Harrigan and I walked up the front steps, and he discreetly checked his .45 under his jacket. It was only when I was standing on the front porch that I realized all my neighbors were out. I saw the elderly couple next door, the four Boyle brothers across the street, the retired veteran a few doors down. Even the milkman, unable to get past the roadblock, parked his green truck and watched. I could only imagine the confusion of seeing a guy about to storm his own apartment.

I looked over to the officers, put up my thumb, and then reached for the door. Thankfully, I didn't have my gun out because the moment I opened it, Jeremiah appeared and made me flinch. He had on overalls but no shirt and his collar bone protruded like a broken stick. He held a broom in one hand and a hammer in the other, and I wondered what menial task required both. He wasn't surprised to see us, but when he saw all the cops, his face dropped.

"Sweet Jesus," he said, which with his brogue sounded more like 'sweetches.'

"Jerry. I need you to step out. Now, please."

He slammed the broom on the floor and cried, "This is my home! I won't be taken from it."

To many, his reaction may have seemed like melodrama, but considering Ireland's marred history of peasant evictions, it was understandable. When I looked at Harrigan, he was trying to conceal a smile. I lowered my voice and spoke in a frank but sympathetic tone.

"There might be a murderer upstairs. He might be armed."

Jerry's fleshy eyes widened, and he rested the broom against the wall.

"I think I'll go to the shop for milk," he said, and he skirted by us.

He was already past the threshold when he looked back and said, "And Brae?"

Harrigan and I turned.

"If you've time later, can you help change a bulb on the second floor?"

"Sure, Jerry," I said. "Go get your milk, okay?"

The old man gave a quick nod and left. Harrigan and I went up the staircase, treading lightly so we couldn't be heard. But the house was ancient and the wood brittle, and anywhere we stepped it creaked. If Kemp hadn't heard the commotion outside, I thought, he knew we were there now.

We came to the top landing and I faced the door. While Harrigan raised his pistol and got ready, I took out the key and gently slid it into the lock. I glanced beside to him and our eyes met in a silent countdown. Then I turned the knob and we burst in.

The anxious anticipation left me the second I saw that the room was empty. The cushions on the couch had been propped back in place and the ashtray was clean. When I walked over to the kitchen, the dishes were all washed and put away. In the hallway, I could feel the dampness from a shower, smell the cologne I always wore. I entered the bathroom and looked in the tub to confirm that it had been recently used.

I came back out and Harrigan was in my bedroom. I watched from the doorway as he searched the closet, the hamper, under the bed, and behind the dresser.

"Maybe he's in the top drawer," I said.

Harrigan frowned.

"I've seen stranger things, Detective."

Kemp was indeed gone and the apartment was spotless. He had even folded up the white towel he used to shower. I checked my valu-ables—a gold watch, three rings, a stack of war bonds, and my dog tags—all stowed in a tin on the bureau. The only thing missing or out of place was Kemp. Part of me was relieved he was gone, and it spared me the guilt of having to arrest a friend who I believed was innocent.

But the blame for his flight would fall on me because I had secured his release.

"You want to tell them or me?" Harrigan said.

"Maybe you should."

I locked the door and we walked down the stairs. As we came outside, someone must have cheered because the whole street erupted in applause. Not only was it unwarranted, but it was also the most absurd reception I had ever experienced as a cop, and I looked around to see if something had happened that I wasn't aware of. When it was obvious that we had nobody in custody, people stopped clapping, and I felt like a false hero.

I went over to one of the officers.

"All clear. There's no one here. You guys can go."

The cop turned around, waved to the others, and they started to get back in their cruisers. Harrigan walked over to the curb and explained to bystanders that there had been a mistake and that they were safe. Slowly the crowd began to disperse until only a few neighbors remained, gossiping on their porches. In the distance, Jerry was coming up the hill holding a large paper bag. As he got closer, I realized he had no shoes on. He walked by without looking at us and didn't even ask about the incident.

"Jerry, you see anyone leave my apartment?"

"I don't see much these days," he muttered as he went up the front stairs, "with me cataracts and all."

"Strange old mick," I said, but Harrigan was already in the car.

CHAPTER 16

BY THE TIME WE GOT BACK TO HEADQUARTERS, IT WAS EARLY afternoon. We parked out front, and I followed Harrigan toward the entrance with the heavy dread of a man going off to the gallows. Like always, he remained neutral about my situation, humble enough to know that violations of protocol or policy weren't his concern. But when we reached the steps, he stopped and turned to me.

"The captain is only concerned for the victims," he said. "It's not you."

"I don't need a pep talk."

"With respect, Detective, all I mean is don't take it too hard."

"What? Getting a censure or getting taken off the case?"

"The first wouldn't happen—the second wouldn't be the end of the world."

Two janitors, finished for the day, came through the doors, and we stayed quiet until they passed.

"If someone else gets whacked," I said, "and Kemp is charged, I'm in big trouble. I got him outta jail."

I could feel myself panicking, and I struggled to keep my voice down. Before he answered, Harrigan looked around the lot to make sure no one was listening.

"Look, you had no idea that was his hotel room. No idea. You didn't ask anyone to clear the charges—"

"But they did!"

"But you didn't ask anyone."

"I didn't have to. When a Detective asks for a friend who's been arrested, the favor is implied."

"The worst that will happen is the captain will take you off the case, until the heat dies down, until Kemp is caught."

"You mean framed?"

His face tensed up, and he took one step closer to me.

"You don't believe it's him?"

"I don't."

"You're willing to put yourself on the line?"

"I am."

Harrigan shook his head, knowing the investigation had just gotten far more complicated.

"I do hope you're correct."

Suddenly, the doors opened, and we looked up to see the captain. He didn't act surprised to see us, and he wasn't visibly upset. He came down the stairs and approached with casual indifference.

"That didn't come off very well now, did it?"

"No, Capt.," I said. "Not well at all."

The doors opened again and a maintenance worker came out to inspect a broken pane. A Sheriff's van pulled in the lot and backed into a spot. Two men in suits got out of a taxi. There was more activity in those few minutes than there had been all day, and Jackson seemed annoyed by it.

"This is like Fenway Park. Let's move."

He nodded and the three of us walked over to a fence that ran between the buildings. A single tree provided enough cover for privacy, and we gathered in a tight circle.

"We've gotta find Kemp. I don't care what we have to do," the captain said. "When's the veterans reunion?"

"Last night and tonight."

"Ok. I need you two to go tonight. I don't expect him to be there. But you never know, these types can be extremely cocky."

Harrigan glanced at me without Jackson seeing, but I looked away. It was an awkward moment, and I was vaguely ashamed for not telling the captain what I believed about Kemp. But now was not the time or the place, so I kept quiet and went along with the plan.

"Sniff around," he went on, covering his mouth with his hand. "See if anyone's heard from him. Make conversation, mingle."

"How do I explain him?" I said, nodding at Harrigan.

"Tell them he's your lover," Jackson said, and we all laughed. "I'll put out an alert at tonight's roll call. Everyone on the beat should be looking for him. We'll need a mug shot."

I cringed when I remembered that Kemp hadn't been photographed. After he was arrested, he mentioned that he was my friend, and the captain on duty refused to book him until he had talked with me. It was an honorable courtesy and something any cop would have done, but it left the procedure incomplete.

"I don't think we have one," I said, and the captain's expression changed.

"What do you mean we don't have one? He was arrested."

"They didn't book him. They kept him in protective custody."

Jackson grumbled, turned his back to us, and walked to the fence.

"This is an outrage, Lieutenant," he said, shaking his head.

I could no longer see his face, but I felt his frustration. He stood there for over a minute before coming back and saying, "But I don't blame you entirely..."

I wasn't absolved, but I breathed a little easier.

"...We're not gonna get anywhere saying a 6-foot white guy with bad teeth and a limp. We need a photo."

He was only giving an example, but the description was comically accurate. Something about the mention of teeth triggered a memory, and I recalled an old photograph of my platoon. In it, Kemp was leaning against a jeep with a broad smile, and his crystal-white teeth gleamed in the winter sun. It was one of a handful of pictures I brought back from Korea, and although it was an amateur shot, it might have been good enough for a wanted poster.

"Capt.," I said. "I have a photo. It's old, but I have one. In my office."

Harrigan gave me an approving nod, and Jackson thought about it for a moment.

"That may do," he said, peering down at his watch. "But it better be in my office in forty-five minutes. I'm going for a stroll."

With that, he walked off and headed out of the lot. Harrigan and I went into headquarters and the building was even quieter than it had been that morning. The few officials who worked on Saturdays were gone, home mowing their lawns, getting their grills ready. We walked by Jackson's office and turned a corner, where I counted off the rooms until we reached mine. The office came with my promotion, but I always forgot the number because I never used it.

I searched for the small brass key on my keychain and opened the door. Inside smelled like an old funeral home, and I could almost taste the mustiness in the air. The boxes I had brought there last fall were still scattered across the floor, stacked against the walls. If someone had accidentally come in, they might have thought it was a neglected storeroom.

As we entered, Harrigan looked at the chaos and winced.

"It's not pretty, I know."

"Pretty disorderly," he replied. "I thought you military men were meticulous."

"Meticulously messy."

He waited at the doorway while I moved boxes around to clear a path.

"Sit, please," I said, and he walked over to a leather chair beside my desk.

He watched with amusement as I tried to tidy up, but it would have taken a day to get the room clean and presentable. I picked up some old reports off the floor and put them in a metal file cabinet. In a Cold Duck wine box, I found a pile of framed citations and commendations that spanned my whole career. When I felt something soft under my foot, I glanced down to see a duffle bag from Korea, its faded canvas stamped in big black letters: JOSEPH H. BRAE. I recalled the meaningless initial a quick-fingered secretary had made in error while registering me at the Roxbury Home for Stray Boys. Somehow it had followed me throughout my life—from my first library card to my draft card—and was the only thing I had resembling a given name.

I searched through the boxes until I found the one with my service memorabilia. Inside it were Marine arm patches, enlistment records, a cracked compass, marching socks, and finally, a small brown envelope. I opened it up, took out some old photographs, and flipped through them. For years, those pictures sat in a footlocker in the basement of my apartment, and I hadn't seen them since I was a rookie. I almost thought the one I wanted was missing until I discovered it at the bottom of the pile. I held it up for Harrigan and he got up and came over.

"I can't believe it," he said, shaking his head.

"Now you know how I feel."

It was a grainy black & white, taken on a frigid autumn morning on the front line. My whole squad, eleven soldiers not counting the photographer, was leaning against a jeep smiling. Because we had just finished a makeshift game of football, most of the men wore t-shirts, and we were all sweating despite the cold. The ground was covered in snow, and in the background, the mountains went on forever.

"See anyone familiar? I asked softly, and Harrigan couldn't take his eyes off the picture.

"That's the man from the car accident."

It was comforting to hear him identify Al Russo, as if the mutual recognition meant a shared loss. I started to choke up when I saw that pint-sized Italian who was afraid of everything but would take on anything. He used to boast that growing up on Valentine Street predestined him for a long and steamy love life. He wasn't Casanova, but before we left for boot camp, he gave a charm bracelet to the Greek girl he had met in high school.

"Who else?" I asked. "Who else do you see?"

He put his finger on the photo.

"That's the man who was hit by the train, right?"

"Well, he was shot. But yeah, that's him. Billy Minerva. They called him 'minnow.' Good guy—simple guy. Liked his booze. Never thought he'd end up homeless."

"And…" Harrigan said. "Is that?"

"Doug Rodrigues," I said. "Man did his feet stink. I was dug in with him for three days once when we were expecting to get hit. Three days…in the cold. And I still almost passed out."

He laughed so hard I could see his teeth, which was a remarkable display of emotion for him.

"That's Paul Munch," I continued. "I saw him last night at the reunion. You might meet him tonight."

"I'd be honored, Detective," he said then asked, "Where's Travis Kemp?"

I pointed to the man in the center of the picture, the barrel-chested sergeant from East Cleveland. He was a born leader and a natural warrior, someone with such presence that others seemed to orbit around him. Kemp didn't really have a smile, but rather a slanted grin that made you think he was smiling. In the photo, his shirt was unbuttoned, and his sleeves were rolled up to reveal big biceps. He always had a tan, even during the most sun-deprived periods of our deployment, and his hair was perfect. He had a rare blend of confidence and charisma, and no one in our unit would have been surprised if he later became a Senator. It was one of the awful ironies of war, and of life, that someone with so much potential ended up a drunk.

"Let's get this to Jackson," I said, stuffing the photo in my pocket.

The captain was still out when we reached his office, so I left the picture on the desk with a note explaining which soldier was Kemp. It may have been old, but the likeness was clear enough, and most cops should have been able to make the connection.

As we exited the building, Harrigan put on sunglasses, and we stopped at the foot of the stairs to chat. Two Asian men carrying knapsacks came across the parking lot and asked us in broken english for directions to the State House. People visited Boston all year, but tourism peaked in the summer, and some days it felt like the city had more foreigners than locals. While I smoked a cigarette, Harrigan communicated with the men using hand signals and overemphasized words. They bowed with wide smiles and walked off.

"I don't think they understood a word I said."

"That's okay because neither did I."

Harrigan frowned and we went to get our cars.

"Those guys were probably shooting at me in the war," I said, but it wasn't out of resentment.

He reached the cruiser first, and I continued toward my own car, a few spots away. As I waved goodbye, he said, "At least over there you knew your enemy."

I opened the door and looked across at him.

"Ain't that the truth."

CHAPTER 17

WHEN I GOT TO BOSTON CITY HOSPITAL, I PARKED ON THE SIDE, IN THE cool shadow of the main building, and listened to the radio. Ruth's break was at five o'clock, and I wanted to surprise her by taking her to dinner. With twenty minutes to spare, I couldn't sit still, so I decided to go around back to the coroner.

No one knew Doctor Ansell's hours because he didn't post them. Yet he always seemed to be in the office, and I never knew a time he wasn't there. There were rumors he slept in the morgue, but knowing Ansell, he had probably started those himself.

When I came to the end of the dark hallway, I knocked twice and waited. A few seconds later the lock turned, and the door opened.

"Detective," the doctor said.

Dressed in a beige summer jacket and fedora, he looked like he was getting ready to leave. In one hand he had a black briefcase, in the other a fat cigar.

"Afternoon, doc," I said. "You busy?"

"Just heading out, but I've a few minutes. Come in."

When I stepped inside, the smoke hit my eyes and I blinked. We drifted toward the center of the room, where Ansell stopped and said, "What's up, kid?"

"First. Thanks for expediting the autopsy."

"I didn't expedite nothin'," he said.

"There's over a week wait time. I checked. You can deny it, but you did me a favor. You did the department a favor."

He thought for a moment then looked up at me.

"Some things are more important than other things. Some things have priority. I'm not sayin' some people are better or some are worse —although it could be true. I'm no judge. But I been in this business long enough to smell revenge."

The glasses magnified his eyes and seemed to increase the intensity of his words.

"Revenge is an awful smell," he went on, "a putrid smell. And comin' from me that's a lot. Look what I have to deal with." He swept his arm across the room, at the gurneys, instruments, implements, and jars of chemicals. "But what I mean, kid, is that it stinks."

"You know something I don't?"

"Not at all. Either we both see it or we both don't. Now, I'm no forensics kook and I'm certainly no sleuth, but come here."

He took me over to his desk and opened the top drawer. He reached under a mess of papers and took out a box. When he lifted the cover, a chill went up my back when I saw a small star attached to a red, white, and blue ribbon.

"The Bronze Star?"

He smiled humbly.

"That's right. My mother thought it was some deformed Star of David. But what'd she know? She was from Lithuania—God rest her soul. I was a combat medic in the war."

"I knew you were a veteran."

"In the big war. Not to say yours wasn't big—it made up for in valor what it lacked in scope. Believe me. I started in North Africa. Landed in Palermo, Anzio, right up the boot—got as far as Lucca. Fell in love with an Italian girl named Gianna." With the cigar between his teeth, he put both hands up to his chest and said, "Big tits, no brains. What a kvetch she turned out to be. But that's another story."

I touched the medal and said, "I never would've guessed."

He looked up with a grin and smacked my cheek playfully.

"Why? 'Cuz I'm short and ugly?—at least that's what my wife says. Hey, we ain't all beauties like you, kid. Believe me, I was there. I learned in three weeks—or one offensive, everything's measured by offensives—what I would've learned in four years of med school. Maybe that's why I became a pathologist, eh? At least here, I don't have to try to save 'em. They're already dead!" Ansell belly laughed and started to put the box away. "So why am I telling you all this?" he continued. "Maybe 'cuz I been around bodies all day and need someone to talk to? If not, it's because we know." He put his hand over his heart. "Only a soldier knows why another soldier dies." As he escorted me toward the door, I said, "You think you know something about the murders?"

"Me?" he scoffed. "No. I'm not a detective. But I'd be willing to bet you do." I was so stunned by his words that I couldn't respond. "If you wanna say goodbye to Rodrigues," he said, "he's in number 42. Keys are in the cabinet by the sink. Lock it when you're done. The front door will lock when you leave. Good luck, kid."

As I walked up the driveway to the main entrance of the hospital, I heard shouting and saw Ruth arguing with a taxi driver near the portico. A small crowd was watching, and I was surprised that hospital security hadn't shown up. I couldn't hear what they were saying, but the man was brazen enough to be in her face, pointing. Although I could feel my temper rising, I stayed cool and went toward them. When she saw me coming, she said, "Oh, Jody, thank God. Tell this jerk to move. He's blocking a wheelchair ramp."

I reached in my pocket and pulled out my badge, gritting my teeth and speaking in a low voice.

"Move the fuckin' vehicle."

Instantly, the man got in his car, started the engine, and drove off. He didn't have to leave the premises, but he did, and I watched as he exited the gate and disappeared into traffic.

"I'm sorry," Ruth said, pushing the bangs from her face. "They do this all the time, no one says anything."

"Don't be. You should've said something, everyone should."

Before I said another word, she locked her arms around my neck and kissed me. She must have lifted her legs too because I felt her entire weight and almost fell forward. I looked to my left and right, slightly embarrassed by the public affection. The front entrance was bustling with patients, nurses, visitors, and all the various employees it took to run a hospital. But the only person that noticed was an old woman with a cane, who looked over and winked affectionately.

"My, that was quite a reception."

"I missed you," she said. "I don't care who sees. Bunch of prudes, these people. They need a dose of lightheartedness."

"You might give them heart attacks instead."

"What are you doing here? This is a nice surprise."

"I was at headquarters earlier, then the Morgue. I figured I'd stop by."

"I'm glad you did. Where're you parked?"

I pointed to the side lot and we headed toward it. I took her hand and we strolled down a pathway and through a fence gate. When we got in the car, she pulled a clip out of her hair and shook her head until it was a bushy mess. She lowered the visor to check her makeup and found an eyelash out of place. As I backed out, she turned to me with puckered lips and said, "You seem tense."

"When am I not?"

"No, you seem extra tense. I could feel it on your lips. Why were you working today?"

"Where would you like to eat?"

"Does that mean you don't wanna talk about it?"

I smiled.

"It means I don't wanna talk about it *here*."

"You pick. I'll eat anywhere. I'm hungry."

I turned onto Harrison Avenue and aimed for downtown. With the radio on, we didn't speak, and I sensed a strange distance between us. She knew something was wrong, but she didn't know what, and I was reluctant to tell her about the case. It was the great dilemma of law enforcement: the people who could have provided the most emotional support were the same ones you wanted to shield from the horrors of the job.

When we reached Tremont Street, we looked across to the Boston Common and saw a clown on stilts striding over the cobblestone, looking for an audience. I beeped the horn and waved and he waved back with a sad smile. Ruth laughed and placed her hand on my leg, and I put my hand on top of it. I took the next right at Temple Place, a narrow lane of records stores, pawn shops, arcades, and eateries.

The workday was over for most and pedestrians scurried along the sidewalks and street, rushing to get home. I saw the sign for Joe & Nemo and was lucky to find a spot out front. The diner wasn't fancy, but it was fast, and Ruth had to be back in an hour. When we got out, she stood on the curb while I fished for a nickel and dropped it in the meter. I put my arm around her, and we walked inside.

We found an open booth overlooking the street, and she put her purse on the sill. The smell of roasted frankfurters, beans, and hot rolls was enough to make a fat man drool.

"I'm starved," she said.

A young woman in a blue apron came over with a notepad and asked for our order. The restaurant had only a dozen items, including drinks, and patrons were expected to know what they wanted. I ordered two hotdogs and Coca-Cola's, and the waitress left without saying thank you.

Before Ruth could speak, I blurted, "I've got problems."

She almost laughed until she realized I wasn't joking.

"What? What is it?"

I first looked around to make sure no one could overhear us.

"Remember the body that was found under the West 9th Street bridge Tuesday?" She nodded and I said, "It was another guy from my unit. Billy Minerva—'minnow' was his nickname. Shot in the head. Happened near the train yard. We think he must've stumbled onto the tracks and got hit."

Her mouth fell open and she leaned back in the booth.

"My God," she said, and I continued, "And then…and then last night—"

"You went to the reunion, I hope."

"I did. I got the call there. They found a body in a seedy hotel in the Combat Zone. Another guy I knew." My voice wavered, I looked down. "Rodrigues was his name. Doug Rodrigues."

She moved forward, slid her arms across the table. She tried to take my hands, but I wouldn't let her.

"I don't know what to say."

Her eyes began to tear up.

"There's not much to say."

"Who…I mean, why?"

"I've asked myself those questions. I don't know. It makes no sense. These guys are all in town for the reunion, I'm sure. It's too much of a coincidence to be a…coincidence."

She made a wry face.

"Is it an old grudge? A dispute? Something about the war?"

"You sound like Harrigan," I said, "and Doctor Ansell." I turned toward the window. "Everyone jumps to the past. I wanna believe it's about now, about the present. But I don't know." I tapped my fingers on the tabletop and sighed. "Part of me doesn't want to know. But I have to know. And we're gonna get the guy…"

The waitress walked up so I stopped talking. She put down a tray of food and drinks and left the bill on the table. I thanked her, and she swaggered back toward the kitchen.

"Were you good friends with these men?"

"None of us were *friends*," I said, and I may have been blunt. "I'm sorry, what I mean is in combat you're brothers, but not friends. It's different. It's hard to explain. Russo was a friend—that hurt the most. But that was different, we had known each other since first grade. That never changes. Minerva and the guy they found last night— Doug Rodrigues—we were tight, but that was years ago. It's doesn't make it easier." I rubbed my forehead and couldn't seem to sit still. "I don't know. I'm confused. Maybe I'm in shock."

I looked down at the hotdog, but I had no appetite, and even the smell of the food was revolting. "I've been trying to forget this shit for years. Now it's in my backyard. I should've taken Jackson's offer—"

"Which was?"

"Recuse myself from the case. To not even deal with it."

She reached for her Coca-Cola and took a sip. She put down the glass and looked me in the eye.

"Ever think there may be a reason this is happening?"

"Aw, Ruth, none of this astrological crap, please. I mean, I appreciate it, but I don't believe in fate or destiny or...what's that word the hippies use? Karma?"

I expected her to laugh but she didn't. She had already eaten most of her hotdog and her drink was finished. Someone else might have been offended, but I found comfort in knowing that she could eat despite my distress. She may have been wild and unpredictable on the surface, but deep down she was a rock, and that was why I loved her. When it came to the barbarity of living, she was more than tough— she was a survivor.

"Eat," she said. "You must..."

I picked up the hotdog reluctantly, taking a bite and chewing it out of habit and not desire.

"...You know this has to have something to do with the war..."

If anyone else in the world had tried to tell me about the war, I would have berated them. If it was a man, I might have punched his lights out. But she was my girlfriend and was probably right, so I shoved aside my pride and listened.

"...Can you think of anything?" she pressed. "Even the most absurd reason why a soldier would murder his fellows?"

"There may be. There're always reasons. Things happened during the war. They always do. But I—" My voice began to crack and taking a sip didn't help. "There's lots I can't remember. Months, in fact." She put her hands under her chin and squinted in curiosity. "I mean, there's lots that I do, of course. But even then, I was drunk a lot."

"Have you been checked for...stress...from the war?"

"You mean *battle fatigue*?" I said, and I could feel myself getting defensive. "No, absolutely not. I don't believe in it. I won't get checked for it. I came back in one piece—"

"That has nothing to do with it," she said firmly. "We're not talking about your anatomy. We're talking about your mind. When you say you don't remember, what exactly do you mean?"

"I mean, it's hard to remember. Some things are clear, others are not. It haunts me. When I think back, it hurts. I actually feel pain."

Ruth stopped to think and then asked, "So you remember, but it's difficult."

I nodded and leaned against the wall, running my hand through my hair, as confused as I was exasperated.

"It's…it's hard to explain," I said with a sigh.

"I'm sorry. I don't mean to be pushy. I'm just worried about you."

"Please, don't be. You're right. I know. I appreciate it. It's just that… this has all come back so quick. I didn't expect it."

Her foot found my leg under the table, and she began to rub my calf. She gazed at me with loving concern, and I started to get aroused. She may have been the only nurse to wear dark lipstick and mascara, and beneath her white uniform, I could see the faint outline of a lacy bra. If her seductiveness didn't save a few men's lives, I thought, then it certainly made their passing more pleasurable.

"Listen," I said. "I'm gonna be busy the next few days, maybe weeks."

"I understand," she said, her lashes fluttering. "But don't forget that Monday is your birthday."

"I forgot."

"I didn't."

"I might be working."

"I'll find you."

I looked down at the table, smiled bashfully.

"I hope so."

CHAPTER 18

I GOT TO THE LENOX AT 8:00 P.M. SHARP AND HARRIGAN WASN'T THERE.
I searched the lobby, the lounge, and even the restrooms, but couldn't
find him. I sat on a burgundy felt chair near the piano and smoked
three cigarettes. There must have been a wedding somewhere nearby
because a group of men wearing tuxedos and boutonnières came into
the lobby. They were laughing and half-drunk and one man took his
friend around the neck, made an inside joke. They were all in their
mid-twenties, and their rowdy camaraderie reminded me of when I,
too, was a yahoo. As a rookie, I hung around with two dozen other
young cops and we walked around like we owned the town.

"Detective?"

I looked over and Harrigan was coming toward me.

"About time."

"I couldn't find a spot."

I got up from the chair, smoothed out my jacket.

"Alright," I said. "Anyone asks, you're my date."

"I'm far too handsome for you, Detective."

We walked across the lobby and down the main hallway, and he
seemed impressed by the elegance of the décor, the gilded frescoes
and silk wallpaper, ornate mirrors and oil paintings.

"Tell me," he said. "Were there negroes in Korea?"

The question caught me off guard.

"What? Yeah. Mostly rear support, some combat units. They didn't end segregation 'til '51." I looked at him and said, "Just tell everyone you're a colonel. We never saw them anyway."

Across from the elevator bank, the doors to the banquet room were vibrating from the band music.

Harrigan whispered, "Are you armed?"

"Of course, but I don't think it matters. Kemp won't be here."

"You're sure of that?"

"Unless he wants to get caught. Ever meet a criminal who shows up where the cops are looking for him?"

"Only the dumb ones."

"Well," I said, reaching for the door handle. "That's not Kemp. Now smile, don't answer questions, and let me do the talking."

Inside the smoke was thick, but the crowd was smaller. Maybe, I thought, one night was enough, and some of the men realized how little they had in common with their old buddies. To be reacquainted with soldiers you had fought with brought up memories both tender and terrible. This wasn't a VFW birthday party in Tulsa—it was a major battalion reunion and something which had probably only taken place once or twice since the war.

As we stood in the doorway, everyone in the room seemed to turn and look. If I was self-conscious, I knew Harrigan must have been jumping out of his skin. We walked over to the bar and the bartender noticed me from the night before.

"Hiya," he said. "What can I get?"

"Soda water and lime," I said, and I turned to Harrigan, "Whaddya like?"

"Ginger ale, please."

"Wanna beer?"

"Thank you, ginger ale is fine."

With no other customers, the man got the drinks immediately and placed them in front of us.

"On the house," he said.

"You sure?"

"Cops drink for free, no hard stuff. My old man was a cop. Forty years on the force."

"What makes you think we're cops?"

"Well," he said, and he started to wipe down the bar, "Number one, your partner has a pistol." I looked at Harrigan and could see the holster hanging under his jacket. "Number two, your buddy was bragging about you last night. Couldn't shut up. He was drunker than a mule."

"Paul Munch?"

"I don't know his name. Big guy with a crew-cut, blonde hair. He had a little incident last night. Surprised you didn't hear about it."

I glanced at Harrigan, who was listening but pretending not to.

"An incident?" I said.

"He tried to hit someone. A captain or a lieutenant. He knocked over a table. Took five guys to hold him back. It was ugly. We don't usually see that kind of thing here."

"Did he get arrested?"

The man shrugged his shoulders.

"Not sure, he was removed anyway."

I took out my wallet and put a dollar tip on the counter.

"Thanks for the drinks."

As I went to leave, he added, "There's the man he went after."

He pointed to the far wall, where Lieutenant Goddard sat with some older men, probably other officers.

"Thanks."

"Anytime, Gentlemen."

Harrigan and I walked through the room, between the tables, and around chairs, and I nodded to men I didn't know. The band was playing a slow waltz, which was awkward for a party without females, and some drunks were dancing solo while their friends heckled from the sidelines. Someone touched my leg and I startled. When I turned around, I saw the smiling face of Private Daniel LeClaire and couldn't believe it.

"Danny," I said, and he got up from his chair. I went to shake his hand, but instead, he grabbed me in a hug.

"Oh, Christ," he said. "Brae, you have no idea..."

"Good to see you, Danny."

His eyes were teary, his face twitched with emotion. His speech was slurred, but it was sincere.

"I can't believe it, man. You look the same. What the hell you been eating?"

"You look the same too," I said, and I was lying. The only way I knew it was him was by the birthmark on his right temple. Otherwise, he looked seventy years old, and if I had passed him in the street, I would have thought he was someone's grandfather.

When I first met Danny LeClaire, he was a lanky redneck from Dallas, Georgia, with a thick drawl and a face full of acne. The men joked that he sounded like he had hot potatoes in his mouth. The only thing he ever drank was water and hard liquor, a taste he had acquired while helping his uncle work a moonshine still during the Depression. He could be restless and hot-tempered, but he was a first-class point man and a good soldier.

"How've you been?" I said.

He hiccupped and replied, "Still breathing. Could be worse. A whole lot worse."

I moved so Harrigan could come forward.

"This is my friend, Harrigan."

"My pleasure," LeClaire said with a bow, and they shook hands.

"Were you here last night?" I asked. "I didn't see you."

"I got here late, real late," he said. "I took the bus up yesterday morning and we broke down in Greensboro."

"Where're you staying?"

"Don't know the name. A little motel in Chinatown. Chinatown, can you believe it? I feel like I'm behind enemy lines."

He laughed out loud, hiccupping again, then wiping his nose. As he did, I noticed the three fingers he had lost to frostbite during the war.

I glanced at Harrigan and said to LeClaire, "Can we have a little chat?"

"Hell, we can have a long chat, brother."

We walked away from the table and to a quiet space near the doors. LeClaire was so drunk he stumbled and I caught him before he hit the wall. I lit a cigarette and offered him one, which he gladly took. We talked for a few minutes about mundane things as I waited for any curious eyes to stop looking.

"I heard Paul Munch had some trouble last night," I said, finally. "You know anything about it?"

He chuckled, raised his eyes.

"He tried to rip Goddard a new one. I can't say I wouldn't have wanted to see it neither."

"Yeah?" I said coolly. "Why is that?"

His face darkened, and I could tell that something troubled him. The blonde waitress passed by, and I called for her.

"Danny, let me get you a drink, for old time's sake."

"Double bourbon," he said, without blinking, "Any brand. Ice, too."

Once she left, I looked back to LeClaire but also felt someone staring. I peered over and my eyes swept the hall, from the bar to the dance floor to the empty tables near the stage. I didn't have to look that far, however, because I noticed Lieutenant Goddard gazing at us from the middle of the room. His eyes were sagging, but not because he was drunk, and he had the smooth grin of someone who suddenly remembers a joke from the past. The men at his table were too busy laughing and smoking to notice.

A couple of minutes later, the waitress returned with the drink, and I handed her a five. Harrigan took the glass off the tray and handed it to LeClaire, who toasted him in thanks. Then LeClaire took two slugs and left enough to sip on while we conversed.

"Tell me," I said. "What's Munch got against Goddard?"

"It ain't just Munch. It's us all."

An eerie tingle went up my back.

"How do you mean?"

"You know, Jody," he said. "You know what I mean."

His hiccups were gone, but he was drunker than drunk, and he began to sway the way people did before they fainted. I knew that if I didn't get him to talk now, he would be passed out in ten minutes. So I moved closer and cornered him against Harrigan.

"No, Danny, I don't know. I wanna know. I want you to tell me. What's he got against the Lieutenant?"

As I tried to catch his eye, he kept looking away, either too intoxicated to focus or reluctant to talk.

"No," he said. "I don't wanna…talk…about…it." His words came out in scattered bursts. "I'm here to…have fun…right? C'mon Jody, just forget it."

"No," I said, and I started to get angry. "I don't wanna forget anything. Tell me. What is it?"

Suddenly, I saw a hand on LeClaire's shoulder, and when I turned, it was Lieutenant Goddard.

"Catching up, Gentlemen?" he said.

I hadn't seen him in over a decade and he looked the same. His skin was clear, his hair full, and he hadn't gained a pound. The Boston accent that he had started to lose in the service was completely gone, and he could have passed for a Midwesterner. If we never liked each other, it was only because he didn't like anybody. Beneath the pretentious grin, I could detect a slight hostility, and I knew the conversation wasn't going to be cordial.

"Danny was saying the music's not loud enough."

Goddard chuckled and said, "He's just gotta clear the bullshit out of his ears, that's all." He looked at LeClaire then to me. "So, sergeant, I'm surprised to see you here."

"Wouldn't have missed it."

"I didn't think you left Roxbury. Are you still in the old neighborhood?"

"Not far. And you?"

He ignored my question.

"Who's your friend?" he said, looking at Harrigan with a phony smile. "I don't remember him from K Company."

"This is Detective Harrigan, BPD."

Goddard curled his lips down as if to say he wasn't impressed.

"Run along Danny, go mix," he said.

LeClaire responded like it was an order, and Goddard watched him as he stumbled back over to the bar for another drink.

"Boy's got troubles," he mused. "Damn war may not have killed us, but it's wounding us every single day." His expression changed and he looked up at me.

"You're a cop?" he asked.

I nodded.

"On duty?"

"I'm always on duty."

Harrigan stood with his arms crossed and an icy expression. I felt the tension growing between me and Goddard and didn't know why. I may have feigned respect for him in Korea when he was an officer and I was an NCO, but I wouldn't pretend to like him now.

"What business do you have here?" Goddard said, crossing the line from tacit scorn to contempt. Inside I was fuming, but I stayed composed because I didn't want to ruin the evening.

"My business is my business."

"Big man now, eh?" he said, taunting me with a smirk. "Big man with a badge? You weren't a big man over there."

"That's history—" I said, and I almost made the mistake of calling him 'lieutenant.' "This ain't Korea."

"You're wrong. This is Korea. Look around." He swept his arm across the room. "It was the high point of their lives. Everything since has been downhill. Drunks, gamblers, derelicts, failures. We may have won the war, but we lost our souls, brother."

I shook my head and refused to look at him.

"You may've lost yours. Speak for yourself. Or can't you do that?"

He moved toward me, close enough that I could smell his cologne and it was cheap. He stared at me with his blue, robotic eyes and said, "Now why don't you run along and leave these men to their misery. Go catch a thief." When I snickered, he leaned in closer, whispered in my ear. "And take the nigger with you."

The first punch landed so hard it made a loud crack, and I wasn't sure if it was his skull or my knuckle that broke. Goddard fell against a table, and glasses and silverware went flying. I grabbed his tie, pulled him toward me, and swung wildly. The band stopped and men rushed over to break it up. Two large hands took me under the ribcage and yanked me away, and when I looked back it was Harrigan. With my arms subdued, I started to kick, and my shoe slipped off and hit Goddard in the eye. For a split second, everyone around us stopped as if astonished by the lucky shot. The commotion resumed but the fight was already over, and a half-dozen men were separating us.

When I calmed down, Harrigan let me out of the arm lock, and I asked someone for water. Goddard straightened out his uniform and walked back to his table, where four or five cronies patted him on the back, asked if he was alright. Two hotel employees burst into the room too late and were quickly assured that everything was under control.

"Detective," Harrigan said. "Let's go for a walk. Please, let's go. Now."

I was ramped up from the excitement; the adrenaline made me jittery. When I looked across the room, I saw Goddard holding a napkin to his nose. He was laughing and joking with the other men, and someone handed him a cocktail like it was a prize for second place. He hadn't even got a punch in, which was unusual because he had a longer reach.

The band began playing, and the room started to sound like a celebration again. While one custodian fixed the table, another swept glass off the floor. Someone I didn't know gave me my shoe and shook my hand. I tried to dally, but Harrigan ushered me into the hallway, and we headed toward the lobby. I must have looked upset because as we passed the lounge some younger women looked over curiously. I adjusted my tie, straightened out my jacket, and went out the exit door.

I got to the sidewalk before Harrigan and took out a cigarette. When I couldn't find a match, the bellhop stepped over and held out a brass lighter.

"Thanks, pal," I said, and he nodded.

Harrigan walked up behind me, and I mumbled, "Sorry."

"Don't be."

I took a puff and turned around.

"That goes way back. I've wanted to do that since the war. Since the first day I met him. I shouldn't have dragged you into it. And I shouldn't have made a scene. I feel like a rat."

We walked to the corner, and I leaned against a light pole. He let me simmer for a few minutes and didn't say anything. I had another cigarette and stared out on all the activity along Boylston Street. Across the street, a group of sailors whistled at a lady on the corner, who giggled then lifted her dress above her thigh. In front of a cigar shop, a black boy squatted on a shoeshine kit with his chin between his hands as if praying for a customer. On the next block, a huckster sat on a mailbox, challenging passersby to a shell game. When someone yelled no, he danced a silly jig, and everyone broke out in laughter.

The city was a circus of nightlife as the young and unmarried ventured out for love, lust, liquor, or some combination of the three. There was an astonishing civility that made me wonder what I had been missing all along. I was born in the slums and worked in the ghettos and rarely got to see all the prettiness of downtown revelry.

"Where was all this when we were young?" I said.

"It was here. Always has been, always will be."

I shook my head, looked down at the curb.

"I was sittin' in a foxhole when I was their age. What a waste."

"You don't really believe that."

"I don't know what I believe."

I blew out some smoke and turned to him.

"Know what I believe? I believe I just made a fool of myself."

"And you know what I believe," Harrigan said, "I believe most of the men in that room wanted to see it happen. Even the men sitting with Goddard. They don't like him—they fear him. You can see it."

"Maybe," I said, spitting into the gutter. "I just don't know what his problem is."

"He's an arrogant man. Very arrogant."

"He always was, even as kids. One of the most arrogant bastards you'd ever meet."

I felt drops on my arm and it began to sprinkle. Fearing a downpour, people started to run for cover, and I watched a group of young women duck into a bar holding purses over their heads.

"You knew him as a boy?"

I nodded and took a final puff before the cigarette got wet.

"All my life," I said. "All my goddamn life."

CHAPTER 19

AL RUSSO AND I ENLISTED IN THE MARINES ON APRIL 1ST—APRIL Fool's Day—of 1950. At the time we were both working nights in a seafood processing plant in South Boston, a job Al's father had gotten us because he knew the foreman. Although it was temporary, we enjoyed the freedom of a paycheck and few responsibilities. I had my sights set on the Boston Police exam in September, and Russo was considering careers that ranged from plumbing to door-to-door vacuum sales. We were twenty years old, with futures as bright as they were uncertain, and we were limited only by the whims of our imagination.

A week after our high school graduation, I said farewell to everyone at the Home—the children, the matrons, the kitchen staff, and even the groundskeepers. With the money we had saved from working at Flanagan's during our teenage years, Russo and I moved into a second-floor apartment above a tailor shop on Washington Street. We may have had our independence, but we had to earn it. And six evenings a week, including holidays, we walked to the corner to catch the bus to work. He carried his work smock in a bag, and I wore mine beneath my jacket. Because we always smelled like fish, passengers would wince and sometimes change seats.

Remnants of snow were still on the ground that spring night when Russo made the announcement that would forever change our lives. We had spent the day in Franklin Park, drinking with some unemployed veterans and playing punchball. As the bus rumbled toward Dudley Square, I sat slumped in the seat with my arms crossed and legs apart. My head throbbed; my mouth was bone dry.

"I'm going down to the recruiter tomorrow."

When he spoke, I was too groggy to listen. At the next stop, he nudged me with his elbow and repeated himself.

"I said I'm going to the recruiter—tomorrow."

I yawned and turned to him.

"What recruiter?"

"U.S. Marines, at South Station. I'm signing up. There's gonna be a war in Korea. I ain't getting drafted."

"Marines?"

"Tomorrow. I'm enlisting."

I sat straight up and looked at him. Despite the hangover, I was now alert.

"You are?"

"Wanna go?"

Instead of replying, I turned and gazed dreamily out the window. There I looked out to Roxbury, that vast country within a city whose buildings and streets bespoke the disillusionment of so many immigrant tribes. It wasn't a place of broken promises because there were none, and even with the arrival of spring, a permanent gloom hung over everything. I may have loved the place, but I didn't like it.

"Yeah," I said. "I wanna go."

He smiled wider than I had ever seen him smile before. He grabbed my hand and shook it until the bus stopped and the doors opened. When I stepped off at Dudley Square, I felt like I had been reborn. Work that night seemed less grueling, and I was inspired by a new purpose that made everything possible.

Early the next morning, still smelling of swordfish and Schlitz, we missed the bus and decided to walk to South Station. The recruitment office already had a small crowd, and we waited in line for over an hour. When we finally made it to the front, a bad-tempered corporal checked our paperwork and told us to wait in another line for a medical examination. The physician overlooked Russo's scoliosis and my flat feet, and by midafternoon we were cleared for service. With orders to show up in two weeks, we left South Station and wandered the streets of Boston looking for a barroom.

What started as a cold beer turned into a three-day bender. Monday morning, Russo and I awoke on a Dorchester beach beside two traveling nurses we met in the subway. Memories of that weekend were a vague patchwork of scenes and situations, and the only thing I knew for sure was that I had spent all my savings.

In the ensuing days, we canceled our lease, quit our jobs at the factory, and said goodbye to friends. Anything of value I kept at Russo's parents' house in a lockbox under his bed. We weren't the only two young men from Roxbury to enlist, and every day we heard of someone else going off to boot camp. It was an exciting time—at least for us—and although people didn't have the same flag-waving enthusiasm of the last war, they treated us with respect.

Two nights before we left for Parris Island, Russo and I went one last time to Whiskey Point. No longer children, we bought beers at the corner market and walked through the streets, drinking openly. When we got to the woods, my boots were soaked from the springtime slush, and Al had torn his jacket. But nothing seemed to bother us, and when I fell over while taking a piss, we both laughed. Enlisting was our first foray into manhood, and we were as drunk from pride as we were from booze. And although we had no concept of the horrors we would later endure, we imagined ourselves as soon-to-be heroes.

When we came to the top of the rock, we discovered that we weren't the only ones celebrating. A dozen or so other young men were standing around a fire, smoking cigarettes and drinking Ballantine Ale. Some were familiar and others were strangers, but they invited us to join them, so we did. With many of them also leaving for boot camp, it was our first taste of camaraderie and we hadn't even held a rifle.

More and more people arrived, climbing over the ledge and

appearing from the trees carrying crates of beer and liquor. There was a strange peace, as groups and gangs, many of them rivals, coalesced in a neighborhood-wide farewell. Fat cigars were passed around—someone even had marijuana, which few of us had ever seen. We sang patriotic songs, sentimental ballads, told dirty jokes. What had begun as a small gathering turned into a rowdy bash, and by midnight the hooting and hollering could be heard for miles.

The temperature plummeted, and even with the alcohol, I began to shiver. I called to Russo, and we went over to the bonfire to get warm. I heard a distinctive voice and looked to see a young man in a service uniform. He was clean-shaven and handsome, with straight blonde hair and white teeth that sparkled in the moonlight. It took a moment for my eyes to adjust, but when they did, I realized it was the boy who had bullied us years before.

He was surrounded by his cronies, street thugs and petty criminals. With square jaws and thick necks, they had that dangerous combination of no brains and no fear. One had a mark on his knuckle that looked like a prison tattoo. I recognized another as the doorman at a private gambling joint on Seaver Street. To leave would have been too obvious, so I stayed low and avoided eye contact.

"Always salute the rank above you, never look down to a Colonel, even if you're taller than him…"

As the soldier bragged on, I heard some oohs and aahs, but not everyone was impressed.

"…when they assign you boots, make damn sure they fit. Don't volunteer for anything, and never smile…"

To my left was Russo, drunk and swaying with a mischievous grin. I wanted to nudge him and tell him to behave, but he was just beyond my reach.

"…If we get into it with the chinks," the young man went on, "it's gonna be a nasty war. We can handle the gooks, not the chinks, no way…" He guzzled some beer and said, "You boys have any questions?"

"Wasn't it gooks who killed your parents?"

Everyone was quiet. Whoever asked must have been fearsome

because the soldier was humiliated, but he didn't strike back. Instead, he stared into the flames with a bitter gaze.

"That's right," he said. "It was. So I've as much at stake in this war as anybody. I'll get my revenge, as much as Uncle Sam will get his victory. Now, any more questions? I'm off to Pendleton in the morning."

When Russo raised his hand, I tried to stop him, but it was too late.

"You know the motto of the Greek army?"

The young man frowned and looked at his henchmen, who were equally stumped. The question was so bizarre that no one knew whether it was serious or a joke. Before the soldier could respond, Russo answered for him.

"Never leave your *buddy's* behind."

I cringed. A few of the guys in the crowd laughed, but the young man and his gang were furious. They all looked over and one of them barked, "Think you're a comedian, you little guinea?!"

He flicked a cigarette and Russo jumped out of the way. Suddenly, a bottle flew toward us across the fire. It spun in the air and went off course, hitting someone next to me in the head.

"Ow, you son of a bitch!"

Holding his head, the victim flexed his arms and sneered, and at that moment, I knew there would be a brawl. Everyone eyed everyone else, assessing their loyalties and planning who they were going after first. Just before it happened, I grabbed Russo by the collar and pulled him away. Then all hell broke loose.

As we scurried across the clearing, we heard shouting, groans, the smack of fists, bottles breaking. The temporary truce was over. I helped Russo over the ledge and we disappeared into the shadows. We crawled down the hill on our hands and knees, and by the time we reached the bottom, we were covered in mud. We made it through the fence and staggered down the street, drunk, filthy, and smelling of smoke. It was early spring, but the chill of winter was still in the air and my hands were numb. In the distance, the noise on the cliff, faint but clear, broke the silence of the night.

"That was close," Russo mumbled.

I stopped and spun around.

"Shut up!"

"Wha—?"

"You gotta big mouth!" I exclaimed.

I shoved him in the chest, and he stumbled backward, catching himself before he hit the curb. He shook off the surprise, wiped his nose, and looked up. In a move I never would have expected, he charged straight at me. I skirted to the side, pushed him away, and he fell smack on the pavement. He got up, stunned and panting, and came at me again, this time swinging. I dodged his drunken punches then wound up and cracked him in the nose.

"Ah, fuck, Jesus, Jody!" he cried, blood dripping down his mouth.

Even though he was hurt, he still hadn't had enough, and he rushed at me a third time. I grabbed one of his forearms and twisted it around and jabbed him in the teeth. His eyes gyrated, his body wobbled, and he fell forward into my arms.

"Jody, I'm sorry," he gushed.

"Shut up."

A neighbor must have heard the commotion because a front porch light went on. I told Russo to put his arm over my shoulder, and I carried him up the street.

"Jody, what are those lights?"

"Those are stars, you idiot."

"Oh."

CHAPTER 20

I AWOKE TO THE SOUND OF RAINDROPS AND THEY WEREN'T OUTSIDE. AS I
sat up in the bed, I saw water sheeting down the wall and a puddle in
the corner by the radiator. The house was old and neglected, so every
storm seemed to reveal a new leak, and it was usually in my apartment because I was on the top floor. Jeremiah did his best to maintain
the property, but an elderly man on a pension was no match for a
wooden structure on a hill in the brutal New England climate.

I took a dirty towel from the hamper, tossed it on the puddle, and
went to the kitchen. I made tea and toast and turned on the television
to catch the news. I had only taken one bite when the anchorman
announced a follow-up to the story about the veterans murders. I
almost choked when the grainy black & white of Kemp flashed across
the screen.

Suddenly, the phone rang. I jumped up from the couch and ran to
the wall.

"Hello?"

"Detective, emergency meeting with the captain. He told me to
call."

"What time?"

"Now," Harrigan said. "Or sooner."

Ten minutes later, I barreled into the lot at headquarters and skidded to a stop. When I got to the office, I heard the captain and Harrigan talking with someone. I pushed the door open, and Officer Suliman was standing beside the desk.

"Lieutenant," Jackson said. "Thank god you're here. Come."

When he waved for me to enter, I took a seat next to Harrigan, and everyone looked like they had just been awoken from a sound sleep. The captain wore a blazer and no tie, Sully's uniform shirt was untucked, and even Harrigan looked somehow disheveled, although I couldn't figure out how.

"Morning Sully," I said.

"No church today, after all, Brae?"

"Someone's going to hell—but it's not me."

The captain cleared his throat to interrupt the banter.

"Officer Suliman has been kind enough to join us this morning," he said. "He's the point man for any backup we'll need in the case. I've made him privy to the details."

Jackson adjusted his glasses and reached for a notepad.

"I got a call yesterday. Someone at the Department Of Justice."

"Washington?"

"That's right. Now..." the captain said, and he looked past me. "Will someone please get the door?" Sully went over and closed it, and he continued. "Apparently Travis Kemp sent them a threatening letter, arrived early last week. It went up the chain of command, as you can imagine, before someone decided to act on it."

Harrigan and I leaned forward at the same time, fraught with anticipation, wanting to know more. I peered over to Sully and he raised his eyebrows.

"It was rambling, at times incoherent. In short, he said he was going to Boston to get justice—"

"Justice for what?"

Jackson put down the notebook and spoke calmly.

"They don't know exactly. An incident."

"An incident?"

"Something that happened in the war. In the letter, he calls it a 'bloodletting.' The man I spoke with was a clerk. He said he would get more info when they open tomorrow morning."

I sat in the chair, deflated and confused, staring at the wall behind Jackson. I didn't look over to Harrigan and Sully, but I could feel them watching me. My stomach gurgled and I couldn't think straight. The wall clock struck eleven.

"Lieutenant," Jackson said, taking off his glasses.

"Sir?"

"Any idea what this is about?"

I listened to the rain outside and my mind drifted. I saw the Korean mountains—snow-covered and lovely—looming at the horizon of my memories. Those days of endless routine, broken only by the chaos of combat, were a long string of indistinguishable moments. Whenever I tried to put them in order, to apply some kind of chronology, they only became more muddled.

"I'm not sure."

Harrigan and Sully looked at each other, puzzled by the response.

"I'm sorry," the captain said, "but that's not an answer."

"There's a lot I don't remember."

He paused and wiped his eyes, as frustrated as an interrogator with a stubborn suspect.

"Can you try, Lieutenant? Did anything unseemly take place during your tenure?"

I laughed inside when he called my tour of duty a *tenure*, and it was another example of how little he understood about the military and its jargon.

"My *tour* was fifteen months, sir. A lot happened. I need more information. Facts, time frame, nature of the incident. Who was harmed, who was hurt, who saw it, and who didn't. For all I know, someone could've beat up a friend of his. Some privates could've assaulted a guy on the line. Things got tense, maybe Kemp snapped. Over there, the smallest slights could turn into big feuds. I've seen it happen. If he needed a reason, he could find it. There were plenty."

I said so much so fast that I was winded. Harrigan seemed relieved that I had been honest, but Sully just looked confused. Jackson sat thinking with his hand over his forehead, and, after a long minute of silence, he finally turned to Sully.

"Sergeant, thanks for your participation. We'll be in contact, soon."

Sully tipped his cap and walked quietly out of the room. When the door closed, the captain stood up and crossed his arms.

"Lieutenant," he said. "I didn't want Officer Suliman present when I said this."

"Sir?"

"We got a call last night. A man by the name of Goddard. He said you assaulted him at the Lenox Hotel. He'll be filing charges when the courthouse opens in the morning."

"That son of a bitch," I said under my breath.

"Speak openly goddammit!"

"I'm sorry. I said *that son of a*—"

"I heard what you said."

He walked around the desk and came over to me.

"Is that true? Did you hit him?"

I glanced aside to Harrigan.

"A couple times," I said hesitantly.

"A couple times? Well, he's got a broken nose, lacerations, possible cheek fracture. We've got a murderer on the loose and now I have to deal with police brutality?"

He threw his hands in the air and shouted, "For Chrissakes, Lieutenant! You're in enough hot water with—"

"The man called me a nigger, sir."

The captain froze and looked at Harrigan. All at once, his anger was replaced by a new rage, and one that wasn't directed at me. He ran his fingers through his hair, breathed deep, and said, "Is that true?"

We didn't have to reply because our mutual nods were confirmation enough.

"No one calls my detectives such rubbish. I'm sorry."

I had never heard him apologize before, and it probably meant more to Harrigan than it did to me. The tension in the room subsided, and Jackson lowered his voice.

"Forget it, Lieutenant. Forget everything I just said. If this escalates, we'll come up with a strategy, a defense. I'll say you were off duty, that's a start. Maybe Goddard will back off. But don't worry about it, focus on the case. You did the right thing."

He walked back behind the desk and said, "So what happened? How'd it get to that?"

"Goddard was the head of my platoon, a lieutenant—"

"Then you two have something in common."

"Hardly," I said. "The ranks don't equate."

It was the second time the captain had shown his ignorance about military matters, and I could see he was embarrassed.

"But we did grow up together," I added. "I've known him most of my life. A real prick. What's worse, he was an officer. He went to officer candidates school after college."

"Why was he a prick?"

"He was an awful lieutenant, full of himself, a real dandy. On patrol, he was the last in line. He miscalculated distances. One night, we almost walked into a KPA position after he ordered us down the wrong path. He was a spoiled brat."

"Spoiled brat, from Roxbury? Hard to imagine."

I chuckled and said, "His folks had money, they owned land. They were an odd bunch, real eccentric. Lived in an old house behind Whiskey Point."

"Why was he at the reunion if he wasn't liked?"

"Arrogance, most likely. It wasn't that he wasn't liked, he wasn't respected. At least among the non-coms. Some of the privates were too green to know. Goddard had his cohorts, like any rat."

"Well," the captain said. "It's not him I'm concerned with now. If those charges stick, we'll deal with it." He looked down at the desk, shuffled some papers around. "I've contacted the Cleveland police, to let them know. We wanna make sure Kemp doesn't run home. As for here, we've got every cop on the alert."

"I saw the photo on the news," I said.

Harrigan must not have known because he looked surprised.

"I had to do it," Jackson said. "I had no choice. The press is no friend of ours, I know, but sometimes they can be useful idiots."

He opened his top drawer, took out a brown envelope, and slid it across the desk.

"Here's the original. Thank you."

"I don't think it'll help," I said, putting it in my coat.

"Pardon?"

"The picture of Kemp. I don't think it'll help."

Harrigan looked over apprehensively. Even in his silence, I could feel him urging me to shut up.

"I don't follow," the captain said. "Why? You think the photo is too old?"

"No, because Kemp couldn't have killed anybody."

I DIDN'T WANT to say it, but I had to be honest and sometimes honesty was a risk. In any criminal case, there had to be complete agreement, if not in fact, then at least in principle. Otherwise, every detective would pursue his own quack theories, and everyone would go off in different directions. Considering the evidence, my opinion was like investigative heresy. But I sincerely believed it.

At that moment, the only thing which could have saved me from a dispute with Jackson was the report of another murder. And it happened. The phone rang and he picked up. He had a short conversation in which he listened and nodded but didn't say much. When he hung up, his face was a shade paler, and he had entirely forgotten my previous statement.

"Take your things, Gentlemen," he said, getting up. "We've got another body."

We hurried down the hallway and out the front doors, where we ran across the parking lot in the rain. Harrigan and I got into my car, and the captain took his own. I turned on the sirens and we raced down Beacon Street toward the South End. Streets that were normally quiet on Sunday were made barren by the storm, and we got to the scene in five minutes. As we turned onto East Berkley Street, I could see police cars and an ambulance in the distance. The medical examiner had already arrived, and I pulled up behind the van.

We got out and went toward three cops who were standing by an alleyway in blue parkas. A small crowd of residents had gathered on the sidewalk, holding umbrellas and watching curiously. Some wore sleepwear under their overcoats—others looked like they had just left church.

"Gentlemen," I said as I passed the officers.

When they saw the captain, they stood up straight and tried to look professional.

"Watch your step," one of them said.

We turned into the alleyway, a narrow corridor that ran along the backs of the brick townhouses and ended at the next street. Beyond we saw the victim, lying on dirty cobblestone with a wet sheet over him. The three of us walked toward the body, stepping over potholes and crevices filled with muddy water. Gutters overflowed; drainpipes were gushing.

As we approached, Doctor Ansell and an assistant were crouched over the corpse in trench coats. Two paramedics stood under an overhang, chatting quietly and waiting for permission to take the body.

"Doctor," I said. "I didn't know you work Sundays."

He craned his neck.

"I'm a Jew for Chrissakes. It's Saturdays I don't work."

"But you worked yesterday."

"Talk to my Rabbi, kid."

"Who reported this?" Jackson asked.

"Not my job," Ansell said. "Check with your people."

The doctor treated everyone with the same contempt, regardless of rank or status, and sometimes it created an awkward tension. I had seen him insult senior officers, berate officials, and mock DAs. When, a few years back, the FBI was working with us to investigate some gangland murders, Ansell told them they were *Full Blown Idiots*. Because he had witnessed so much savagery in the war, he viewed manners and decorum as absurd human pretensions. And although he may have been gruff, he was a true democrat, which meant that he would talk to a prince the same way as a pauper.

I leaned over his shoulder and watched him work. The victim's face was covered, but his left arm was exposed, and Ansell was taking blood. He must have sensed my presence because he looked back and said, "Listen, kid. I'll do my work, you do yours."

"I thought I was."

He huffed and shook his head. I backed away and went under a doorway, where I reached in my coat for a cigarette. Harrigan was walking back and forth, scanning the ground for clues, unimpeded by the rain. I had just lit a match when the doctor whistled for the paramedics, signaling that he was done. As I went over to the body, he got in my way.

"Wanna save yourself some nightmares?"

"Too late for that."

"Don't look. You seen one, you seen 'em all. I have his identity, that's enough. Give yourself a break. It's Sunday."

Harrigan came up and stood beside us.

"What's the method?" I said.

"Same as before, kid. Same as before. Back of the head. Bang! One shot."

I put my hands on my hips and sighed.

"Would I recognize him?"

"Maybe, maybe not. Pretty swollen. He's been sittin' for a while."

I thought back to Russo, Minerva, and Rodrigues. Maybe I didn't have to look. After seeing one, the rest was just morbid self-indulgence, and why add another grisly memory to a mind that was full of them. As Ansell stood looking up at me through his wet glasses, I stared over at the anonymous victim. The paramedics had him on a stretcher and were waiting for me to decide before leaving.

"You know who it is?"

"I do," the doctor said.

"You sure?"

"I have his wallet, his license."

I waved to the paramedics and they lifted the stretcher and headed to the ambulance. I looked at Ansell, waiting for the answer and at the same time not wanting to know. I listened to the raindrops tapping on the roofs and porches and thought of all the funerals I had ever attended. For some reason, it always rained during funerals, and the dismal gloom seemed to reflect the great tragedy of human suffering. It never made me sad, but it always made me wonder.

With the paramedics gone and everyone else beyond earshot, Ansell was finally ready to tell me.

"Paul H. Munch."

CHAPTER 21

IF THE HOTEL HOLLOWAY WAS SEEDY AT NIGHT, IT LOOKED SINISTER IN the gray haze of the drizzly afternoon. The stone exterior was cracked and crumbling in parts; the window frames were all rotted. The old gutters were splintered, and dirty rainwater splashed onto the street below. Like most buildings in the Combat Zone, it was dilapidated and probably would have collapsed had it not been attached to the adjacent structures.

Harrigan parked in front of a hydrant and we got out. Without the neon of the sex shops and burlesques, the street had a pitiful squalor. Some businesses were open, but many were not, and the only people hanging around were vagrants, drifters, and a few hookers.

We walked to the entrance of the Holloway and I opened the door. In the small lobby, a black transvestite was filing his or her nails on a stained settee. To the right, the red-headed clerk from the night of the murder was sitting behind the counter reading a copy of Worlds of Tomorrow. The moment he saw us, he put down the magazine and got up.

"Morning officers," he said.

"We've got some questions."

"Sure, I'll try to help."

I hesitated and looked at the person on the settee. Harrigan walked over, politely showed his badge, and the patron went up the stairs.

"You gave information on the occupant of the room Friday night?"

"Yes," he said. "From the ledger. I showed them it. Travis Camp or something."

I leaned over the counter and stared at the young man. Seated on a stool, he tilted back and the wood creaked. I could tell he was scared so I reassured him with a formal smile.

"Were you working the night he checked in?" I asked.

"Yeah, yeah, I checked him in."

"Did you see him again after that?"

He looked up in thought.

"No, no, I don't think I did. But I'm not always here."

"Would you remember him?"

"Sure," he said, nodding nervously. "I think I would."

I reached in my coat and took out the black & white picture from Korea. I held it to the young man's face and watched for a reaction.

"Look at them good. Was it anyone in the picture? Take your time. Think."

A single bulb hung from an electrical cord above us and cast a smoky light upon the photograph, giving it a warm patina. It was only a decade old, but it could have been a daguerreotype. While the clerk examined the picture, my eyes swept across the men, and I felt sadness as if for the first time. I saw the overconfident grin of Travis Kemp, the squinting frown of Billy Minerva. Al Russo looked like he had to use the bathroom, and Doug Rodrigues was gazing off somewhere, probably at the clouds. When I thought of all the horrors we suffered, it was nice to know we had good times too.

The employee eventually looked up.

"Um, definitely not. I mean, it's hard to tell. This is old. But I'd remember him, I'd recognize him."

"You're sure?"

"No, sir. I'm sure-sure. I'm an artist. I remember forms and faces."

"An artist," I said, and I glanced back at Harrigan.

"Yes."

"How 'bout showing us your artwork?"

———

THE SKETCH WAS NO PICASSO, but it was detailed enough for me to know it wasn't Kemp. What the clerk depicted was a man of medium height, with a slight frame and thin lips—none of Kemp's characteristics. It was more of a cartoon than a drawing but was proof enough that the person who registered that night was somebody else. The clerk also remembered that he had no luggage and that he had asked for two sets of keys. I was biased, of course, but when Harrigan became skeptical of the evidence too, I knew I was right. No one with any brains would rent a room under his name and then kill someone in it. Maybe the pressure to make an arrest had gotten to Jackson, I thought, because he had given in far too easily.

Harrigan and I raced south along Washington Street, through a dozen soggy intersections. The windows were fogged up so every few minutes, I would reach across him and wipe a circle in the glass. We turned onto Albany Street, the last road before the Expressway, and into the industrial corner of the South End. We passed block after block of boarded-up warehouses and factory buildings. The only businesses left were a few printing companies, a bargain clothing outlet and variety stores that catered to the Greek and Lebanese holdovers. Otherwise, it was a no-man's-land of urban desolation, a manufacturing graveyard, a place so bleak it made skid row look vibrant. In other words, it was the perfect location for a homeless shelter.

We pulled over and parked along the curb beside a rusted meter that hadn't worked in years. I looked across the street to see four or five men huddled in a doorway smoking. Above them was a wooden sign, the lettering too faded to read. When Harrigan and I got out and walked over, they moved to the side. They were a hard-bitten lot, with long beards and weather-beaten faces. One of them had on a military jacket that I recognized as Marine-issue.

I knocked on the door and someone mumbled that it was open.

We went in and found a reception area with a couple of ladder-back chairs, a throw rug, and a ceramic pedestal ashtray shaped like a bird fountain. To our left was a counter, and in the office, I saw a heavy-set black woman, seated with her back to us, typing on an old Remington Rand. When I tapped the bell, she turned around and smiled.

"Hello."

She got up from the chair, walked over, and I politely showed her my badge.

"We have some questions about a man who was staying here."

"Oh my. Please wait, I'll get—"

Before she could finish, a man peeked his head out from the back room then came over.

"I'm Lance Sears, the director. How can I help?"

"Detective Joseph Brae," I said. "This is Detective Harrigan. We have some questions."

"I'll do my best."

Sears was so tall that even Harrigan had to look up to him. He had big eyes, an oversized jaw and he hunched like someone who had done manual labor for too many years. From a distance, he might have been intimidating, but up close he was a gentle giant.

"A 'William Minerva' was staying here," I said, and it was somewhere between a question and a statement.

With his hands on the counter, he paused and looked at us. He seemed strangely relieved, almost like he had been waiting for this moment.

"Let's chat in my office, shall we?"

He told us to come around through a door, and we followed him into the back room. What he called an office was not much larger than a utility closet with a desk. It had only one window, which looked out to the brick exterior of the next building, just inches away. The walls were covered in news articles of summer outings, Thanksgiving banquets, Easter dinners, and fundraisers. There were inspirational stories about residents who had gotten good jobs; obituaries of men who had died too young. A framed photograph showed Sears and Governor Volpe, smiling and shaking hands.

"Please," he said. "Sit."

I looked down to see two wooden stools that were probably purchased at a flea market. Harrigan and I sat awkwardly and tried to get comfortable.

"I apologize for the tight quarters," he said, cracking his knuckles. "Now, what can I tell you about Minerva that you don't already know?"

"Let's start with what you do know?"

"Well, we got a call from the St. Francis House in Providence, maybe two weeks ago. They said one of their residents would be coming to Boston to attend a reunion. They asked if he could stay here a few nights. I said 'of course.' It's all pretty common, we do the same for our people if they have to leave town. It puts them in good hands. We know they're safe."

"Did you meet him?"

"Briefly, the day he arrived. I was coming in; he was going out."

"When, exactly, was that?" Harrigan asked, notepad in hand.

Sears reached for a blotter and opened it. He flipped a couple of pages, ran his finger down the sheet.

"It was...um...July 18th," he said, and then he looked up to us. "Yep, that would make sense. Last Monday. I was at an event for the mayor. Got back late afternoon. We passed in the lobby. I didn't recognize him. And I know all the men. I welcomed him, we shook hands, he said thanks—"

"Any idea where he was going?"

"I don't, I'm afraid. To meet a friend, that's what he said. I didn't ask where. We don't track our residents. All we require is that they be back by 9:00 p.m."

"To meet a friend?" I said, giving Harrigan a sidelong glance.

"That's all he said. I got a call Thursday from BPD. Said he was found dead. Found under a—"

His voice wavered, he stopped. His face tensed up and he looked away. He had only met Minerva for a moment, but I could tell the loss was hard. In the short silence, we all contemplated the tragedy of such a lonely death as the rain tapped softly against the sill.

Finally, he sighed and said, "Wish I knew more, Gentlemen."

"And his things?"

"Still in his locker, on the second floor. Why don't we head up? I'll give you a tour."

Harrigan and I followed him out of the office and down the corridor. We came to a cafeteria, where a dozen men sat moping at a table, picking at food and smoking cigarettes. Their glum moods changed the moment they saw Sears, and everyone turned to wave. We continued to the rear of the building, and he showed us the library, a small room with shelves full of donated books. Most had frayed bindings and stained dust jackets, but they were arranged with meticulous care.

We walked up a narrow, creaking stairwell, and Sears had to duck the whole way. On the second floor, the lavatory and shower facilities had just been remodeled by the son of a former resident, and it smelled like fresh paint. The dormitory rooms all had three shared beds, and only a few had windows. The hallway was lined with steel lockers that reminded me of high school, and every unit had a piece of yellow masking tape with a name written on it. We passed several men—all ages, colors, and persuasions—and everyone called Sears 'Capt.,' although I knew the rank was merely honorary.

We stopped at the last locker, and he fished in his pocket for the keys.

"Nothing's been touched, I can assure you. I have the only set."

"And what if you're not here," I joked.

"I'm always here."

When he opened the door, we saw a large green duffle bag hanging on a hook. Out of respect, I didn't rush for it but let him take it out and open it. Inside we found a blue gabardine jacket, plaid shirt, black pleated pants, and a pair of monk strap shoes—an outfit that wouldn't have matched at a costume party. There were also socks, a towel, two packs of Kent cigarettes, and an old toothbrush. I felt something hard, and when I reached into the coat pocket, I pulled out a silver flask. As I handed it to Harrigan, I noticed the stub of a train ticket too.

"Not the bus?"

"That's right," Sears said. "I forgot. He walked here from South Station. He told me a friend bought him the ticket."

"The train from Providence ain't cheap."

"About twice the price," Harrigan added.

I looked up to Sears.

"Thanks. This was helpful."

We put the bag back in the locker, where it would remain until either a relative claimed it or it was needed for evidence. Sears led us down another stairwell, and we came out to the reception area. It must have been close to dinnertime because the desk clerk was putting her coat on to leave. With nothing else to say, Sears shook our hands and escorted us to the door.

Before we walked out, I turned to him, almost as an afterthought.

"You do good work here."

"We do work," he replied humbly, "and hope for goodness."

CHAPTER 22

IT WAS DARK BY THE TIME I GOT TO RUTH'S HOUSE, AND SHE WASN'T expecting me. I parked down the street and walked to the back of her building, where I knocked on the drainpipe and waited. The rain had ceased, but the alley was filled with dirty water, and my shoes got soaked. The temperature had fallen, and a thin fog engulfed the city, creating an air of mystery that was all too appropriate for what was happening. I had never seen fog in Boston during the summer, before or since.

She opened the door so gently I didn't hear it.

"Well, well," she said.

She had on a long pink nightgown and flat slippers that made her shorter.

"Can I come in?"

"You may," she said, "quietly. Sylvia is creeping about."

We walked up the stairs to her apartment and she closed the door. All the lamps and the TV were on, and the room smelled like cream of mushroom soup. She had just finished eating, and an empty bowl was on the table beside a half-full wine glass. When I sat on the couch, she sat a few feet away and didn't speak. Her coldness made me feel unwelcomed.

"I hope you don't mind—"

"Of course not," she said.

She took a sip and faced the television. Walter Cronkite was on the evening news, and somewhere below I could hear a tenant using a hairdryer. At the commercial break, I turned to her.

"Why the silence?"

"No silence."

The news came on again, and she sat with her legs curled beneath her, her eyes focused on the television. She finished the wine and walked over to the kitchen to pour another glass.

"Have you eaten?"

"Many times before," I joked, but she didn't laugh. "No, not tonight."

"I have some fresh bread and soup. Want some?"

"I can get it," I said, and I went to get up.

"Don't bother."

She got a bowl from the cabinet and poured hot soup from a pot on the oven. She tore a piece of bread from a long French loaf and brought everything over to the coffee table.

"Thanks."

I had only taken one bite when she turned to me.

"Why didn't you tell me about Travis Kemp?"

Bent over with bread in my mouth, I couldn't reply. I swallowed quickly and said, "Tell you what?"

"Don't play games with me," she snapped. "He's been all over the news."

"Ruth, I—"

"He's suspected of killing those men. You knew it and didn't tell me?..."

She got up from the couch, stood at the center of the room.

"...We had dinner with him. We ate with a murderer—"

"Kemp is not a murderer!" I said, and I jumped up.

"They found a body in his hotel room. He hasn't been seen since. He shows up out of nowhere and suddenly these men start dying?"

As I went toward her, she stepped back.

"You have no idea what you're talking about!"

"Apparently I do. This man's trying to kill off everyone he knew in the war." I followed her around the coffee table, but she kept evading me. "He's a sociopath. Can't you see it? Remember when I mentioned combat stress? Well, honey, this is it in action!"

When she finally got close, I grabbed her wrists and looked her dead in the eye.

"He is NOT a killer. Stop blathering about things you don't understand. You weren't there. All you know is what you hear on TV. Put down the alcohol for once and—"

She pulled one of her hands free and smacked me across the face. Instantly, my eyes shut, and the sting radiated through my cheek and nose. For a moment, I was dazed. When I opened them, she was hunched over, her bottom lip quivering, tears falling to the floor.

"I'm so sorry," she moaned.

But I couldn't look at her. I walked to the coat rack, took my jacket, and headed for the door. She ran over and tried to block me from leaving.

"Please. Don't. Don't go. I'm sorry. You're right. I don't know. I'm just scared for you, that's all."

I shrugged her off and walked out. She followed behind, begging me to stay and apologizing over and over again. As I came down the last set of stairs, Sylvia was in the foyer dusting a vase.

"What are YOU doing in this home?"

I ignored her and reached for the door. Ruth descended so fast her nightgown had come undone, and her bra and panties showed. Sylvia arched her back and stamped her foot, as appalled as she was indignant.

"This is scandalous!"

"Shut up you crusty old bitch! Shut your goddamn mouth!"

As I walked out to the street, the shouting broke the tranquility of the Beacon Hill evening. It was a violent spat, much like that between a mother and her teenage daughter, and I could still hear their voices when I got to the car. A parking ticket on the windshield was the final slight in a day that began bad and ended worse. I spun the tires as I pulled out and sped off into the night with no destination. My mind raced and I was shaking. I smoked half a pack, but cigarettes seemed to have lost their calming effect. I turned on some soft music, but that didn't help either.

When I ended up in Roxbury, I couldn't remember driving there. I turned down Valentine Street and passed Al Russo's house, where I noticed a light on in the kitchen. I went a few more blocks and came to the vacant building of the Roxbury Home for Stray Boys. All the windows were shattered—every door pried open. With litter on the ground and graffiti on the walls, it had a neglected hollowness that broke my heart in two.

I continued along Washington Street and went past Whiskey Point, which loomed over the houses like a black void. Although the cliff wasn't visible, I knew it was there. I could feel its presence —always.

Eventually, I came out to Blue Hill Avenue and saw Pat Connors tavern. It was one of the last Irish pubs in the area, most of the others having closed or moved. Roxbury was a mixed area, but it was quickly turning black, and the indications of an uneasy racial transition were everywhere. Long-time stores had closed, the homes and businesses all had security bars, and the elderly weren't out after dark. It was a strange desolation, like the calm before a storm, and the streets were empty.

Pat Connors had no windows and two doors, one for entering and one for getting thrown out of. Half of the patrons were cops and the other half criminals, and both comingled under a gentlemen's truce which had been in place for over thirty years. When I walked in, I saw about twenty people—all men—scattered around the bar and two pool tables. The room had so much smoke even I was repulsed, and there wasn't enough light to read a newspaper. It reeked of stale beer.

Everyone looked over, and a few guys called my name, but I ignored them and went to the bar. Behind the counter, Sully was pouring pints and mixing drinks, and he didn't even notice when I took a stool. He had started as a teenage barback when the place opened in '33 and had been working there in one capacity or another ever since. I knew he had just gotten off a shift because he was still wearing his police uniform pants.

"Hey, Sully," I said.

He looked up surprised.

"Brae? What're you lost?"

"Was in the area, thought I'd stop by."

"Can I get you a tonic or something?"

"Ice water's fine."

I heard the crack of a cue ball followed by cheers, and I knew that someone had made a good shot. I looked in the mirror behind the bar and saw myself for the first time in days. I had stubble on my chin, black circles under my eyes. I was worn out.

Sully filled a glass with ice and water, topped it off with a lemon, and slid it in front of me.

"No charge for a lieutenant."

"So, you'd charge if I was still a sergeant?"

"Probably not. But you wouldn't get the lemon." He leaned over the counter, looked at me with concern. "Seriously, what brings you here?"

"Just needed to think."

"Not much of that goes on here," he said, nodding to two men arm wrestling in the corner. "Are you okay? I mean, you look beat. What's got you? Lack of sleep, lack of sex?"

"Always the first, never the second."

I took a big sip and asked, "What'd you think of the meeting today?"

He looked around then lowered his voice, almost to a whisper.

"I think Jackson's getting a lot of pressure from the top. They gotta get this guy. Everyone's talking about it."

"What's your take?"

"I'm not supposed to have a 'take.' I'm just a street cop. You're the experts. I can only go on what the captain says."

When I took out my cigarettes, the box was empty.

"Sully, you got a smoke?"

He reached into his chest pocket and handed me a Lucky Strike. I opened my matchbook, but the pack was damp, and the tips crumbled like wet chalk.

"How 'bout a light?"

"Want me to smoke it for you too?" he quipped.

"You'd catch fire with all *that* cologne."

Sully frowned and slapped a lighter on the bar counter. On the underside of his gold bracelet, I observed the names of his two daughters. The last time I saw them they were infants, I thought, and they must be in middle school by now.

"What if I told you Kemp never rented a room at the Hotel Holloway?" I said.

Someone called for a beer and Sully held up his finger.

"I'd believe you."

"What if I said Kemp would never kill a fellow soldier?"

He grabbed a pint glass, paused before filling it.

"I'd say that's subjective. If you said he didn't rent the room it means you have proof. If you say he would never murder, you're making an assumption about his character, his heart, his soul. That's sticky territory. We've all seen the loveliest people do the most unlovely things. Ain't that right?"

The man called for a beer again and Sully said, "Shut your trap Gaudet before I send you home."

"But I'm on the clock."

I heard laughter behind me—someone heckled the customer. Sully topped off the beer and slid it down to the man, who dropped a dollar on the counter and saluted.

"I wish you were right," he continued. "But then that leaves the department at square one. And that's a lot of pressure. You won't like when I say this, so don't be offended. But we're lucky most of the victims are from out of state. You think the pressure's bad now, imagine the outcry if they were all from Boston? Heartbroken wives, their kids crying, the honor guard playing taps at the funeral." He made an exaggerated shudder. "Ugh! What a tragedy. There'd be a goddamn manhunt."

"So what? You mean these guys are less important?"

"Don't say that," he said harshly. "Watch your mouth, I ain't saying nobody's worthless. No one knew these guys, that's all. They're all from somewhere else—"

"Al Russo's from Roxbury. He's not from somewhere else. Born and raised here." I tapped my fingers hard on the bar. "There wasn't any public outcry over him."

Sully sighed, made a sympathetic frown.

"Look, Brae, we're arguing over something we both agree on. But it's a fact, and it's an ugly fact, that these guys were undesirables—homeless, drunks. If people cared, the creep might've been caught by now. It's a shame and a damn shame at that. Look how long it took for the networks to pick up the story. Four vets murdered in a week and they don't air it 'til Sunday?" He raised his voice and said, "Who the hell watches TV on Sundays?"

"Not us," someone remarked, "'cause we're all in here drinking, Sully. And speaking of it—"

He rolled his eyes and then walked away to get some drinks. I put my elbows on the bar and again stared in the mirror. It was cool inside, but I felt sweat on my forehead, and I wondered if I had caught a summer flu. Sully returned and filled my glass before I could ask for more water. When he said something and I didn't respond, he glanced over with a worried look. I asked for another cigarette, and he tossed me the whole pack. And for the next hour, I sat smoking and thinking, caught in a hypnotic daze that was somewhere between bliss and oblivion.

When I next looked up, it was close to midnight and most of the patrons had gone home. The lights were on, the pool tables were quiet, and the jukebox was off. A high school kid in a white smock was mopping up the floor. In one of the booths, an old man was singing 'It's a Long Way to Tipperary' out of tune. Somewhere else a drunk was snoring. Every night had an end, I thought. Even this one.

At the far end of the bar, Sully was by the register counting bills. Although he didn't know it, I could see him in the mirror and he was watching me.

"You were in the war," I said.

He didn't hear me, so I repeated myself.

"You say something Brae?"

"You were in the war, right?"

He walked over, looked at me curiously.

"I was in *a* war."

"Then tell me. Why would a soldier kill his comrades?"

He put his hands on the counter.

"Because he's nuts, I guess. You sure you're alright, Brae?"

I stamped out my cigarette and leaned over the bar.

"All these years later, why?"

"I don't know why. You need to go home and get some rest. You're talkin' strange…and you look like hell."

I chuckled to myself and shook my head. In the mirror, I saw Russo and Minerva and Munch and Rodrigues—all the men I had served with but not seen in years. Maybe I had abandoned them, I thought. I was overcome by a bitter remorse that made me want to take my glass and throw it at the wall. My body was still, but inside I was erupting.

Sully turned around and went back to the register. But when I called him, he came right over.

"Yeah, what's up?" he said.

"Get me a drink."

When he reached for my water glass, I grabbed his wrist and stared into his eyes.

"A real drink."

He yanked his hand away and gazed down at me.

"Now you know I can't do that."

"I want a drink. This is a bar. Now get me a fuckin' drink."

The veins in his forehead were pulsating—his jaw was tense.

"We're closed."

I looked up at the wall clock and it read 11:55.

"Not for another five minutes."

Behind me, I heard the door open, but I didn't turn around.

"Sure, Brae," he said, his temper rising. "Want a fuckin' drink? I'll get you one."

He reached for a beer glass and started to pour from the tap. As I watched the golden liquid stream out and fizz, I was mesmerized. He dropped the drink in front of me and I handed him a five.

"That's gonna cost you a lot more than that," he scoffed, and he walked away.

I watched my hand go for the cold glass like it was in slow motion. The moment I touched it, I felt a hand on my shoulder.

"Aren't you on duty, Lieutenant?!"

I turned around to see Harrigan and Jackson, dressed in long trench coats and fedoras, and I knew it was raining because they were all wet. I gave them a grim smile and mumbled hello.

"You take that drink and you're fired," the captain said. "One sip— if the froth gets on your lips. I'll sign the paperwork tonight if I have to. Your choice."

Harrigan stood beside him in silent agreement.

"I...didn't...know," I stuttered. "I didn't know I was—"

"You're always on duty in my department. ALWAYS! Now let's go."

He nodded to Sully, who was leaning against the wall holding a bar towel. Of the three or four men left in the pub, not one noticed or cared enough to acknowledge the incident. Anyone there at closing time on a Sunday night was a drunk, and drunks were aware of only two things—themselves and their alcohol. As we walked out the door, I took one look back and saw how dismal it all was.

Outside it was pouring. A warm but strong wind whipped up awnings and made the trees sway. Litter rolled down the sidewalks and into the gutter, where the rainwater carried it away.

"What the hell are you trying to do?" Jackson said. "Kill yourself? Kill me?"

"I need off this case, Capt. I...I...I—"

He shook his head.

"Too late for that, I'm afraid. You had that opportunity a week ago. You're in now. We need you."

"What? Why?"

"Something came over the telecopier after you left today. From the clerk at the DOJ. Eight letters."

"Letters?"

Harrigan said, "Letters from Kemp. Various dates, from '54 to last year."

"There were more, too. It was just a sample."

When two men came out of the bar, the captain lowered his voice and said, "It seems Kemp's been writing the DOJ for ten years, trying to get them to launch an investigation into an incident—"

"I know, I know," I interrupted. "But what incident? What the hell is he talking about?"

"The earlier letters don't specify," Harrigan said. "But the later ones do."

Jackson looked at Harrigan and then me. His face was tense, distressed—even sad.

"This isn't going to be easy to hear. But if not now, when?" He glanced up and down the dark street before continuing. "Kemp alleges that some civilians were murdered in cold blood. 'Butchered' was a word he used. He said a squad was ordered to fire on a village, to destroy it. There's no record of the event, at least not in the official files."

I should have been shocked by the claim, but for some reason, I wasn't. Many things had happened during the war, and the facts were sometimes worse than the rumors. Just because I couldn't recall something didn't mean it didn't happen.

"Do you know anything about this?"

"I don't remember," I said. "I just can't remember. I want to, but I—"

"Okay, okay. I understand."

I was relieved by the captain's words because they meant that he believed me.

"We can talk about it tomorrow. Harrigan will drive you home."

"I've got my car."

When he repeated himself, I knew it was an order.

"And get some rest. Take a bath, relax. If you remember anything, call me. The phone is beside my bed." He paused and said, "I know this isn't easy, Lieutenant. All I'm asking is that you try."

"You know Kemp wouldn't do this," I said.

He looked at the ground then slowly peered up. I could barely see his eyes under the rim of his hat. "I don't know anything yet. For your sake, I hope not. But I can only go on the evidence."

Harrigan said, "I showed him the sketch."

"The hotel employee shouldn't quit his day job," Jackson said. "That drawing is about as nuanced as a stick figure. I've seen better sketches from a five-year-old."

"The clerk said it wasn't Kemp. I showed him the photo."

"That photo isn't reliable. We both know it. It's fourteen years old, taken by an amateur in the glaring sun. It's the best we have, but it's hardly good. That's probably why Kemp hasn't been picked up yet. I'm sure of it."

I looked down Blue Hill Avenue at the rain-damp street and wondered where Kemp could be. His car was in the tow yard, and the gun the police found the night of his arrest was seized. His face, as murky as it was, had been flashed across the television to a half-million households, and the police in Cleveland were on alert. Maybe he was out there, I thought, lying dead behind a dumpster or in an alleyway. If he wasn't the killer, then he was certainly on the hit list. But Kemp could hide and he could elude. He may have been a failure in civilian life, but he was a remarkable warrior.

The captain patted me on the shoulder.

"Now go. Be at headquarters early."

With that, he pulled up his collar and began to walk away.

"How'd you know?" I said, and he turned around. "How'd you know I was here?"

"Ask your partner."

I turned to Harrigan for an explanation.

"Sergeant Suliman called headquarters. Headquarters called the captain. The captain called me."

"That snitch," I mumbled to myself.

"He was concerned, said you looked unstable. He was afraid you were going to do something stupid."

I nodded once, spoke with a sullen regret.

"And I almost did."

CHAPTER 23

I ONLY REALIZED YEARS LATER THAT THE WAR WAS THE GREAT DIVIDING line of my life. Whenever I thought back, I imagined myself as two separate people—the starry-eyed kid who left for Korea and the cynical man who returned eighteen months later. I could never seem to reconcile those two selves and, faced with a choice of who I was to be, I abandoned my past and opted for adulthood. Yet I always had a sentimental connection to my youth, and no matter how hard I tried to forget, I was drawn to it like a child to his mother. Maybe that was why I went back to Whiskey Point.

At the time, Al Russo and I had only been back a few months and were just starting to adjust to civilian life. He returned to the fish processing plant in South Boston, and I rode out the summer with my small savings, renting a room on Seaver Street and waiting for a call from the Boston Police. We spent nights cruising around in a beat-up Buick convertible that Al's father had bought him as a gift for not getting killed. If we weren't sitting on the hood at Nantasket Beach, we were driving through the city blaring rockabilly. We went to parties, chased women, and drank in every VFW Post from Mission Hill to Manomet. Dressed in leather jackets and Levi's jeans, we were reliving the youth that had been stolen from us. We were the cat's meow.

The night before I went into the police academy, Al stopped by to surprise me. In the backseat, he had a case of beer, a frosted cake, potato chips, and some Cuban cigars. It was the end of August and the evening was cool, but we drove around with the top down, talking, drinking, and reminiscing. Much of the neighborhood had changed since our youth. The vacant buildings had been torn down or boarded up, the shops all had different names, and the stop signs I used to climb were now traffic signals. The penny candy store that Russo and I used to hang out at for hours at a time was a Caribbean food mart, and the YMCA had been converted into a Baptist church. Most traumatic of all, at least for me, was that the Roxbury Home for Stray Boys had closed.

It was only when I thought back to that time that I realized all the ways Al had changed since the war. For a guy who was chronically timid, he would now fight at the drop of a hat, something I learned one night at a diner when he challenged a gang of greasers. Unlike the false courage of his youth, Al was now willing to back it up. He drove fast, looked everyone in the eye, and always carried a gun. Where I had mellowed after the war, he had become more daring, and some days I was nervous to be around him. Maybe the strangest thing of all was that he started calling me 'Brae' instead of Jody.

"Let's go to the cliff," he said as we pulled away from my apartment.

"No way."

"C'mon, Brae, just like old times."

"Let's go to Castle Island. It's crawling with broads."

"Let's go to the cliff, it's crawling with ants!"

He laughed and hit the gas.

"We're going to Whiskey Point."

I rolled my eyes but didn't argue, remembering it was I who had first taken him there. Before I knew it, we were speeding down narrow lanes and side streets, the same intricate route we used to take by foot. When we turned onto the dead-end that abutted the woods, I felt the thrill of mischief.

A neighborhood that had once been Jewish and Irish was now mostly black, and people watched suspiciously as we passed. We parked at the end of the street, and when Russo asked about the fire hydrant, I told him not to worry because I was *almost a cop*. We grabbed the beers and food and walked over to the fence. I pushed aside the weeds and was surprised to see that the hole was still there. Once on the other side, we opened some beers and lit the cigars. As I looked around, the woods were not as endless as they once were, and I could see streets and houses through the trees.

We started toward the hill, drinking, laughing, and reminiscing about all the wild things we used to do when we were young. Each time he finished a beer, he would whip the bottle at a tree, and it would shatter.

"Now how 'bout some real stuff?"

He reached into his side pocket and took out a bottle of Cutty Sark. I knew he already had had some because the cap came right off. Tilting his head back, he took a giant swig and his cheeks puffed out. His eyes closed, and he winced as the sting of alcohol rippled through his body. Then he raised the bottle and made a toast.

"Whiskey for Whiskey Point!"

He handed it to me and I drank. I already had a buzz, but hard liquor was a different sensation altogether. Where beer affected the mind, whiskey affected the soul, and it only took a few minutes before I felt like I was floating in a dream.

"Have some more," Russo said, and I did.

"Let's get up there before we can't."

It was starting to get dark, so we headed up the cliff, stepping carefully on rocks, avoiding roots and loose dirt. Maybe it was our military training, but the ascent wasn't nearly as difficult as I remembered. We got up in no time, and Russo was the first to go over. As he did, his smoldering cigar fell, and I caught it just before it rolled into a nest of dried branches. I handed him the beers, cake, and chips, and then lifted myself over the top. When I stood up and looked across the clearing, I was amazed.

While most things from my childhood looked smaller and less impressive, Whiskey Point was the same. Its gray shale surface, jagged and uneven, culminated at a peak that was so magnificent it should have been snow-capped. Along the far side of the rock was the cliff— at some points visible, some points not—which preceded a straight drop to the bottom. In the distance was the city, the harbor, eternity.

I heard hissing and turned to see Russo standing at the edge and peeing into the wind.

"Careful," I said.

He zipped up his pants and smirked.

"Careful of what? You lost your mettle, Brae? This would've been a road bump in Sobaek."

Suddenly, he began to skip along the rim, leaping from rock to rock with his arms outstretched. Every few steps he would turn and taunt me, daring me to chase him or to come close to the edge. When he had circled the entire rock, he came over and collapsed beside me.

"Gimme a drink," he said, panting. "God, I missed this place."

I handed him the bottle and he took a big slug. He held it up and yelled, "Here's to Whiskey Point, the Jirisan of Roxbury!"

The echo over the cliff made me realize how deep his voice had become over the years. We passed the bottle back and forth until it was empty, and then we each had another beer. Sitting on the rock and facing the horizon, we puffed on cigars and contemplated our lives. I was stone drunk, as was he, and the lights of Boston rippled beyond like the heat wave of an oasis.

"Remember the time we found the dead body?"

"Wha?…" I said, my eyes drooping.

"The body, at the bottom of the cliff. Remember?"

"How could I forget?"

"You can forget. I can't."

"What the fuck does that mean?"

My words were slurred, and I had trouble following the conversation. I had the urge to lean over and go to sleep.

"You can forget things, you always could. You remember your parents?"

"I've told you before, man," I said with a hiccup. "No. I was five fuckin' years old when I got to the Home."

"You remember Korea?"

I laughed to myself.

"Like it was yesterday," I said.

"You remember the night we went on recon down the river to check out some villages?"

It was now so dark I could only see the faint outline of his face.

"There were lots of nights."

"No, this was a particular night. A God-awful night. We split up. You took 2nd squad across a bluff. I went with 1st to the village."

I heard humming in my ears, started to get dizzy. Worried that I would pass out, I stood up.

"What the fuck are you talkin' about?"

"You remember, Brae. You heard it."

"Go to fuckin' hell—"

I stepped back and saw him standing in the moonlight.

"Don't tell me to go to hell, you were there. You heard it. You were five hundred yards away. Why don't you ever talk about it? I think about it every day. Don't tell me…" As he got excited, he began to speak with the same squeak he had as a child. "…How can you forget and I can't? Because you're lying! Don't tell me you don't remember!"

I walked toward his shadow and said, "Shut up, you—"

Before I could finish, he clocked me in the jaw and I was stunned. I almost fell backward but regained my balance and went at him. He hit me again, this time in the nose, and warm blood oozed into my mouth. He grabbed me around the waist and tried to take me down. I could barely see him, but I could feel his movements, and he was quicker than me. I must have slipped because I felt a sharp pain and realized I was on the ground. When he got me in a headlock, I grabbed him by the hair, gouged his eye with my thumb and he shrieked. We rolled over the rock, swinging and kicking, caught in a fury I couldn't explain. The last memory I had was running through the woods, the chirp of the crickets all around.

———

I AWOKE ON MY BACK, staring at a ceiling. The crown molding was covered by thick cobwebs; the plaster was cracked and stained. I felt dampness around my crotch and knew that I had pissed my pants. My head pounded, and my face was sore to the touch. All I could smell was vomit.

I lay there for a few minutes, listening to my breath and trying to recall what happened the night before. But I couldn't. I slowly peeled myself off the floor, one limb at a time, until I was standing. When I looked around, I saw that I was in the empty room of a ramshackle house. Moss was growing in the cracks of the floor; dead leaves were piled up in the corners. There were rat droppings everywhere.

The sunlight came in through the glassless windows like a phosphorescent beam and I was blinded. I held a hand over my eyes and went toward the door. Outside was a beautiful day—the sky was clear, and the birds were singing. I walked out onto the lawn and realized I was at the old house near Whiskey Point. It was vacant—completely abandoned. With an overgrown yard and weathered clapboard, it had the look of an Appalachian farmhouse that had been deserted long ago and left to rot.

Although my wristwatch was broken, I could tell by the position of the sun that it was well past noon. I cringed in self-disgust because I had missed my first day at the police academy. I stumbled across the clearing and toward the woods, the only way I knew how to get back. With my soiled clothes, battered face, and blank expression, I must have looked like a zombie. People pointed and children stared as I staggered through the streets. Someone even pulled up in a car to ask if I needed help. I finally made it to a phone booth but collapsed before I could use it.

A good samaritan called the police and an ambulance showed up. When Officer Suliman arrived, I explained that I was supposed to be at the Academy. Still drunk and slurring, I begged him to help me. He picked up the payphone and called Jackson, who was a lieutenant at the time, and they had a short conversation. As the paramedics wheeled me away, Sully told me to see the lieutenant when I got out of the hospital—to tell him the truth and not to lie.

It was the last time I ever drank.

CHAPTER 24

I WOKE UP DRENCHED IN SWEAT, AND IT WASN'T FROM THE HEAT. MY room was dead quiet, and the air was dry and comfortable for the first time since June. I rubbed my eyes and yawned. Even before I looked at the clock, I knew I had overslept, but I wasn't concerned because I had worked all weekend.

I got up and went into the bathroom, where I splashed cold water on my face and took a piss. I had just turned on the shower when the phone rang.

"Hello?"

"Afternoon, Detective," Harrigan said.

"Afternoon? What time is it?"

"12:03."

"Damn it. I'll be there in fifteen minutes."

'Wait," he said, before I hung up, "not headquarters."

Everything he did or said was an understatement, and I could tell by his tone that something had happened.

"Is it?"

"I'm afraid so."

"Where?"

"Chinatown, Tyler Street."

I hung up and ran into the bedroom, where I combed my hair and threw on a suit. I grabbed my wallet, keys, and .38 and rushed out the door.

The streets of Chinatown were narrow and crowded. Trucks were double-parked from end to end, delivering supplies to the many small businesses. There were tea houses and restaurants, butcheries and grocers, and places with exotic names like the Lotus Inn and the Lantern House. People drifted into the street without looking; children ran by my windows. More than once I had to brake, but I never got fast enough to hurt someone because traffic flowed like the Yangtze.

When I turned onto Tyler Street, a trash vehicle was blocking the road, so I hit the horn. Residents and shopkeepers all turned to look, and a burly garbage man stared me down. I held out my badge, beeped again, and he waved in apology. He pulled the truck over, and I could see two police cars and an ambulance in the distance. I raced to the end of the block and Harrigan and Sully were standing on the sidewalk.

"This is never gonna end," I said to myself.

I parked in front of a loading dock and got out. As I came upon the scene, I saw a body in an alleyway, lying flat and covered in a white sheet. An officer was in the street directing cars and another one was in a cruiser talking on the two-way. I looked grimly at Harrigan but spoke to Sully.

"Who reported it?"

"A woman who lives in the house," he said. "She went to take the garbage out and found this."

"Bullet wound?"

"One to the head, one to the back."

"Two? He's getting sloppy."

"And unethical," Sully said, motioning like he was pulling a trigger. "In the back. The guy was running away. A coward's shot. Even gangsters know that. You don't shoot a man in the back. Unless he's screwed your wife—"

"There's no honor among thieves. Or murderers."

Harrigan remained quiet, but I could see in his eyes that he was uneasy. His hands were in his pockets, something he never did unless he was upset, and he had his back to the corpse.

"Something wrong?" I said.

"Better go look, Detective."

Without another word, I went over to the body. A few feet away, the paramedics were seated on a garden wall eating lunch like it was a picnic. Their indifference made me sick, but until the medical examiner arrived, they couldn't do much beyond confirming that the victim was dead. They looked up when I passed by but otherwise didn't acknowledge me as I knelt to examine the corpse. Even with the sheet, it was obvious the man had tried to escape his killer. His arms and legs were frozen in a running position, and I thought of those human statues in Pompeii that were preserved in form by the ash. He had probably slid a few feet along the pavement because the tops of his wingtip shoes were scuffed.

If I learned anything from combat, it was that a person could get used to the most abhorrent tasks. I had already seen the bodies of four old comrades, and each time was less traumatic than the previous. Maybe it was gallows humor, but I even tried to guess who it would be this time. I snapped the cloth back and observed a birthmark on the side of the head, just behind the right eye. I had only seen this once before, and I didn't have to look any further to know it was Danny LeClaire. I put the sheet back and walked away.

It was only then that I understood why Harrigan was shaken. He had met LeClaire at the reunion, and whenever you knew someone, no matter how little, it made the loss personal. Watching a person go from living to dead in only a few hours was like a fast lesson on your own mortality.

"LeClaire," I remarked, and Harrigan just nodded his head.

"I heard you two bumped into him Saturday night," Sully said.

"We did. He was drunker than a skunk."

"You're not surprised?"

"What? That he was drunk or that he's dead?"

One of the cops called to Sully and got his attention. I lit a cigarette and gazed off to the Expressway above the houses.

"I'm not surprised by much anymore," I said, but he wasn't listening.

I heard an engine and turned around to see the medical examiner coming down Tyler Street. As he drove up, he beeped the horn and shouted for Sully to move his cruiser. Ansell was behind the wheel again, accompanied by an intern, and the moment our eyes met, he mouthed some words I couldn't understand. It took him three tries, but he finally backed the white van into a spot.

I looked at Harrigan.

"I guess we go see Jackson."

"I've got my car. I'll meet you there."

I said goodbye to Sully and went to leave, but then stopped.

"Hey," I said to him.

"What's up?"

"Thanks for last night."

I could tell by his expression that he was tempted to say something sarcastic. But instead, he looked over with a sincere smile.

"You're welcome, Brae."

I GOT to headquarters before Harrigan, and Jackson's office door was closed. When I knocked, he didn't answer but I could hear voices inside. I stood in the hallway and waited, nodding to coworkers who passed by and thinking of Danny LeClaire. I heard the clip-clop of heavy shoes and looked to see Harrigan approaching with something in hand. As he got close, I realized it was a sandwich.

"Glad you brought me something," I said under my breath.

"I'm sorry, I didn't know."

"I'm sorry you didn't ask. I'm starved."

Suddenly, the door opened and the Police Chief came out, followed by a young female assistant. She was pretty, with dark hair and blue eyes, much like I imagined Ruth at twenty-one years old. She walked behind her boss, either out of deference or because she couldn't keep up, clumsily carrying an attaché and other things. Neither said hello, although she tried to smile, and they whisked by us and stormed down the corridor.

The captain called us in and we sat. My chair was warm, and I could smell the remnants of light perfume. We waited while he wrote something down, which gave Harrigan enough time to finish his lunch. Finally, Jackson stapled some sheets together, put them in the drawer, and looked up.

"How are you doing today, Lieutenant?"

"As good as can be expected."

"That's all we can ask," he said with an ambiguous grin. "Nothing more."

The statement was a bit philosophical, even for him, and already I was worried. He reached for a document on the desk and held it with the delicacy of an artifact.

"You'd both better brace for this," he said.

Harrigan and I glanced at each other.

"Got a call from Cleveland this morning—CPD. They were kind enough to do some background on Kemp."

I felt my heart beating—my palms began to sweat.

"It would seem," he continued, a phrase he always used to soften the hard reality of what was to follow, "that Kemp terminated the lease of his apartment on the fifteenth—halfway through the month. Gave no reason, according to the landlord."

"How about work?" Harrigan asked, and it was a good question.

"No job. Hasn't worked in years. Or there's no record of him working. He was on 100% disability for injuries sustained in the war."

I jumped in, "I can understand that."

"Can you?"

"I was there the night he got hit, during a mortar attack. He got it bad, real bad. That's why I thought he died. I was sure he died."

The captain kept his eyes on me while he reflected on what I said.

"100%? Pretty extensive, eh? I mean, it doesn't get much worse. I would assume that designation is for someone who's incapacitated, like a paraplegic."

"He has difficulty walking, he limps. He lost range of motion in his back and shoulders. Suffers headaches, has digestive problems."

"I see," Jackson said. "Well, I also heard from someone at the DOJ. Chief Counsel. He's familiar with Kemp's grievance. He said years ago, before his tenure, it was investigated. They found no record of any crimes against civilians in that sector, during that time period."

"No small wonder," I said. "What 'time period' would that have been?"

He looked down and ran his finger along the report, searching for the date amid all the dense detail.

"Fall of 1950, last week of October."

"October, October, October," I said, rubbing my chin. "We were on the Han River. That was pretty hot."

"Hot?"

"I mean cold. It was freezing. The sector was hot. Lots of back and forth. Skirmishes, mortar fire. Figuratively hot."

"Of course," the captain said. "I don't know if anything happened or not—I wasn't there. But Kemp is convinced something did."

"He doesn't name any names?"

"Not a one."

"I don't get it."

A jackhammer rang out somewhere nearby and I startled. Even Jackson flinched, something he never did, and I knew he was disturbed by the case. The tension between us was still there—it was subtle, but I could feel it. Even if he could be convinced Kemp wasn't the murderer, he wouldn't believe he was entirely innocent.

As for me, I understood Kemp better than his own mother did, having served with him for fifteen months on a mountainside. And if I knew anything, it was that he was a good soul. He was that big-hearted soldier everyone loved and wanted to be around. He was the man who would dress up as Santa Claus for a holiday fair; who would hand a vagrant a crumpled five-dollar bill; who would take out the trash for an elderly neighbor; who would wonder about his misfortunes but never ask why. Travis Kemp may have been a drunk, but his only sin was that he loved too much and cared too little.

The captain stood up and closed the window, and the clamor of the construction went away. He straightened out a framed photograph on the wall of President Johnson, posed in a navy pin-stripe suit. Then he returned to his desk and cleaned his glasses off with a napkin, holding them up twice to look for smudges. With the discussion at a standstill, he did what any good superior does—he changed the subject.

"On another note, Goddard filed charges against you this morning in district court. Assault and battery."

I was more embarrassed than indignant but knowing that Jackson was on my side made it easier to hear. In my thirteen years on the force, I had never received a complaint or grievance from a civilian. Accusations of abuse could dog an officer for his whole career, even if he was exonerated, and for a detective reputation was everything.

"I'm sorry."

"If what Goddard called Harrigan is true, your response was justified. Not technically, but morally. No judge will disagree. This isn't the Jim Crow south."

He shook his head with a bitter disgust.

"Now, were there many witnesses?"

"One less since this morning," I said, and I wasn't being snide.

Harrigan said, "There was a room full."

"Who saw Brae's assault? Who overheard what Goddard called you?"

Before Harrigan could answer, Jackson turned to me.

"There may be a hearing. You understand that?"

"I do."

He leaned back in the chair, clasped his hands behind his head. With the window down, the room was getting hot, and I was starting to get uncomfortable.

"We need a list of everyone who attended the reunion. Who organizes these things?"

"Paul Munch was a coordinator."

"Well," Jackson said. "He'll be no help."

"The Lenox might have a list," Harrigan suggested.

I then remembered the battalion newsletters I received once or twice each year.

"I might have the names. Let me check my office."

The captain hesitated, then spoke.

"I have a meeting this afternoon. If you can get a roster, I want you to take it to the Lenox. See if any of the men are staying there."

"My guess is they're gone. Most were from out of state. They would've left."

"Try," he said. "We may be grasping at straws, but at least we're grasping."

HARRIGAN and I walked silently down the corridor until we got to my office. It was the second time I had gone there in a week, which was a record. Inside, the room was stuffy because the shades were drawn, something the janitor must have done while cleaning. The boxes were just as I had left them—piled-up, tipping over, scattered around, and dusty. Harrigan stood at the entrance with his long arm stretched against the doorframe.

"Only you could find something in here."

I looked back and said, "Trust me, everything's right where I want it."

I knelt beside the crate which had my war paraphernalia. I opened a brown shoebox and inside was a stack of leaflets. Throughout the years, I never read those mailings, but I saved and stored them with the attention of a curator. Even when I moved, I would write to the P.O. box of the vets organization and give them my new address. I always pretended not to care, but my actions said otherwise.

I flipped through the bulletins, newsletters, and notices, some of which went back to the summer of '53. Most were sealed, but some were not, and I got nostalgic reading all the old addresses from my rookie years. Caught up in the hustle of young adulthood, I moved around like a gypsy then, sharing apartments with other cops and never staying anywhere too long.

It wasn't hard to find the most recent newsletter because they were organized by date. I reached for the one from May and tore it open. Inside was a single page, two-sided document which bore the battalion insignia at the top. As Harrigan looked over my shoulder, I skimmed through and searched for anything about the event. It began with a welcome statement from the organization commander. Next were some personal announcements from members, including deaths, the births of grandchildren, and address changes. I turned over the page and the entire back was dedicated to the upcoming reunion. At the bottom, in the last section of the bulletin, was a notice in small print:

ANY MEMBER FROM COMPANY K, 1st *Platoon, who would like to attend the reunion but lacks the means, please write to:*

Travis Kemp
  P.O. Box, 443
  McLean, Virginia, 22101

ALL EXPENSES WILL BE PAID. *Semper Fi.*

WHEN I HELD it up for Harrigan, he winced, as surprised as he was confused.

"We need to get a trace on this ASAP," I said. "Call the PD in McLean. See if they can contact the post office."

He quickly jotted down the address, and as he started to leave, he stopped.

"I thought Kemp is from Cleveland?"

"He is."

CHAPTER 25

I GOT TO MY APARTMENT AROUND DINNERTIME AND NOTICED A BLUE
Ford Falcon out front. My street was always crowded, and I could
never tell one car from another, but this one was about three feet
from the curb and slanted. I stepped into the vestibule and heard Irish
music coming from Jerry's apartment. When I reached the top landing, I saw that the doormat was slightly crooked. I may have been
blind to larger details, but I always noticed the little inconsistencies,
especially around my house. I didn't need any more clues to realize
that someone had been there. I took out my .38 and put my finger on
the trigger guard but not the trigger. My nerves were already on edge,
and I didn't want to cause an accident because I was paranoid.

I put the key in the lock and turned the knob. I pushed the door
open and stuck the pistol into the room, aiming slightly downward
just to be safe. When nothing looked out of the ordinary, I stepped in
and walked across the floor. I sensed a faint smell of smoke and went
over to make sure the oven wasn't on. My mind told me someone had
been in the apartment; my gut told me they were still there. I went
around the corner and the bedroom door was closed. The burning
odor grew stronger, and I was sure it was coming from in there.

Holding the gun out, I stood at the side of the door and tapped it open.

From my angle, the room looked empty, so I lowered the .38 and crossed the threshold. As my eyes came around the door, I was stunned. Laying on the bed and dressed in skimpy pink lingerie, was Ruth. On top of my bureau was a white cake with several glowing candles.

"You gonna shoot me, birthday boy?"

I looked down and shook my head, laughing sheepishly, feeling like a fool. I walked in and sat at the edge of the bed. She was ravishing. Her hair was bushy and wild, and she wore lipstick that was so red it glowed.

"How'd you get here?" I said.

"I borrowed a car from my roommate. The blue one out front.

"Borrowed? You don't have a driver's license."

"Driver's licenses are for teenagers," she said. "Besides, my boyfriend's a cop. Now go blow out the candles before I do."

I went over to the dresser and looked at the cake. Written in thick red frosting were the words: HAPPY BIRTHDAY, LOVE ALWAYS, RUTH.

"Don't forget to make a wish."

I turned back with a suggestive grin.

"I don't think I have to."

I took a deep and exaggerated breath and blew the candles out in one fell swoop.

"Where's my gift?" I joked.

She unsnapped her bra and her breasts popped out. I climbed on the bed and put my arms around her. She kissed me and I kissed her, and we fell into a fit of impassioned smooching that probably could have been heard outside. I put my tongue into her mouth and my hand down her leg, and she moaned. My clothes seemed to fall off my body, but somehow her panties and garter got tangled and required extra attention.

We were both naked for only a few seconds before she was on top of me and the mattress was bouncing. Like a Ouija board, the bed moved from one side of the room to the other and miraculously ended up back in place. The noise of our lovemaking was so loud that when it all stopped, I fell onto my back and heard ringing in my ears.

"Oh my God," I said, and I wasn't praying.

"Happy birthday."

"I forgot. I'm so sorry."

"You won't forget again."

I was still panting when she reached down and rubbed my thigh. She worked her hand farther up my leg, and I was surprised to experience a second wave of arousal. She straddled me and we started to kiss, and, in a few minutes, we were back to where we started. I hadn't had such stamina in years, and I knew that if anything could make a birthday special, it was being reminded what it was like to be young.

"Jesus," I said, lying on my back, out of breath. "You little devil."

She smiled but didn't say anything. She snuggled close with her eyes half-open and I could feel her heart beating. A salty breeze came in through the window, and I started to yawn. We must have laid there for over an hour in each other's arms, thinking and dreaming, and I even dozed off once or twice. In the comfort of her feminine presence, I rested easy and forgot about the investigation.

Bang! Someone or something hit the front door and we both jumped.

"What the hell's that?" Ruth said.

"Stay here."

I got out of bed and threw on a t-shirt and pants. When I reached to the dresser for my gun, she put her hands to her mouth, and I thought she was going to scream.

Bang! The second blow was harder than the first and I felt the floor shake. I left the bedroom and tiptoed across the floor, where I put my back against the wall and listened. Just as I held up my gun, I saw Ruth standing in the doorway in her long nightgown, her face tense with alarm. I waved her back, but she shook her head defiantly —she wouldn't go.

I turned toward the door and yelled, "Who is it?!"

On the other side, I could hear an inaudible murmur, like someone talking in their sleep. Whoever it was then bumped into the door and the hinges rattled. My trigger hand was steady, and I was ready to shoot, but I restrained myself and called out one last time.

"Who is it? Identify yourself!"

"Jody," I heard, and the tension in my hand released.

The voice was strained and muffled, but I had no doubt who it was. I turned the knob and opened the door to see Kemp, looming in the darkness, swaying unsteadily.

"Help, Jody. Help me, please…"

I put my arm around his back and brought him in. I lowered him to the couch and looked at Ruth.

"Water! Get some. Hurry!"

Kemp's lips were parched, and his face was so red it was purple. His eyes were going back into his head like he was having a seizure, and I worried that he was. Ruth came back with a glass of water, and I held it to his lips. He tried to drink, but most of it spilled, and it took a few tries before his mouth was moist enough to speak.

"Jody," he said, gasping. "I'm sorry."

When I stood up to hand Ruth the empty glass, she looked at me and her face dropped. I gazed down and saw a red splotch on my undershirt.

"He's bleeding," I said. "He's bleeding, help me."

I pushed Kemp farther back on the couch, and he sank into the cushions. I took off his coat, and Ruth unbuttoned his shirt. I ran my hands along his chest and arms but couldn't find the source of the blood. It was only when I checked his entire torso that I noticed a dark stain on his gray pants. Kemp put his hand on his right leg and tried to say something. Ruth and I pulled off his trousers and saw a bullet hole on the side of his thigh. It was small but bleeding severely.

"Christ! It might be an artery."

Ruth didn't panic. She inspected the wound with her hands.

"I don't think so, I really don't. I don't think that's arterial bleeding. It would spurt. Let's turn him over."

As we moved him, he groaned a little but was otherwise cooperative. She looked under his leg and said, "There's an exit wound. At least the bullet's out. Still, we need to get him to a hospital."

"No," Kemp muttered, and I was relieved to know he was alert. "Please, you can't. I can't." I could tell by his voice that he was determined not to go, and I didn't bother arguing. I looked at Ruth and said, "More water, please." While she went over to the kitchen, I leaned into his ear and said, "What happened, Trav? I need to know. Who was it? Tell me. I'm listening."

Our eyes met, but he didn't answer. When Ruth returned, he took the glass himself and drank.

"We need to stabilize him," she said.

"I've got a medical kit in the closet. It's from the war, maybe it'll do."

She went into the bedroom and a minute later came out with a small canvas pouch. She opened it and inside were bandages, compresses, a box of ammonia ampules, and some antiseptic. As I held Kemp's leg up, she cleaned the wounds and wrapped a dressing around them. In the light of the table lamp, I saw dozens of scars from his wartime injuries.

"Kind of ironic," he said with a grin.

"Yeah. Isn't it?"

Ruth knelt beside him and held his wrist to get a pulse rate. All emotion was gone, and she tended to him with the clinical dispassion of a triage nurse. I was always proud of her, but at that moment she shined like never before.

"He seems stable," she said. "But you have to get him to a hospital. It could get infected or worse."

"Thank you," Kemp said, but she wouldn't look at him.

She may have believed that I believed he was innocent, but overall she was skeptical. Television was a powerful thing, and once something was portrayed one way, it was hard to convince people otherwise. I didn't blame her for her suspicion—all she knew about Kemp was that he rented a hotel room and that someone was murdered in it.

She went into the bathroom to wash the blood off her hands. As the water was running, Kemp put his hand on my arm and spoke in a low, raspy voice.

"Jody, I can't go to the hospital. Not tonight, not tomorrow. Please, understand."

His fingernails dug into my skin.

"Okay, take it easy," I assured him. "As long as you're stable, as long as you're not gonna bleed out on my floor. But we need to talk."

I pulled my arm out of his grip and went to get some more water. Ruth came out of the bedroom fully dressed, with her purse and a wool blanket.

"Cover him," she said, and she tossed me the blanket. "In case he goes into shock. Keep him warm. Wipe the wound with antiseptic every hour. Watch out for fever and vomiting. If he spikes, you'd better get him to the emergency room quick."

"Where're you going? "

"I have to get the car back. I need to go."

She stepped up to me, gave me a peck on the cheek, and looked into my eyes.

"Be careful, please."

"Thank you," I said. "I'll call in the morning. Drive safe."

"I will."

She walked across the room without looking at Kemp. Beneath her summer dress, I could detect the faint lines of her lingerie. Even in a crisis, sex was so overpowering that it made all other concerns secondary—if only for a moment. We had just been together, yet her body was as alluring as ever, and I imagined her nude. After she strutted out, I closed the door and listened to her heels click down the stairs.

"That's quite a lady you've got there."

When I looked at Kemp, he was flopped on the couch with his chin in his chest. His eyes were sagging and his breathing low, but he seemed better.

"Thanks."

"You think she's too good for you."

"Shut up."

"She's not, Jody. You deserve her."

I ignored him and went into the bedroom. I came out with a pillow and the birthday cake, which I put in the refrigerator. When I walked over to Kemp, he tried to sit up, but I told him to relax.

"How're you feeling?" I said.

"I've been worse."

"I'll check the wound in a bit."

"Thanks."

I went to the door and slid the deadbolt. Behind the couch was a heating pipe that ran from the floor to the ceiling. As Kemp dazed off, I moved toward it with a pair of handcuffs. I clasped one cuff around the pipe and closed it with a cough to mask the sound. Then I leaned over, put the pillow behind his neck, and told him to lie back. As he did, I grabbed his wrist and cuffed it.

"What the?…"

He sprung up, as if by instinct, and his arm twisted behind his back. He screamed in agony and fell back to the couch with the confused panic of an animal that has been suddenly caged.

"Jody?!" he cried. "Why? What's this for? Jody?"

I stood before him with my arms crossed.

"I'm sorry, Trav. This is for my safety and yours."

"How you figure?"

"We've got some things to discuss, and I need you to listen."

He raised his eyebrows and said, "Well, you've got my attention."

He started to cough so fiercely I thought he was choking. I grabbed the glass off the table and gave it to him. He drank it all in one gulp and mumbled a sarcastic thank you. I paced the room, moving in wide circles, my eyes on him at every point.

"First, why'd you disappear Saturday morning?"

"I went for a walk."

"You're lucky you did, pal, because there was a posse here looking for you."

I raised my voice and tried again.

"Now how about the truth?"

"You want the truth. I didn't want you involved in this. That's the truth."

"Didn't want me involved?" I laughed. "I've got five homicides in one week, all guys from our unit. One was shot in a room rented under your name—"

"That's a damn lie!" he snapped. "Any amateur can sign someone's name at a five dollar a night fleabag."

"I'm not sayin' I believe it Trav. I'm just sayin' it happened."

With his right arm raised behind him, he appeared like he was taking a pledge. The position looked painful, but if he stayed back on the couch and didn't move, he wouldn't have any pressure on his shoulder. He may have winced once or twice, but I knew it was his pride that was hurt the most.

"You show up out of the blue. I haven't seen you in fourteen years."

"Fifteen," he said. "It's fifteen years last month."

"Whatever it is. You show up and men start dying."

By now I was shouting, stomping my feet as I walked. When I heard a door open on the second floor, I remembered the tenants and lowered my voice.

"I'm not blaming you, but it's quite a coincidence, ain't it?" I leaned forward, brought my face close to his. "Ain't it?"

He peered up with shame-filled eyes.

"I didn't want you involved, Jody. I swear."

"Well, pal, I am. And you'd better come clean. Or the next conversation I have is with headquarters, and those street cops don't care if you live or die!"

Suddenly, the argument ceased and the room fell silent. I didn't know why, but I just stopped shouting, and Kemp just stopped shouting back. In the distance, I could hear cars and busses along Huntington Avenue. I went over to the window and forced it open as wide as it would go. Paint chips from the sash fell in my hair, and I shook them out. I lit a cigarette and looked across the neighborhood, over the endless rooftops of the triple-deckers. The streetlamps hissed, and in the shadows of the small yards and alleys, I could hear squirrels and rats scavenging.

After a few minutes, Kemp broke the stalemate.

"Jody," he said softly, "none of this had to happen."

"But it did." I flicked the butt out the window, turned to him.

"And you need to explain it."

"It's complicated," he said, wiping his face with his free hand. "I don't know where to start."

"How 'bout the beginning?"

"You ready to go that far back?"

"As far as I have to."

"Ok. What does it matter now? Make some tea. I'll have a cup. And can you get me another bandage? I'm dripping."

Leaning against the wall, I looked at him with bittersweet sympathy. I didn't know whether he was a prisoner or a friend or some strange combination of both.

"Yes, sir," I said, and I made a halfhearted salute.

I turned on the kettle and went into the first-aid pouch to get a clean dressing. When he pulled down his trousers, the wounds were red and swollen but the bleeding seemed to have stopped. I took off the dirty bandage and put on a fresh one, wrapping it snugly around his thigh.

"Ever think you'd be doing this?"

"What? Tending to a dead man?"

"I *was* dead, you know?" he said. "When they brought me to the MASH I had no pulse. Vitals were flat. My blood pressure was 40 over 20. I bought the farm."

"You're a fuckin' miracle."

Just as he laughed, the kettle whistled. I went over to the kitchen, got two teabags from a jar, and poured the water. I handed one cup to him, and I took a seat at the other end of the couch. He stretched his injured leg over the coffee table, groaning as it straightened out.

"Remember the night we got hit?" he reflected. "The night I was wounded?"

"How could I forget."

"That was a big risk for the gooks, right? They only had a few companies scattered on the other side of the Han River. We'd been picking them off with reconnaissance all month, remember?"

"Go on."

"Why'd they do it? Why'd they shake up the hornets' nest? Ever wonder?"

I took a sip and said, "It was a war. The enemy attacks you, you attack the enemy."

"No, Jody, it was more than that. Think back a week before the attack."

"I'm thinking."

"Command sent us down the hill. Our orders were to check out some villages, remember? Just before the valley—at the river bend. About a mile of rice paddies. Then some hooches, remember?"

Anyone else could have described that period and it would have been a blur. But hearing Kemp's voice somehow unlocked the memories of those particular days, and I started to see things I hadn't seen in years.

"I do," I said, nodding. "I remember that night. It was a new moon. Couldn't see a damn thing."

"Bingo. Command thought the gooks were using civilian houses for observation. Sent 1st and 2nd squad down there to check it out..."

I gazed ahead and began to dream. Visions of that night and many more began to flood into my mind, and I felt like I was reliving them.

"...We went down single file, about two dozen men. Goddard led the march..."

I remembered how surprised I was that Lieutenant Goddard was with us because he never left the line.

"...When we got to the river bend, Goddard ordered us to split up. You continued south along the ridge with 2nd squad, and I went west with Goddard and 1st squad."

My lips moved. I began to mumble something.

"What?"

"Rice paddies," I said, staring across the room. "We got tripped up in the rice paddies. Worse than a fuckin' minefield."

"Those paddies were your salvation. Let me tell you. We marched another five hundred yards..." Kemp's voice now trembled; he breathed heavy. "...We came to some hooches. Maybe a dozen. Little wooden things. Looked like huts. Dingy little huts. Dirty little things..."

I recalled those tiny peasant hamlets that were everywhere in Korea. Many were hardly fit for habitation, yet often housed families of six or more.

"...Goddard had us spread out. There wasn't a light for miles. They must've been sleeping—all of them. No candlelight—nothing. Goddard orders me and LeClaire to watch the perimeter." Kemp turned to me and our eyes met. "There was nothing in these hooches, Jody, I'm telling you. Nothing. We start moving through, some animals start getting antsy. Goats, sheep. The villagers knew we were there. But they kept quiet." He hesitated for a moment before continuing. "I reached a fence and couldn't go anywhere. I looked back, back up the hill. This place was nothing—nothing. You couldn't see our line if you were on stilts. KPA wouldn't have wasted their time. There were no forward observers. Command was paranoid. I'm telling you, paranoid."

I remembered hearing the radio transmissions the night of the operation. When we finally got through the rice paddies, we came to another village at the start of the valley. Aside from the smoke of cooking fires, there was no movement or activity. We secured the area, looked for any indications of an enemy presence, and headed back.

"I had a cigarette," he said, "and stood looking out across the river. LeClaire was probably ten yards to my west. I heard the hoot of an owl and looked up, but it was too dark to see."

His voice was now shaking so much he began to stutter.

"Suddenly, I hear noises. Sounds like wood breaking. Goddard ordered the men to bust down the doors. They went hut to hut. Just kicking in doors. Women started screaming, old men were shouting. It was mayhem. Gooks running everywhere..."

When I looked over, he was curled up in the corner of the couch, his cuffed hand back and his free arm around his gut.

"...It felt like an hour—it was probably less than a minute. Fuckin' chaos. Then suddenly, suddenly...I hear shooting. Someone opens up with the Browning. Others start firing. Keep in mind, I'm at the perimeter. Any strays come my way..."

Next thing I knew my head was in my hands, and I was shivering like a child. In an instant, it all came back to me, and I was seized by a terrifying remorse. Even if Kemp went no further, I would have known the rest of the story because I was there. I wasn't in the village, but I was with my squad ¾ of a mile south, and we heard the blood-curdling cries of the villagers that night.

"When the guns stopped," he continued, "everything went quiet. It was quieter than before. It was a weird quiet, like when your ears are filled with water. Occasionally a woman would whimper, but it only lasted a second. Goddard called for everybody to fall in, and we did. He looked nervous—I could see it in his eyes. But you know what?"

He turned to me and I just shrugged my shoulders. I was still willing to listen, but the suspense was over because I knew.

"It was a thrilling nervous—a giddy nervous. Same way you felt as a kid when you did something bad and got away with it. It was like that."

"Then what?"

He looked away disgusted and said, "Then we marched back. We marched back in the dark and no one said nothing."

"Someone must have talked. You don't wipe out a village and not say anything."

He shook his head side to side, emphatically.

"It was the strangest thing I ever experienced. It was like we were all part of something so evil, so heinous, that just mentioning it would mean we were all going to hell—or to the stockade."

"I heard the shots that night," I said. "My squad heard it from across the rice field."

"Then why didn't your men say anything?"

It sounded like a counteraccusation, but I knew Kemp didn't mean it that way.

"I don't know. I really don't. There's so much I don't remember, months in fact. Maybe there were other massacres—I don't know. If I wasn't drunk, I was petrified, if I wasn't petrified, I was drunk." I rubbed my hands together and looked him in the eye. "Korea for me was one big blackout. Like a nightmare you can't remember, but know you had."

"Not anymore, I'm afraid."

"Ain't that the truth."

It must have been midnight, but it seemed much later. Outside the window, the city lights reflected off the sky to create a black and translucent void. Bats flapped between the houses, and somewhere a tabby cat cried out. I was beginning to nod off, but the conversation wasn't over—everything hadn't been revealed. I forced myself awake and said, "Let's get to now. Let's get to the present."

"That's the hard part in all this."

I laughed out loud, but he didn't see the humor.

"You know, Jody," he said with a sigh, "for lots of years I pretended it didn't happen. For a lot of time, I ignored it. But a conscience is a stubborn thing—"

"But you didn't pull the trigger."

"No, you're right. I didn't. But I kept my mouth shut and that's the same in some ways. Hear no evil, speak no evil. I may not be a good Christian, but I'm a good man. The guilt eats into you, a little each day. You can stuff it down, but it comes up."

He tilted his head back and said, "You know, I listened to the cries of those villagers every night since the war? Every goddamn night." His eyes got teary; he began to choke up. "When my wife left me, I could accept that. But when she took my little girl, I knew what those people felt. I knew what we had done. I knew real loss, real grief."

"You have a girl?"

He nodded and a tear fell down his cheek. He wiped it away with his thumb.

"My baby. She'd be about…uh…twelve last month. She used to say when she was little…" He started to giggle. "…that I was her hero. Can you imagine? Me? A hero?"

"Maybe you are?"

He dropped his head in his chest and began to convulse, his eyes closed, his face scrunched up in despair.

"Not after what I've seen, man, not after what I've done, there's no making up for that."

I slid down the couch and put my arm around his shoulder. When he looked up, I said, "It's never too late to be a hero."

He put his free hand over his eyes and sobbed like I had never seen a grown man cry before. In some ways, I was envious because I was empty inside. I let him go on until he was dry, then asked, "What did you do about it? What've you done?"

He dried his eyes with his shirtsleeve.

"I wrote the Department of Justice, asked them to open an investigation."

"Did you tell them what happened?"

"I told them something happened. I told them when. I didn't give details."

"Then you're protecting Goddard."

"No!" he said. "It ain't like that. It's not my duty to snitch on another soldier."

"How do you expect them to investigate when you didn't name a crime and you didn't name a suspect?"

"They could check records; they could interview witnesses."

"They're all dead!" I said, and the words hit me like an epiphany. A chill went up my back and suddenly I understood why, and all the events took on a strange coherence. But I didn't tell Kemp because I had to let him finish—I had to maintain the momentum of his confession.

"I guessed the truth would come out. I guessed that justice would prevail, as they say."

"And when it didn't?"

He gritted his teeth, stared straight ahead.

"Then I would make it prevail."

I got up from the couch and yelled, "You sick bastard. And you thought murdering them was justice?"

"No. No. No. For Chrissakes, Jody, give me some credit. I may be crazy, but I'm not nuts. I'm not gonna kill a whole squad for what a lieutenant made them do. I came to Boston for Goddard and Goddard only."

"And he panicked."

"He did more than panic. He lost it. The man's a psychopath, brother. Look at my leg. He was aiming for my skull."

"What happened? Where?"

"Hold on," he said. "Let me back up. I got Goddard's address from the Association, and I wrote him last winter. I told him he needed to come clean. We needed to deal with this. If he admitted his part and the DOJ didn't want to pursue it, then fine. We could all wash our hands. But I wasn't gonna let him live the rest of his life thinking the lives of two dozen Korean men, women, and children meant nothing."

"And he didn't agree?" I said sarcastically.

"I can only do my part. This is about me." He thumped his chest and said, "When I heard about the reunion, I wanted to confront him. I brought a gun, I won't deny it. And I may have shot him. I've got nothing to live for—"

"Don't say that," I said. "Please."

"It's true."

"Don't say it, even if you think it's true. Just don't say it. Not in my house."

"As you wish," he said softly. "When I got here, I called every hotel in town—couldn't find him. I must've gone through the phonebook ten times. I knew a bunch of the guys were staying at the Statler. I asked the receptionist if I could leave my name, in case Goddard showed up. When I said Travis Kemp, know what she said?"

I shook my head.

"She said...she said someone with that name was staying at the hotel. Can you believe that son of a bitch? Can you believe the balls? He was registered under my goddamn name!"

"Where does Goddard live?"

"Where? Out of state somewhere. Has been for years. Somewhere south. Virginia, I think. Yeah, Virginia."

"You sure?"

"I keep in touch. I may not have been heavy into the Association… and I'm sorry I lied to you about it…but I keep in touch with guys from K Company. I always know what everyone's up to."

"Not this time," I joked. "You missed this one."

He looked down at his leg and said, "He didn't miss me. If I had my gun there'd have been a shootout. I was taking him out dead or alive."

"What happened?"

"When I found out he was staying at the Statler, I went to confront him. This was…" He squinted in thought. "…Monday—same day I left you the note at police headquarters. I waited in the lobby of the Statler all day looking for him. I sat and had some drinks. Finally, I spotted him coming out of the elevator. Couldn't believe my eyes. Wasn't even sure it was him. He looked so good, so fit. Like a lawyer or something. A real dandy. Blue eyes—blonde hair. He should've had a surfboard." I smiled and continued to listen. "I didn't confront him, though. I followed him instead. I was drunk, I admit it. Thoughts were going through my head. It was like I was hunting him. I followed him outside. He gets in a cab—I get in a cab. Tell the driver to follow. We drive for ten minutes and finally, Goddard's taxi pulls up to a home-less shelter, somewhere on the south side—"

"The South End," I corrected.

"Right. He gets out and goes inside. I told the driver to wait. Five minutes later Goddard comes walking out with…you know who?"

"Billy Minerva."

"The spittin' image," he said. "Goddard has his arm around him. They are laughing. I told the cabbie to take me to my hotel—the Kenmore Inn. What else could I do? I told you, it's not the men I'm after, it's Goddard. I thought it was strange. Minerva always hated him."

"You know Billy was found dead the next day?"

Kemp reacted with the casual regret of someone who just found out their team lost in overtime. I knew he wasn't being cold, but that he just had no more sorrow to give.

"I didn't know. If I had known, I would've stopped him then and there. I needed Goddard alone, that's all. Alone."

He leaned forward for his tea, which by now was cold, and took a sip.

"I waited for him all day Tuesday, but nothing. That's the night I met you and Ruth in the restaurant."

"Were you following me, too?"

"I had to be cautious, Jody."

"You should've worked for the CIA."

"They take drunks?" he joked, then he continued, "I waited in the lobby Wednesday and again, nothing. Same on Thursday. I was starting to think he left town. Finally, Friday rolls around, the first night of the reunion. I was parked across from the Statler eating a sandwich, having some beers. I see Goddard come out. He's got on a long coat—looked like wool. Strange for this time of year. He doesn't get into a cab but starts walking. I follow him down Stuart Street. I had to pull over a few times so I wouldn't pass him. He gets to the red-light area—"

"The Combat Zone."

"And how appropriate," Kemp said. "I thought he was going to get some tail before the reunion, something to loosen him up a bit. He turned down this narrow street, lots of strip joints, peep shows. Real shithole. He goes into a building, I guess a hotel. I figured it was a whorehouse. I park across the street and wait. By now I'm blotto. I've had two six-packs and a couple of nips. It was probably eight o'clock, and I wanted to get to the reunion. It just got dark. The streets were quiet. It's always that way, in those seedy areas. Everything is calm for a few hours after sunset. Must be dinnertime for degenerates…"

I laughed quietly to myself, thought of the Hotel Holloway.

"…I'm just ready to leave," he went on, "to go to the reunion when I hear a shot. Just one. Sounded like a firecracker, but I knew it was a pistol. There was no one on the street, just some bums. But they didn't notice. I was nervous, real nervous. I started to sweat. I kept my eyes on the front door. A minute later, Goddard comes out. He looks up and down the street and starts to walk. I panicked. I started the engine and peeled out. I had my gun in my right hand. I pulled up to him. Our eyes met. He knew it was me, man, he knew it…"

I lit a cigarette and offered it to him, but he didn't want it.

"…He runs across the street, goes into an alley. I reversed and hit a car. So I gunned it to the next street—"

"Essex Street," I said.

"Probably, I don't know. I pulled up to another alley and saw Goddard running behind the buildings. I figured I might be able to cut him off. I went half a block and took a hard left, down a street, but it was really an alleyway. I'm speeding down it when from out of nowhere, I see him standing next to a fire escape and pointing a gun. I ducked and punched the gas. I hit a curb, and my car bounced off a wall. I plowed straight into a dumpster. I don't know if he squeezed off a round or not. All the glass shattered, and smoke was coming from the radiator. I was dazed. Cops came in seconds, thank God."

I stood up to stretch my legs, and he asked for more water. As I walked over to the sink, I got lightheaded and had to grab the refrigerator handle. I could have attributed it to everything I had just heard, but it was more likely from exhaustion and lack of food. I got a bigger glass from the cabinet, filled it with cold water, and sat down again.

"Here," I said, giving it to him. "Now where does all this leave us?

"Thanks. I don't know about *us*, but I've been on the run for three days."

"This whole town's looking for you."

"They're looking for the wrong guy. The cops are hunting me and I'm hunting Goddard. Like a goddamn spy movie."

"Where's Goddard?"

"Don't know," Kemp said, shrugging his shoulders. The movement must have disturbed the wound because he winced. "He checked out of the Statler…or Travis Kemp did. I thought he might've gone back to Virginia. I saw the news Sunday morning, old picture of me."

"I gave it to them."

"God, I looked good back then," he said, and he sounded serious. "I stayed in my hotel, didn't leave. That night I read in the paper that another body was found."

"That was Paul," I said. "Paul Munch."

"Poor bastard. I knew then Goddard was still in town, Jody. I knew he hadn't left. His work wasn't done."

"He hadn't killed every witness."

"Bingo," he said, for the second time.

I stamped out another cigarette and cleared my throat. I looked at him and said, "That nutcase was trying to get rid of any witnesses. Even if the DOJ ever decided to investigate, there'd be no one to corroborate what happened."

"It sounds crazy," he said. "But it ain't, really. Goddard may be a lunatic, but he's a clever one. But I was on to him. And I had to get him before he got away with murder, twice. I scoured the city Sunday night, going into every gin joint and dive bar I could find. It was useless, though, and I knew it. I didn't have my gun, but I had my hands. And I was gonna strangle the bastard if it was the last thing I did."

"You must've been drunk—"

"I was."

"Because finding one man in a city this size is looking for a needle in a haystack."

"True, but I didn't have to find him—he found me. Tonight, I got off the bus around six o'clock and walked over to my motel. It was dark. The parking lot was dead quiet. As I went for my keys, I heard a car door open. I turned around. I saw a long coat, in summer. I knew it was him. I had just got the key in the door when I heard a shot, then another. Both went wide. I opened the door and dove inside. But something hit my leg. I got in and closed it. I watched through the curtain as he sped out. It was a green DeVille—a Cadillac, if that helps."

"You bet it does. So you got a cab?"

"No," he said with a smile. "I walked here."

"You walked from Kenmore Square to Mission Hill with a bullet in your leg?"

"It only hurt if I stopped. If I kept moving, I was okay. I didn't think it was serious because I could walk. It was only when I climbed your stairs that I began to lose consciousness."

The story ended where it had begun—at my doorstep. We sat for the next few minutes thinking, reflecting, wondering. I yawned and kicked off my shoes because my feet hurt.

"Now will you let me out of these?"

I looked over to Kemp and remembered that he was shackled. He had been so uncomplaining that I forgot about it entirely, and I was embarrassed I hadn't freed him sooner.

"Oh, right. Sorry."

When I tossed him the key, he caught it with one hand and unlocked the cuffs.

"Nice to be a free man again," he said.

"We're not out of the woods yet, brother. Let's check that wound and get some rest."

He leaned back and I helped him pull his pants down. As I undid the bandage, I could see that the blood had coagulated, which was a good sign. I took a tube of iodine gel from the first-aid kit and rubbed some on the edges of the entry and exit holes. He gritted his teeth and hissed from the sting, but I knew he could take it. He had been through much worse and the pain of a single bullet to the thigh was nothing compared to the shrapnel wounds he had suffered in Korea.

"You want something to eat? Some crackers?"

He glanced at me with a guilty grin.

"To be honest, I could use a drink."

I looked at his glass of water on the table.

"A real drink," he emphasized.

"You know I don't drink."

"You got anything around the apartment. Anything?"

He was so desperate I thought he would drink rubbing alcohol or mouthwash if he had to. But I did have something in the house, a pint of B&B Liqueur a colleague had given me at a work Christmas party. I agonized over whether to tell him, and it was a dilemma on so many levels. The booze would thin his blood, and if his injury ruptured during the night, he could bleed to death. But if he didn't get a drink and he went into delirium tremens, he could die just the same. It would bother my conscience either way, so I decided to give him the liquor. If risk couldn't be avoided, I'd rather err on the side of comfort.

I told him not to move and went into the bedroom. I opened a trunk in the corner and fished through piles of miscellaneous things until I felt the bottle. It was a work of art, dark green with a crest stamped on the collar and a white foil cap. Kneeling down, I curled it in my hands and was conflicted.

Addiction on its own was no crime, and few were the men who returned home from the war without some kind of obsession. For Kemp and me it was alcohol, for others it was opiates, sleeping pills, or pain medication. Things that brought about euphoria in the average person would only make a vet feel normal. For those who didn't have chemical habits, there was always sex, gambling, and the endless pursuit of money. I couldn't begrudge Kemp for his dependence unless I admitted my own drunken oversights in Korea. Giving it up at twenty-three may have saved my career, but by then the damage was done. We had all paid a winning price for a war that was a draw at best.

I came out of the room, and he uttered, "Halleluiah."

I was going to toss it, but instead, I handed it to him gently.

"Don't drink yourself to death. I need your help. We're back in the battle. Together."

He held the bottle like it was a golden chalice.

"Just a few swigs," he said, "to take the edge off, to help me sleep."

"Then good night."

I headed for the bedroom, and when I got to the doorway, he called over in a hushed voice. I turned around and he raised the bottle.

"Thanks, Jody. Consider this me drinking so you don't have to."

I shook my head with a somber smile, not sure whether he was being sincere or just overdramatic. As I went to reply, I hesitated, but by then he had already taken off the cap and was drinking. I walked into the bedroom and shut the door.

CHAPTER 26

I AWOKE THE NEXT DAY TO THE SOUND OF BIRDS. THE MORNING sunlight came into the room through the half-drawn shade and created a soft haze. I lay there for over an hour, listening to the world outside and imagining a place where crime did not exist. I immediately thought of Ireland and of Ruth and of our time together. Aside from Korea, I had never traveled abroad, and going there was like finding love in midlife. When this was all over, I told myself, I would take her back and ask her to marry me.

Kemp grunted in the next room and I came out of the daydream. I got up quietly and went to the kitchen to make tea. He was asleep on the couch, snoring, and I tiptoed over to check his leg. The stain on his pants was dry, so I knew that the wounds had scabbed over. When I put my hand on his forehead to check for fever, he stirred but didn't wake up. I checked the bottle of B&B and just a little was missing. The fact that he had been honest about taking only a few sips confirmed my trust in everything he had told me the night before. If a drunk was going to lie about anything, I thought, it was booze.

I heated the kettle but didn't let it whistle. I leaned against the counter and sipped my tea with some British shortbread cookies. As I watched Kemp sleep, I thought back to our time together in the war.

He had been as tall and fit as an athlete and had a natural confidence that made everyone want to be around him. If anyone deserved to be head of 1st Platoon, it was him and not Goddard. Without a college degree, however, he had no chance of becoming an officer and, like me, his life had been predetermined by the disadvantages of his background.

"What're you looking at?"

His eyes were cracked ever so slightly—he had been watching me the whole time.

"Not much," I said.

I realized with some regret that the insult wasn't sarcasm because it was true. He made a snorting laugh and wiped his mustache.

"Want some tea? Water? I have biscuits—or cookies. British biscuits are really cookies."

"Sure."

He didn't specify so I got him water *and* tea and a few shortbread cookies. I put his breakfast on the coffee table and he sluggishly got up.

"Damn I feel like mud."

I wasn't familiar with the expression, yet somehow it made sense.

"You need some clothes?" I asked.

He raised one eyebrow.

"Think I'm gonna fit into anything you wear?"

"Let me see what I've got."

The buzzer rang and I froze. Kemp stopped eating and we both looked at each other. I ran into the bedroom and threw on pants and a shirt. For some reason, I also grabbed my gun and stuffed it in the back of my waistband.

"Don't move, keep quiet," I said as I went for the door.

He nodded and I went down the stairs. Through the frosted glass, I could see a tall figure on the porch. I took out my .38 and pulled back the lever. I didn't know why I was scared, but I was, and I had to trust my instincts. I turned the knob slowly and when I opened the door, it was only Harrigan.

He was surprised by the handgun, but he didn't flinch.

"My gosh, Detective, expecting trouble?"

"I've got company."

"I thought as much," he said, glancing back. "I saw the car."

I looked past Harrigan, and, to my horror, the blue Ford Falcon was still out front. In that instant, my heart sank, and I imagined my whole world lost.

"Ruuuuuttttthhhhh," I shrieked.

HARRIGAN RACED through the streets with the sirens on, swerving around cars and busses, blowing through traffic lights. I sat in the passenger seat limp, my head bobbing back and forth with the motion of the ride. For the first time in my career, I felt helpless, and I was paralyzed by fear. All I could think about was Ruth and her wild innocence. The only way I knew I hadn't lost my mind was because I still worried about my own sanity.

"Hang in there, Detective."

He kept one hand on the wheel and another free just in case. He had been wise enough to take my gun when I almost collapsed at the front door. My only hope now—and it was a long shot—was to beg Jackson to marshal the entire force for a manhunt.

We skidded around the corner and into the headquarters lot. Startled police officials and other employees leaped out of the way, ducked between the cars. Harrigan didn't bother to park; he pulled up to the front steps and left it running.

We flew up the stairs and into the building. Our shoes glided across the freshly polished floor, but we aimed for Jackson's office and burst through the door.

"What's the meaning of this?!" he barked, rising from his chair.

"Capt.," I said, hysterically. "He's got Ruth. Ruth's been taken. She's kidnapped."

"Shut the door," he said to Harrigan.

The captain came over, put his arm around me, and put me in the chair.

"Where's his sidearm?"

Harrigan patted his hip and Jackson nodded as if to say 'good job.'

"Lieutenant," he said, kneeling beside me. "Calm yourself. You need to be calm, or we can't do anything." He turned to Harrigan and said, "Some water, please, hurry."

I looked at the wall with a blank gaze. Terrifying scenarios ran through my head, visions of things unimaginable. When Harrigan returned, I took the cup with a trembling hand and drank.

"What the hell happened?" he asked Harrigan.

"I went to his apartment. Ruth's car was parked out front. That's all I know."

"She…" I said stuttering, "…she borrowed a friend's car and came over. She left last night. Her car is still there." I gripped the captain's arm and stared into his face. "Kemp showed up last night. He told me everything. Goddard is the killer."

Still crouched, Jackson froze and looked over at Harrigan with a sidelong glance.

"Where's Kemp now?"

"At my apartment."

"And you left him there?"

"He's injured, his leg. He can't move."

He stood up, and I could tell he wasn't pleased.

"Then you'd better be right—damn right. Get Officer Suliman on the phone. No, run down to his office. Get him here, now!"

I had never seen Harrigan move so quickly—he was out the door in the flash.

"Listen," Jackson said. "I need you to tell me everything that happened last night."

"Ruth came by. She surprised me. I came home, she was in my bed. There was a birthday cake. We screwed…" The last statement was an unnecessary detail, but I wasn't thinking straight. "Kemp showed up at my door, about eleven, maybe later. I don't know. He was shot."

"Shot?"

"In the leg. Goddard shot him in the parking lot at his hotel. He walked to my place."

"Why? Why did Goddard shoot Kemp?"

I rubbed my face nervously, tried to slow my thoughts long enough to answer.

"Something that happened in the war—"

I heard footsteps come into the office but didn't turn to see who it was.

"We know," the captain said. "The letters from the DOJ. Then Kemp was right?"

I nodded my head.

"Yes, but I didn't remember. I couldn't remember. Until he told me. Then it all came back, I swear." I tilted my head back and agonized. "I think I'm going crazy."

"You're not. It's okay. Please, tell us what happened."

"We were out on patrol, to inspect some hooches." When Jackson frowned, I explained, "Hooches are houses or huts. Our orders were to see if the gooks had any lookouts. The squad split up. I went south with a fireteam, Goddard took Kemp and the rest..."

I noticed then that Harrigan, Sully, and two other cops were standing around me listening.

"...We got tangled up in some fucking rice fields." My voice began to quiver and break. "Suddenly, there's machine gun fire coming from the village, probably over a thousand rounds." I looked up to the captain and felt my eyes get teary. But I got a hold of myself and continued, "Goddard ordered his men to level the place. Kids, old woman—even the cows and pigs were taken out!"

"Alright," the captain said gently, "alright." He patted my shoulder and I exhaled in relief.

The room went dead quiet as everyone reflected on the tragedy of something that had happened years before in a remote Korean valley. The incident was surreal, as much as the retelling of it, and the memories were now so sharp I could recall distinct sounds and smells. I didn't know whether I had suppressed or ignored it, but I was sure I had lived with a latent guilt that would have someday destroyed me. Unlike Kemp and the others, I had been spared because I forgot, or I had forgotten so I could be spared.

Jackson looked over to Sully.

"The search is off for Travis Kemp. Get the word out."

Sully told one of his men to send an alert, and the officer left the room.

"Now," the captain said. "Why Goddard? Why now? Why all these years later?"

"He's killing off the witnesses. He panicked. He knew Kemp was pushing for an investigation and he lost it."

Harrigan said, "That might explain Saturday night. He wanted to get hit in front of a hundred witnesses."

"Maybe he was looking for a hedge," Sully wondered.

I scoffed and said, "I can't be bribed with an assault charge."

"No," Jackson said, "but he might've been trying to distract you, shake you up a bit."

He walked over to the window and stared out across the parking lot. We all knew the clock was ticking, and the subdued urgency put everyone on edge. I was so distraught I took out a cigarette and tried to light it. When Harrigan went to stop me, the captain looked back and said, "No, it's fine. He can smoke. He needs it." It was a precedent even I was not prepared for, and I was as flattered as I was embarrassed. Jackson was no Bible-thumper, but he viewed smoking only second to drinking in order of sinful vices. Sully must have assumed the exception applied to everybody because he lit one up too.

"Lieutenant," the captain said, still gazing out the window. "How many men witnessed this?"

I surveyed the memory, studied the logistics.

"There were twelve in my squad," I said. "Three fire teams. Mine didn't go to the village. We went south. So that would make eight."

"We have five homicides, which leaves three. Goddard is one. Kemp two." He turned around with dramatic abruptness. "Who is the last man?"

I thought back to the soldiers in my unit, trying to put names to faces and faces to names. Halfway through my tour, 1st Platoon began to suffer casualties, and men started to leave the unit, either in body bags or to the MASH. The roll changed as replacements were brought in, and it was difficult to recall who was where and when.

As I sat thinking, Jackson opened his top drawer and took out a copy of the photograph I had given him.

"This might help," he said.

I leaned forward to look. They were all there—Al Russo, Minerva, Rodrigues, Munch, LeClaire, and Kemp. Sergeant Rankin was on the end, but he had been ordered to stay back the night Goddard led the march. I counted the men with my finger, one by one, then looked up.

"Seven."

"Who's missing, Lieutenant? Who's not there?"

He was onto something—someone in the squad was not in the picture. All eyes were on me as I struggled to recall who it was.

"Who took the photograph?" the captain asked.

Suddenly, I saw a face. Only one man in our unit owned a camera —a clunky Kodak Brownie Hawkeye—and I knew who it was. It was the first piece of hope I had had in hours, and I blurted out, "Malachi Oveson! An RTO. He was our radioman."

Sully came forward and asked, "How can we find him? Any idea where he lives?"

I looked at him and Harrigan and recited old doggerel the men used to chant on the line.

"Malachi Oveson, *The closest he ever got to a lay was being born in Hooker, OK.*"

When I laughed, it somehow gave everyone else permission to laugh too.

"Hooker, Oklahoma? Must be a hell of a place."

Jackson said to Sully, "Can you get on that?" and before he was done, Sully was out the door.

"Now listen to me—both of you." The captain spoke in a quick, forceful tone. "We've gotta move delicately here. If Goddard has Ruth, we can't get him nervous." He looked at me directly and said, "I know you understand. I'm thinking out loud here. I think it's best to hold off on an APB until we see if we can locate Oveson. Do you agree?"

Honored that he was consulting me, I acknowledged him with a grateful nod.

"If Oveson is still in Boston," he said, "and if he hasn't been whacked yet, we may not find out where he is for hours—maybe not at all. Go back to your place, see if Kemp knows anything. Watch him close, he may be our wildcard. I'll call you as soon as I hear anything."

As Harrigan and I got up to go, Jackson extended his hand to me. We shook and he didn't let go.

"You gotta be tough—tougher than ever before. Tougher than the war, even."

He tried to catch my gaze, but I kept looking away.

"Can you do that, Lieutenant?" he added. "Can you do that for yourself, for the department, for all of us?"

I paused then looked up.

"Yes. But if he harms Ruth, I'll have to kill him."

CHAPTER 27

THERE WAS SOMETHING AMATEUR ABOUT RACING THROUGH THE STREETS of Boston without an objective. Nevertheless, the frantic pace created the illusion of progress and that was better than no progress at all. Harrigan kept the sirens on and the gas pedal pinned as we drove back to Mission Hill. When we turned onto my street, I saw the blue Ford Falcon, alone and waiting, much like I imagined Ruth to be. Harrigan parked behind it and we got out.

"Let's look around."

We circled the car from opposite sides, looking for clues or anything out of the ordinary. The doors were all locked, which told me she hadn't even gotten to them before Goddard got to her. The windows had no handprints, nor did the chrome. I looked underneath and along the curb, but saw only a few wrappers and cigarette butts, most of which were mine.

"Detective," Harrigan said, and when I turned, he was standing by the fence looking down. As I walked over, I observed dried blood on the pavement and was almost sick.

"Please, God, no," I mumbled.

"Wait," Harrigan said, crouching over to examine the stains.

He followed the blood trail up the front stairs and onto the porch.

In the sunlight, I could see that it was fresh blood, no more than an hour old considering the heat. I sighed in relief.

"It's Kemp, it's gotta be."

I went over and unlocked the door, and we ran up to the apartment. Inside the cushions were scattered on the couch, and the teacups and ashtray were on the table from the night before. I looked down and small drops of blood went from the couch to the bathroom and back to the doorway. The first-aid pouch was open, a clump of bloody bandages beside it. Kemp hadn't been as tidy as the first time he fled my place.

I bit my lip and shook my head in disbelief.

"He's gonna try to be a hero."

"He might have his own plans."

"I can't believe it," I said "He was hit bad. And he's still bleeding. That wound gets upset and he could bleed out."

"Maybe it's his last mission."

Suddenly, the phone rang, and I ran over to the wall.

"Hello?!"

"You've got a good punch."

I looked at the receiver and said, "Who the hell is this?"

"An old friend," the voice answered, and I immediately recognized Goddard. I felt my blood pressure rising, but I fought to stay calm.

"What do you want?"

"No," he said. "What do *you* want?"

I turned to Harrigan and mouthed that it was him. He tiptoed out, and I knew he was going to alert headquarters on the two-way.

"Where's Ruth?"

"She's safe, Brae. Very safe."

"Why'd you drag her into this?"

"She's just a pawn," he said. "Nothing more. I've no interest in hurting her—or anyone else for that matter."

When he paused, I could hear traffic in the background.

"You know, Brae," he went on, "I had you in my sights—"

"What the hell are you talking about?"

"I had you in my sights and didn't pull the trigger. And you know why?" He gave me time to answer, but I didn't. "Because you spared my life once, so I spared yours. We're even. Consider that a debt repaid."

In those few seconds, I thought back to the day Al Russo and I first went to Whiskey Point. I recalled the older boy with the wooden sword who bullied us into a fight. I saw him falling off the rock, and I remembered grasping his hand at the last moment. Never could I have imagined that that small event, tucked back into the far corners of my childhood, would be the thing that saved me.

"I would've done it for anyone."

"I don't doubt it. You're a stand-up guy, Brae. Quite a success. I remember you running around the streets in dirty knickers and knee socks. Now look at you. Not bad for a kid from the Roxbury Home for Stray Boys."

"You've got a good memory," I said.

"I don't forget, if that's what you mean."

"Is that why you can't let go of what you did to that village?"

"What I did? What I did in that village?" His voice got tense, deliberate. He acted like he had been insulted, but it was much more than that. "No, my friend, you've been listening to the wind. It wasn't me that ordered those men to fire. It was Kemp—"

"You're lying!"

I squeezed the phone and gritted my teeth. If I could have reached over the copper and strangled him, I would have.

"It's the truth. And you know it. You're after the wrong man. I'm innocent."

"Killing five men is innocence?"

"Killing five men is justice. I won't hang for the sins of someone else."

"But why? Why'd they have to die?" I asked, stalling for time.

He laughed.

"They didn't have to. They plotted against me. They're with Kemp, and they'll lie on the witness stand."

"No, no, they wouldn't. I knew those men. They wouldn't. There's no conspiracy, you're nuts."

Harrigan crept back into the apartment and motioned something with his hands—the call was being traced.

"Who do you think they'd side with? A second lieutenant or their own sergeant? Who Brae, tell me, go on?"

"I don't care about them, I want Ruth."

"And you'll have her if you listen. If you're smart. If not, she'll die..." Clutching the receiver, I leaned forward and pushed my forehead into the wall. Never before had someone else held my entire life and future in their hands.

"What do I need to do?"

"Nothing," he said, and I was baffled. "Absolutely nothing. Isn't that easy? You don't do anything and your darling comes back alive. You two can live out the rest of your lives in romantic bliss. But if I see one cop—if anyone comes after me—you'll never find her."

His voice brightened and he continued, "I'm gonna leave town. I'm gonna disappear. I'm gonna put this all behind me and you should too. In a week or so, I want to watch the news and hear that the case is cold. Now if Kemp had died...or if he dies...then that'll make things convenient for both of us. Right? The evidence is in place—he died in a shootout while avoiding capture. That happens and justice is truly served. If not, I wanna be off the list, permanently—"

"And if I make that happen?"

"Keep an eye on the mailbox. I'll send you a postcard. I'll give you her location. Then everything will be as it was. This will be over for all of us."

I held up my finger to Harrigan and he nodded.

"Give me some time," I said. "It's gonna take time. A couple of days to work things out. I gotta talk with some people, see if we can squash this."

"You better hope you can," Goddard said, and he hung up.

I hit the receiver against the wall, over and over, until it made a hole in the plaster. Harrigan ran over and grabbed my arm.

"Please, don't. Let's call headquarters and see if they got the trace."

I handed him the phone and walked over to the window, where I lit a cigarette and stood shaking. I listened to his conversation but couldn't follow it. The idea that Kemp could have ordered the assault that night left me with a frightening uncertainty. I wasn't in the village —I didn't witness what happened. Like everyone else in my fire team, I had only heard the shots and assumed the squad had met some resistance. Maybe it was an accident, I thought, an accident Kemp had regretted his whole life, an accident that had turned him into a drunken wreck. I was more confused than ever.

Harrigan hung up and called over to me.

"They got it!"

"Where?"

"Howard Johnson's Motor Lodge, Southeast Expressway."

We dashed down the stairs and out the front door. As we did, Jeremiah was climbing the front steps, a cane in one hand and groceries in the other. He moved out of the way to let us pass and said, "Can you and this fellow help me move a sink?"

"Maybe later, Jerry," I said as I opened the passenger door.

He watched us with a long face as we made a U-turn and took off down the hill.

In minutes we were speeding along Columbus Avenue toward the Expressway. In the distance, the Howard Johnson's Motor Lodge loomed over the smaller buildings around it. I picked up the two-way and used a code mayday to tell any officers in the area to stay off the premises. Before we reached the parking lot, I turned off the sirens, and we rolled into a spot near the entrance. We got out and walked with casual haste, not wanting to alarm anyone or be noticed.

Inside the lobby was quiet, and I nodded to a bellboy as we walked over to the front desk. A young woman in a beehive hairdo and navy suit smiled and said, "May I help you?"

I took out my wallet and showed her my badge.

"We're detectives with BPD. We're looking for a man named Goddard, Thomas Goddard."

"Let me check the guest list," she said, and she opened up a binder.

I tapped my fingers anxiously on the counter as she scanned the pages. She must have gone through four or five two-sided sheets before she finally looked up.

"I'm sorry. I've checked back a week. There's no one by that name."

"May I?"

"Of course," she said, and she spun the book around.

I ran my finger along the pages, reading the meaningless names and dates and searching for what I did not know. I was ready to give up when my eyes caught the words 'Travis Kemp' scribbled in cursive next to room 404. If Kemp's claim that Goddard had been registering the victims under his name was true, then this was more proof. I pointed it out to Harrigan, and he acknowledged it with a subtle nod.

"Thank you," I said, and we hurried toward the elevators.

The doors opened on the 4th floor, and we walked along the corridor, counting off the numbers until we got to the room. It was quiet—no guests were around—and the only sound was the faint laughter of children playing in the pool outside.

Harrigan and I used hand signals to communicate. He would stand out of view against the wall beside the door, and I would knock. He didn't have his pistol out, but he had his hand on it under his jacket, and if anything went wrong, he was ready. I took a deep breath, closed my fist, and knocked. I waited a few seconds then tried again. Still, no answer. Suddenly, a janitor stepped out of a utility door at the end of the hallway.

"Hey, can you open this?" I called out.

"Is that your room?"

When I shook my head no, he started to walk away, but I whipped out my badge and yelled, "Boston Police. Get me in here, now!"

He rushed over and reached in his pocket for a giant set of keys. He clumsily sorted through them until he found the master. As he turned the lock, Harrigan took out his .45 and stood waiting. The knob turned and the door swung inward, and the shades must have been drawn because the room was pitch dark. I pushed the door open wider, and the light from the hallway seeped in. And there, lying on the carpet with a bullet hole in his temple was Mal Oveson. The moment the janitor saw the body, he cried, "Oh my Lord," and made the sign of the cross.

I knelt down and checked for a pulse, but Oveson was dead. I could tell the blood was fresh, and his heart must have recently stopped because some still dribbled out from arterial pressure. When Harrigan flicked a light switch, we saw a modest efficiency room that couldn't have been more than twenty dollars a night. The sheets were a mess, and a tray of half-eaten breakfast was on the dresser. By the door was a black suitcase with a coat draped over it. Oveson must have been getting ready to leave when someone knocked at the door —the last door he would ever open. Because he had come so close to escaping his fate, his death was somehow more poignant.

We heard footsteps, and I turned to see three officers in the doorway. One had his hand on his gun, and the others looked ramped-up and ready for action.

"Who sent you?" I snapped.

The first officer said, "Call just came over the radio. I was doing a detail on Albany Street." He looked back at the others and added, "I saw them when I pulled up. Two more cruisers are out front..."

When I looked at Harrigan, he knew I was ready to explode. I had asked headquarters not to send backup, and now the place was crawling with cops. If Goddard was lurking somewhere near, he would know that his call had been traced and that I had no intention of honoring his deal. I saw the presence of the officers as a threat to Ruth's life, and although I didn't blame them, I was furious. As they stood waiting for me to do or say something, I glared at them and stormed out of the room.

I leaned against a car in the Howard Johnson's parking lot, quietly fuming and feeling helpless. The front entrance was a circus of spiraling emergency lights from cruisers, ambulances, and news vehicles. Curious patrons congregated by the lobby entrance, and I watched as cops interviewed hotel staff and other possible witnesses. The medical examiner's van was parked and idling, but I didn't see Doctor Ansell.

The scene was complete madness, and the news broadcast from

Sunday had put the whole city on alert. It was sad to think that five unrelated murders wouldn't have been a headline, but a killing spree caught everyone's interest. When a young reporter came over and asked if I was staying at the hotel, I told her I was just there to meet a friend.

I watched Harrigan break from the crowd and walk towards me. He wasn't wearing his jacket, and his white shirt was soaked with sweat.

"Leave me to the sharks," he said.

"I would've been the one biting, believe me."

He leaned against the car too, and together we watched the excitement from a distance. I lit a cigarette and took a long drag.

"You're disappointed," he said.

"I can't believe they sent backup. I asked them not to. They shouldn't have done it."

"You're right, Detective."

"Then why did they?"

"Maybe it was an oversight."

Beyond the motel, the yellow glare of the setting sun burst from the horizon in streaks and flares.

"No," I said, shaking my head. "That was no mistake. That was intentional."

Vehicles left and new ones arrived, and the activity showed no signs of winding down. As with any crime scene involving a murder, a patrol car would be on-site for twenty-four hours, and the news trucks would remain at least until morning. The aftermath of a homicide was like a long wake.

"Detectives," someone said, and we turned to see Jackson wending through the rows of parked cars.

"I'm surprised I found you two in this bee's nest." He faced me and said, "Now, you're sure it was Oveson?"

I flicked my cigarette, blew the smoke out my nose.

"*Oveson*," I said, "No 'r'. Yeah, it was him. Clear as day. A bit older, a little heavier, but the same radioman I served with."

"This is a setback. But we should've expected it."

I tried to conceal my bitterness, but I could tell Jackson knew something was wrong.

"Are you alright, Lieutenant?"

"Captain, with all due respect, why'd they send the cruisers? I asked them not to."

He walked up, stood directly in front of me.

"It wasn't my choice," he said.

In his voice, I sensed the awkward regret of someone forced into explaining the mistakes of another.

"It was the chief. He made the decision. I was against it."

"Thanks."

Then he looked at Harrigan and said, "Take him home and stay with him. We'll do the paperwork in the morning."

Jackson patted me on the arm with a tense, yet tender smile.

"We'll find Ruth. If I have to turn this city upside down and shake it. We'll get her back safe."

CHAPTER 28

I DREAMT AGAIN OF WHISKEY POINT—THE SECOND TIME IN A WEEK. IT was a windy fall night in '56, and I was working the second shift. I had been on the force three years but was still considered a rookie. My partner and I had just finished listening to the Celtics beat the Rochester Royals on his Motorola handheld when a call came over the radio about a fire on a cliff in Roxbury. The fire department had been dispatched, but the shift commander wanted patrolmen on-scene in case it was arson.

As we sped down Washington Street, I told my partner to turn right down a dead-end street, but he insisted on a different route. We circled around and came up the backside of the hill, a narrow lane of old homes and three-deckers. He drove slowly along the curb, his flashlight pointed at a long hedgerow. When we saw a dark opening, he stopped, and I was amazed to see the entrance of a road. With overhanging trees and thick vegetation, it was as secret as Batman's batcave. We turned and went up a long, unpaved driveway covered with leaves and fallen branches. The cruiser bounced over the potholes and depressions. At one point we bottomed out and the muffler scraped the ground.

At the top, we came out to a wide lawn, where I saw the abandoned home behind Whiskey Point. In all my years going there, I never knew it had a driveway, and only a child's mind could conceive of a woodland house without a way in.

We parked by the tree line, took our flashlights, and got out. The stench of smoke was all around, and in the distance, we could hear sirens, still a mile or so away. My partner had brought us that far, but my pride was redeemed when he didn't know how to get to the cliff. I told him to follow and we walked through the woods, where we could see the glow of flames. I hadn't been to the rock in several years, but a lifetime of experience had etched its topography into my brain, and I could have found it blindfolded.

We went down a small ravine, up the other side, and through some thorn bushes which were low enough to step over. We ascended the shallow side of the hill and saw the rocky crag ahead. As we approached, I heard the crackle of the fire as well as voices—the culprits were still there. I whispered something to my partner and he got his handcuffs ready. Not knowing who or what to expect, I took out my billy club. When we were within a few yards, we looked at each other and then burst onto the clearing.

"Don't move!"

Seated around a small campfire were three men about my age. They were a ragged bunch, with filthy clothes, long beards, and weather-beaten faces. They were startled, but they didn't try to run.

"You know this is private land?"

One of the men shook his head; the others just gazed at the fire.

"Put it out," I said, and when they hesitated, I yelled, "Now!"

They crawled to their feet and started to kick dirt and rocks into the fire. One of them poured a beer on it, and the smoke went everywhere.

"Get it good. Any of those embers blow into the woods and the whole hill's gonna catch."

They weren't defiant—they didn't grumble. Once the flames were out, they even stamped on the ashes with their boots.

I looked around and saw a familiar squalor. Scattered across the rock, nestled in the cracks and crevices, were beer cans, cigarette packs, food tins, and wrappers. There were empty boxes of Hi Ho Crackers, corn curls, chicken bones, and even the moldy remains of a loaf of Wonder Bread. Add to that the smell of urine, booze, and smoke and it felt like a hobo's den.

"Get those bottles, put them in that box," I said. "Pick up some of that litter."

The rock had more graffiti than I remembered. I was touched by the names of friends and lovers, the hopes and grievances, the rage of young innocence. In the shadows I saw, but only for a moment, myself as a boy, sitting on the ledge and staring out to the stars. It was a time and place I could never go back to, but that I yearned for nonetheless.

"What've we got here?"

I turned around and two officers came out of the woods. They walked with a seasoned self-confidence that told me at least one of them had rank. When I saw the sergeant's stripes, I stiffened up.

"They're cooperative, sir," I said.

"I'll be the judge of that."

He walked over to one of the men and said, "You have any ID?"

When the guy mumbled no, the sergeant said to his partner, "Bring that flashlight over here."

He proceeded to search him, pulling out packs of matches, beef jerky, handkerchiefs, and pennies. In his back pocket was a hand-stitched leather purse that looked like it was from an Indian reservation. Inside it, the sergeant found an old library card.

"Winston Lothrop? That's a mighty highfalutin name for someone living off Sneaky Pete and dog food." He laughed to himself and asked his partner, "Don't we know that name?"

He didn't wait for an answer. Instead, he looked at the men and said, "You boys have been sleeping in that old house back there, right? You know we have trespassing laws in this city? Know what the penalty is for vagrancy?"

His partner asked, "What is it, Sarge?"

"Beats me, I'm not a judge."

All three men stood side by side with their heads down, enduring the ridicule with quiet dignity. The fire pit was now smoldering, and only a few glowing embers remained.

"Damn squatters," the sergeant said. He approached the second man and began going through his pockets. "How 'bout you? What blessed appellation did your fine parents bestow upon you?"

"Howdy Doody."

The others chuckled, and even I found it hard not to laugh.

"Oh, what do we have here?" the sergeant said, and he took out a tin of Ultrex Platinum condoms from the man's coat pocket. "Maybe you *are* a cowboy." He put them back and said, "You can keep these, pal. You're gonna need them in jail."

Finally, he turned to his partner and said, "Cuff these two."

We heard the sirens of the fire trucks as they came up the driveway of the property. While the officer put on the handcuffs, the sergeant looked at the last man and said, "And you? What's your name?"

The emergency lights broke through the forest and flashed across the rock. In that instant, the man peered up, and my heart sank.

"Russo," he said. "Al Russo."

The only thing I recognized were his eyes, two olive-brown orbs, piercing and bloodshot. His face was obscured by a mass of tangled hair and a beard that was like a lion's mane. He had only spoken three words, but in his voice, I detected a deep and permanent despair. If someone had asked the last time I saw him, I would have said a decade ago because it seemed that long. But when our eyes met, I recalled the night before I entered the police academy, the night we had gotten drunk and fought.

The sergeant turned to me.

"Hand me your cuffs, will ya?"

He must have noticed my surprise because he frowned.

"What? You know this man?"

I stared at Russo and he stared back. The things he'd said that night had haunted me ever since, but I had stuffed them away with all the other unwanted memories from my youth and from the war. At twenty-seven years old, it was hard to face the past when you had only recently left it. Much like the time we found the dead man at the foot of the cliff, I was given the choice between doing what was right and doing what was easy. And once again I chose the latter.

"No," I said flatly.

I gave the sergeant my cuffs, and he locked Russo's hands behind his back.

"I need you two to go into the old house back there. If you find anything—sleeping bags, blankets, food, clothing—take it all to head-quarters, toss it in the dumpster."

He grabbed Russo by the arm and looked over to his partner, who was guarding the others.

"C'mon Sully. Let's get these tramps back to the station and booked."

THE MOMENT THEY LEFT, three firefighters came out of the woods holding extinguishers. When they saw that the blaze was nothing more than a campfire, they looked almost disappointed. Nevertheless, they sprayed the remaining ashes with water, and we all walked back down the shallow side of the hill.

We came out to the clearing by the house, and the firemen put away their gear. The two trucks backed up, turned around, and disappeared down the driveway. To get to the house, my partner and I had to step over huge clumps of weeds and dead grass. The structure had deteriorated since I was there years before. The shutters were all torn off, the gutters were gone, and one of the three chimneys was completely missing—either collapsed or scavenged for the brick. As we got to the door, I could hear the wind howling through the vacant rooms and hallways.

My partner pointed the flashlight inside, and the place looked like an extension of the wildness around it. Leaves were piled against the walls, and the floor was covered with pinecones, pine needles, dead grass, and twigs. Huge portions of the ceiling had fallen, and the exposed joists—no more than rough-hewn timbers—were splintered and moldy. Everything of value had been stripped and stolen. There were holes where light fixtures had been; the door and window hardware was all gone. Most remarkable of all was the graffiti, old and faded, suggesting that the house was too rundown even for vandals.

We split up and went in opposite directions, searching the house for any signs of habitation, looking for the men's belongings. While my partner went upstairs, I walked down a hallway and looked in the first room. The only way I knew it was a kitchen was because there were remnants of a drainpipe on the floor. All the cupboards had been taken off the walls, probably used for firewood, and the appliances were gone. I glanced in the pantry to see a few rusted cans, broken plates, and an old Butter-Nut coffee jar.

"Brae!"

I ran out of the kitchen and to the second floor. He called again, and I followed his voice up a narrow staircase that led to a finished attic. At the far end, I saw him standing before a large oak door.

"Ever see anything like it?"

It had two iron crossbars, one near the bottom and one near the top, the type of bolts found on an old barn or warehouse.

"Never seen a door that locks from the outside," I said.

The latches were snug, but we forced them open. Inside, the space was more like a large closet than a room, and when I flashed the light, I saw shelves on one wall and a small window. There were three sleeping bags, pillows, some wool blankets, and scattered clothing, all frayed and dirty. On the shelves were piles of newspapers and a red candle. We had found their lair.

"This is it," I said. "Grab that sack. Put as much as you can inside it."

My partner took an old kit bag from the corner, and he began to collect the items. I tossed the clothes and pillows in the sleeping bags and rolled them up. It was too much stuff to carry, so we took the things they couldn't live without—the quickest means of eviction. In the corner, I saw a tan canvas rucksack that had a missing strap and no frame. I turned it over and the letters 'US' were stamped on the front flap. It was a Marines standard issue.

"Ready?"

When I turned around, my partner had the duffel bag over one shoulder, the sleeping bags under both arms, and a half-gallon of Canadian Club whiskey in one hand. He held up the bottle with a big grin.

"Not bad stuff," he said. "These guys were living high off the hog."

"Lucky them."

"We'll split it."

"You can have it."

I glanced around for anything else worth removing, but most of it was junk. As I went to go, my partner asked, "What about that?"

I looked at the military rucksack and said, "Naw, we'll leave that here."

When we exited the room, I shut the door but didn't bolt it. It made no sense to lock a door from the outside, and after fifteen months of combat and five years on the force, I was loath to add any more absurdity to the world.

I offered my partner help, but he was determined to lug it all, and he waddled like a weighed-down refugee. We got as far as the stairs before one of the sleeping bags caught a nail, and the whole cache, with the exception of the liquor, tumbled to the second floor. We picked everything up and continued on. Once outside, we walked across the lawn and loaded the things into the trunk of the cruiser. As we drove away, I rolled down the window and heard the sound of crickets.

I had always hoped that would be the last time I would ever have to go to Whiskey Point.

CHAPTER 29

"I KNOW WHERE SHE IS."

Harrigan ran into the bedroom.

"Did you say something, Detective?"

I sat up and rubbed my eyes. With all that was happening, I couldn't believe I had napped, but I did.

"I know where she is," I said. "What time is it?"

He looked at his watch.

"9:23."

I almost asked whether it was a.m. or p.m., but one look toward the window, even with the shade down, told me it was nighttime. I jumped out of bed and got dressed, putting on my pants and shirt at the same time, buttoning each with a separate hand. As I rushed to get ready, Harrigan sat against the dresser, his arms crossed and watching.

"Where is she, Detective?" he said, a hint of doubt in his voice.

"An old house. At the top of a hill…in Roxbury."

"Whiskey Point?"

"You know it?"

"Of course. Behind Washington Street."

"You've been there?"

"Once," he said. "As a child. We got attacked by some white kids. They called us niggers and threw rocks at us."

"That was probably Goddard and his gang. He lived up there," I said. "Call headquarters. Have them send support. I don't know the address. There's a driveway on a street behind the hill."

I opened my top drawer and fished through the underwear and socks.

"Where the hell's my gun?"

"At the station, in your locker. I took it from you this morning, remember?"

"No."

While he went to use the phone, I reached under the bed for a walnut case. I blew off the dust and unlocked it with a skeleton key. As I opened it, the black carbon steel of my M1911 glistened against the yellowed newsprint I had wrapped it in over a decade before. The pistol looked as new as the day it was issued, and it still smelled of gun grease. I never discharged it in Korea and kept it only as a memento, but there couldn't have been a more fitting time to recommission it.

I grabbed my coat off the floor and ran to the front room, where Harrigan was waiting by the door.

"We gotta make this count."

"We will, Detective," he said. "We will."

AS WE DROVE to Whiskey Point, my thoughts wavered between Ruth and Travis Kemp. I wondered if she was there, and I wondered if he had given the orders to shoot that night. I didn't believe Goddard would harm her, yet I couldn't be sure, and the uncertainty was gut-wrenching. But any man sane enough to remember being saved as a child was capable of gratitude and maybe even compassion. As for Kemp, his mere survival had been a mystery all along, and nothing would have surprised me.

The constant back and forth chatter on the radio made it sound like the whole force was on its way. I knew that if we didn't arrive before they did, the cops might stumble onto the scene unknowing and startle Goddard. As with any hostage situation, one mistake could mean disaster. The closer we got, the more terrified I became.

Soon I could see the hill, rising over the neighborhood like a black cloud. I had only gone to the cliff from the property entrance once, and that was the night we arrested Russo and his friends for vagrancy. I realized too late that I didn't know how to get there. I shouted at Harrigan to go left, then right, then left again, and each time we ended up lost. The backstreets of Boston's slums were a nightmare of repetition, and everything looked the same.

By some stroke of luck, we came out to a dark road, and I recognized a long hedgerow.

"This is it."

He cut left and went up the hill. As we neared the crest, we saw flashing lights and a cop car parked haphazardly by the driveway opening.

The officers had gotten there first.

"Speed it up!" I shouted, and Harrigan punched the gas.

The tires spun and the car lurched forward. We skidded to a stop behind the cruiser, and he got a flashlight from the glove compartment. We jumped out and headed up the driveway. As we walked, I heard him cock his gun, so I did the same. We stumbled up the rutted ground, pushing aside branches and overgrowth, walking blind in the dark. Our only guide was the pale beam of the flashlight. Mosquitos buzzed in my ear; crickets chirped in the shadows.

Once our eyes adjusted, we quickened the pace. I even tried to run, but my foot hit something and my ankle buckled.

"You okay?" he asked.

"Just twisted it."

The driveway turned sharply two or three times as it wound up the side of the hill. We went another twenty yards and I was out of breath, but we finally came to an open expanse. And there, looming in the distance, was the old house.

"Hurry," I said.

Suddenly, we heard a noise and stopped to listen. Harrigan

pointed the flashlight toward the edge of the woods, and something metallic reflected. We heard the sound again, and I had no doubt it was a human groan. As we got close, Harrigan held up the light, and we saw a police uniform. It was Sully.

"Jesus, Sully," I said, "what happened? What's wrong? Sully, talk…"

Harrigan bent down and patted his body, searching for an injury in the dim light.

"He's shot," he said. "Right here." He pointed under his ribcage. "And here too."

When I looked in Sully's eyes, his pupils were unresponsive, and he gargled like he was choking. I tilted his head back so he could get some air, but it didn't seem to help. I felt his pulse and it was slow. I knew if the paramedics didn't come soon, he would die.

"Stay with him," I said. "I gotta keep going."

Harrigan shoved the flashlight into my hand.

"Be careful, Detective."

I took one final look at Sully and our eyes met. He was only semi-conscious, but I knew he recognized me, and that was all that mattered. I held his hand and squeezed it once. Then I got up and continued on.

I crept across the lawn with my gun out, crouching down and watching for movement. When I got to the house, I tapped the front door open and shined the light. Sweat rolled down my sideburns; my heart pounded. I stepped into the foyer, and my foot hit a piece of wood. The sound echoed throughout the first floor, and something moved in the corner. It could have been a rat, but when I pointed the flashlight, I saw a blue patrolman's uniform.

I ran over, got down beside him, and whispered, "What happened? Where're you hurt? Show me."

He was a young man—a rookie—and I could tell from his crisp outfit that he hadn't been on the force long. I searched for a bullet wound but couldn't find one. When I flashed the light in his eyes, I saw a deep gash on the side of his head. He had been bludgeoned.

I leaned in closer.

"Where is he?" I said.

The officer moved his lips but didn't speak. With the little strength he had left, he raised one arm and pointed toward the door. And in one agonizing breath, he uttered, "Woods."

I took off my coat, wrapped it up, and put it under his head. Then I loosened his collar and said, "Don't move. Help is on the way."

When his eyebrows twitched, I knew he heard me. I patted his shoulder with a grave smile and went out the door. I ran across the clearing to the edge of the forest, where I stared into the thick vegetation and listened.

Beyond was Whiskey Point, that remote aerie of crime and vice that parents damned and children dreamt of. Since I could remember, it stood dark and mysterious at the center of my universe like some sinister Mt. Olympus. Life had a strange symmetry, I thought, and if God didn't have a sense of humor, he certainly had a sense of irony. I lost my heart on Whiskey Point, and now all these years later, I was trying to save it.

The woods were denser than I remembered, and everywhere I stepped, my feet sank in a bed of twigs, leaves, and weeds. They bent and snapped, and the noise seemed to reverberate through the night as if to announce my arrival. I kept the flashlight off and navigated by the glow of the moon. As I came around a large oak tree, I got caught in a thorn bush and the prickles scraped my neck and arms. A moment later, I slipped on a stump and banged my knee. At every turn, I encountered a new obstacle that made me believe that some force or fate was out to stop me. And for that same reason, I knew I was going in the right direction.

Soon the terrain sloped upwards, the trees started to thin out. I was almost at the cliff. A light swept across the woods, and I heard a radio. More backup had arrived. Whether the officers saw me or not, it became a race for glory like the Fall of Berlin, and I was determined to get there first.

In a single lunge, I came over the ledge and landed on the clearing. There I looked up and saw two men wrestling arm-in-arm at the summit of Whiskey Point. They seethed and growled, spinning around with the jaw-snapping fury of a dogfight. A cloud shifted, and the moonlight shone down eerily over the rock to reveal, for the first time, the silhouette of Kemp and Goddard. The vision held a dramatic beauty that wasn't lessened by its barbarity, and I was at once captivated.

My shirt was torn open and blood from the thorns trickled down my chest as I staggered forward, my pistol raised. I called out, but my voice was strained, and the best I could make was a dry screech. I was fifteen feet away when the policemen also came out of the woods with their guns drawn. For a split second, all parties stopped and looked at one another like off-cue actors on an overcrowded stage. Then an officer yelled halt and fired a warning shot that boomed across all of Roxbury. I screamed for them to hold back, but in the murky confusion of the insect-buzzing night, everyone was a criminal and everyone a cop.

"Trav, don't!" I shouted, pointing my gun at Goddard, unable to get a clear shot.

The two men stood at the edge of Whiskey Point, embraced like battered fighters in a ring, each committed to the other's defeat in a stalemate of wills that burned with a savage hatred. They swung and they spat and they swore, their faces swollen and their knuckles bashed to a pulp. It was the final battle of an ancient war, a feud that had begun in a valley in Korea and would end on a precipice in Boston.

"Jody!" Kemp cried.

When I looked at him, I saw a man who had been half-dead for years, and who lived only in the memory of the wife he had lost and the daughter he longed to be with. Whether Kemp had lied or whether Goddard had ordered the killing or whether I had been too shell-shocked to remember any of it mattered little. The scores of a thousand sins would be settled on that rock, and the treachery of a Korean night would be forgiven or forgotten—whichever came first.

My trigger hand trembled, but my body was perfectly still. I turned my ear to Kemp, to listen and to let him know that I was his friend—always.

"Jody!" he called again, and that beautiful baritone rang out over the trees. Tears of blood streamed down a face that was ravaged yet strangely peaceful. He looked over and our eyes met.

"It's never too late to be a hero!—"

In one motion, he pulled Goddard toward him like a lover, howled a terrifying sound, and jumped off the cliff. The officers rushed over, as did I, and we all went to the edge. Crawling on my hands and knees, I peered over the side into the darkness and heard only the chirp of crickets.

The patrolmen stepped away, and soon more personnel came out of the woods and gathered in the clearing. I couldn't move, and I lay flat with my eyes closed, gripping the rock until my fingernails broke. I was relieved that Goddard was gone, but I had come for Ruth, and her whereabouts or condition was something I was afraid to discover.

I overheard a call on the radio, and someone said my name. A young officer walked over and stood looking down at me.

"Sir?" he said, and I craned my neck. "You'll be happy to know your girlfriend has been found and she's okay."

I put my head against the ledge and the tears of a wonderful joy ran down my cheeks. Without her, the world would have been meaningless. Without her, I would have ended up as broken as the men from 1st Platoon. I had been spared twice—once in Korea and now again on Whiskey Point.

"Lieutenant?" the officer said, leaning over. "Do you need assistance? Are you injured?"

"Naw," I said, wiping my eyes. "I'm fine."

I pushed myself off the ground and crouched on all fours. I was closer to the edge than I had ever been, and it was dangerously dark. I climbed back to the level part of the rock, and several officers shook my hand as I passed. I thanked them all for their good work and headed into the woods alone. Flashlights were everywhere as men continued to make their way to the scene of the fall. I wasn't in the mood to talk, so I stayed in the shadows and avoided them.

The journey back wasn't nearly as difficult, and when I reached the house, there were more vehicles than I could count. I saw cruisers and unmarked cars; ambulances and paddy wagons; fire engines and ladder trucks. Half of Boston's emergency response services were there, and they were still coming. A police helicopter circled above, and it made me think of the night I put Kemp in the chopper—the first time he died.

"Lieutenant?!"

As I stepped out of the woods, Harrigan called to me, and everyone stopped to look. I was too exhausted to speak or answer questions, so I averted my eyes and wandered past two dozen cops and firefighters. Some people congratulated me, but most were considerate enough to stay away and give me space. I went straight up to Harrigan and said, "Where is she?"

He pointed to an ambulance with its back doors open, and somehow I found the strength to run. I heard Ruth's voice, and when I looked in, she was waving her arms and yelling at a paramedic. As eager as I was to hold her, I had to stand back and watch.

"I told you!" she yelled, "I'm okay! Now let me the hell out of here before you go out on a stretcher!"

The paramedic was trying to get a blood pressure cuff around her arm, and she kept swatting him away. The poor man was flustered, and he looked like he didn't know whether to beg for her cooperation or give up altogether.

I forced a cough and she turned. Her face beamed, and I hopped in the ambulance and put my arms around her. We hugged for almost a minute, and each time I pulled away she pulled me back. When she finally let go, she had tears in her eyes but was remarkably composed.

"Were you hurt?" I asked.

"No—"

"Please don't lie to me."

"Not in the slightest. He treated me quite well, actually."

She insisted she was unharmed, but a subtle trembling in her shoulders told me she was shaken. If she wasn't traumatized, it was only because Goddard made her feel safe, and for that I was grateful. When he said he had the chance to end my life but didn't as payback, maybe, I thought, he was talking about her. Perhaps from the moment he took her he knew it was only for ransom and never for revenge.

"Where'd they find you?"

"In a room. A horrid room."

"Did it lock from the outside?"

She looked up surprised.

"Yes. Yes, it did. He said his parents used to lock him in there for days. I know it sounds crazy, but he had a heart. I knew he wouldn't hurt me."

"Thank God you were right. You need water? Are you dehydrated?"

"Yes, no," she said, and she laughed. "I mean, I'll have some water. But I'm not dehydrated. I'm fine. Will you tell this guy?"

The nervous paramedic looked at me and said, "I was ordered to check her vitals. I'm sorry."

"You're off the hook, pal. If anyone asks, tell them Lieutenant Brae said so."

He poured a cup of water from a canteen and handed it to her. She took a couple of sips, and I could tell she was thirsty. When she was ready, I thanked the man and helped her out of the ambulance.

Just then the captain came up with the chief of police, who didn't have his usual entourage of assistants, assistant assistants, and senior officials. He was a linebacker-sized man with thinning brown hair and big jowls. He hunched forward when he walked, and he always had the expression of someone who was late for something important.

"Fine job, Lieutenant," he said, and it might have been the first time he ever spoke to me. "I'm gonna recommend you for a commendation."

"Thank you, sir."

Jackson shook my hand with a warm smile.

"I'm glad you're okay. I'm glad Ruth is okay. Can we have a word?"

I turned to her, and she said, "Please go, I'm fine."

Before I went, I looked over at Harrigan.

"Can you watch her?"

"I already was, Detective."

Jackson, the chief, and I stepped away and stood in a circle behind a fire truck. It wasn't much privacy, but it was secluded enough to let us talk without being overheard.

"How'd you know where to look?" the captain asked. "I mean, that was a needle in a haystack. We pulled Goddard's address. He's been in Virginia for years."

"He lived here when I was a kid. I remembered it last night."

"Well," he said. "I'm glad you have your memory back."

"I remembered something else. It might be of interest." I glanced over my shoulder, lowered my voice. "A long time ago—I was eleven or twelve—I found a body at the foot of the cliff—"

"What year was that?" the chief interrupted.

"Maybe '41 or '42."

"Right," he said, looking at Jackson. "I investigated it. I was a detective at the time. The man was reported missing by the family but wasn't found until a few weeks later."

"Do you know who he was?"

"He was a 'Goddard.' The grandfather, I think. I forget his first name."

"What happened?"

"Not much. It was determined to be an accident. The old man suffered dementia and was a bit of a kook. He was in the Spanish-American War. Probably thought he was charging up San Juan Hill."

I smiled and asked, "Why's that?"

"He was in the cavalry during the war. We found a wooden saber on the cliff."

"A sword?" I said, and the chief nodded. "Thomas Goddard had a sword when we were kids." My voice grew eager, my words more direct. "Do you remember what happened to his parents?"

"I do. They were murdered. Shot during a robbery."

"Do you see a pattern?"

When the chief paused, the hair on the back of my neck stood up.

"I get what you're saying," he said, "but that was a robbery gone bad. We got the killers—they confessed. They worked at the father's shoe factory. Two Oriental men, Chinese or Korean, I can't remember. They cased the place, camped out on the cliff back there."

My face dropped in relief. It was strange to suspect someone for something they didn't do but be doubtful of something they did. I knew then that Goddard didn't kill his parents, but I was also certain he had ordered the slaughter, probably as revenge for the former. He may have been a monster, but he wasn't a devil, and in the perverse logic of Boston's street corner morality, there actually was a difference. Or in the parlance of Travis Kemp, maybe *he was crazy, but he wasn't nuts.*

An officer came up from behind and surprised us all.

"Is Lieutenant Brae here?"

I turned around and he asked, "Can you show the ME where the bodies are?"

"I'm afraid your work's not done," the chief said.

When I glanced at Jackson, he said, "Go. We're finished. Thank you."

I walked over to the medical examiner's van and found Dr. Ansell and an intern getting the equipment ready. Two paramedics were there to assist, and they stood holding stretchers, waiting for the word. I recognized one of the young men from the night of Doug Rodrigues' murder. I had treated him harshly and shouldn't have, so I waved and he replied with a timid hello.

Ansell was in the back of the van, frenzied and sweating, talking to himself or anyone else who would listen. When he saw me, he said, "You finally got him, kid. I knew you would. When I heard your lady was missing, I was scared to death. Couldn't sleep. I was praying for you, kid, and I'm not much of a believer."

"Word travels fast."

He climbed down from the van and turned to me.

"When you been in this business as long as me, people tell you things. They tell you what's happened but also what *might* happen. I got a call from headquarters. People were worried, kid. If something bad happened—and there's no use sayin' what that bad thing is—then people needed to prepare for it. You know? For your sake. You have a habit of making your peace after someone's gone. You like to talk to the dead. You came in to see your old comrades. You said you were investigating, but I knew otherwise. Can I blame you? No. I've been talking to the dead for twenty years—sometimes they talk back. But if you came down to my place, to make an identification or to see some-body—and we don't have to say who that somebody could've been—then I was asked to make that person look good, as good as I could. And you know what I told that guy, the one on the phone?"

"What?" I said with a tender smile.

"I told them if you came down to my place, you weren't fuckin' getting in."

I thought of Ruth and the notion that she could have been hurt or worse. I didn't know whether I would have had the strength or courage to identify her, but I was glad to know someone was watching out for me.

"C'mon boys," he said. "Let's get 'em before the wildlife does."

"Doc, the terrain is pretty rough. Wanna just let us do it?"

He put a bag over his shoulder and scoffed.

"Kid, I climbed Monte Cassino with Krauts shooting down at me. Don't tell me about rough terrain. Besides, Crenshaw here couldn't spot a corpse in a Karloff film. He's from New Jersey, if that tells you anything."

The intern made a sheepish frown and looked away. Then the five of us marched single file into the woods like an expedition party. I led the pack, wading through the darkness with tired eyes, searching for the foot of the cliff. Despite all the equipment, we had only one flash-light, which became more crippling the farther we strayed from the sirens and headlights. I kept to the east of Whiskey Point, the most gradual way down, and we descended a small ravine.

As we walked, bugs circled our heads, things darted in the bushes. The air had a stewy humidity that felt like a jungle, and I itched all over. Finally, I saw some open space behind the trees and knew we were nearing the bottom. When we came out of the forest, we were at the base, and I looked up to the mighty rock face, towering and jagged. It was no less magnificent than when I had come here twenty-five years before, and I was pleased that some things from my child-hood hadn't changed.

"Here we go," one of the paramedics said, sweeping the flashlight. And there on the ground, flat against the dirt and facing upwards, were the bodies of Travis Kemp and Thomas Goddard. They were separated by only a few feet, as if Kemp didn't let go until they hit. I walked over and pressed my fingers against his neck, just to be sure. I looked into his face and saw a man who was finally at peace.

"Rest well, good buddy," I said, and I forced his eyelids shut.

Behind me, Ansell was going through his bag trying to find something.

"Where's my goddamn stethoscope?" he said. His assistant tried to help, but he smacked his hand away. "Get away, you pansy. It's a rhetorical question. Don't touch my things."

I went over to Goddard and looked down at him. His eyes were open, and blood trickled from the side of his mouth. His nose looked broken, and his cheeks were red and swollen from the fight. As I went to leave, I noticed that his fists were still clenched. I felt somehow sorry for him, although I didn't know why.

BY THE TIME we got back with the bodies, many of the vehicles had left and things were settling down. There were no more flashing lights or frantic two-way radio conversations. Patrolmen lingered on the lawn waiting for their shifts to end; agents scoured the premises looking for evidence. Two men from the Bureau of Criminal Investigations came out of the house carrying notebooks. Workers from a building security firm were unloading sheets of plywood, preparing to vandal-proof the property. Maybe, I hoped, the incident would bring attention to the place, and someone would buy and restore it. It may have been derelict, but it had a historic grandeur that was rare among the drab three-deckers and tenements of Roxbury.

Ruth was in the backseat of Jackson's car, and the door was open. Harrigan stood a few feet away, his arms at his side and his expression stern, guarding her like a centurion. With the excitement over, I began to notice a pain in my ankle, and I had a slight limp.

"Are you hurt?" Harrigan asked as I approached.

"I'll be fine, just a sprain," I said. "How about Sully?"

When he shook his head, my body went numb. I stared at him for a few more seconds, hoping I had misread the gesture, hoping that what was true was not. The captain walked over and stood quietly beside us.

"Are you sure?" I said.

"It was just announced."

"And the other officer?"

Jackson said, "He has a severe head injury, but he'll probably live."

Ruth got out of the car and came over to me. She put her arm around my back, her head on my shoulder. I could tell she had been crying—perhaps for Sully, but maybe for herself.

I looked at the captain.

"How'd they get here so quick?" I said.

Had Ruth been any other civilian, he might not have discussed the confidential facts. But because she had worked at headquarters before becoming a nurse, she was a safe confidant.

"A call came into headquarters before yours, just after nine. Said there was gonna be trouble. He didn't give an address but explained the location."

"Kemp."

"Had to be. From what we gather, Sully and his partner showed up. His partner got to the house first and went inside. Goddard must have been watching. He hit him over the head with an old baluster. Then he ran outside and saw Sully. Shots were exchanged. Kemp must have stumbled on the scene then—"

"Stumbled is right. He had a bullet hole in his leg."

"We believe Goddard ran out of ammo or his gun jammed because it was found on the lawn. Kemp went after him. The rest is history."

"That it is," I said. "That it is."

"Think we should get you checked out?" the captain asked.

I looked down at my torn shirt and soiled clothes.

"You think I wanna go into City Hospital looking like this?"

Ruth made a wistful smile, Harrigan was stone-faced, and Jackson didn't even acknowledge the joke. Too much had happened, and everyone was drained. Humor may have been a good remedy for stress, but it was no substitution for grief.

"Brae," someone said, and I turned around to see the doctor waving me over from his van window.

"Just a sec," I said, and I hobbled over.

"Know what time it is, kid?"

I shook my head.

"12:06. That means it's Wednesday. Wednesday the 27th."

I just stared with a blank indifference.

"July the 27th," he said. "The ceasefire. The war ended thirteen years ago today, kid. I don't know if that's coincidence or irony..." He reached out, patted me on the shoulder. "...but it's definitely propitious. You can look that word up later."

At that point, not much could have surprised me, but Ansell beat the odds. I was too stumped to reply, so I looked at him and started to laugh uncontrollably, the first real laughter I had had in days.

"Let's hit the road," he said, turning to his assistant. "And for Chrissakes watch out. If you drive like you work, we'll end up backing into someone—" The doctor looked at me and winked, "And that'd be irony."

As the van reversed, I saluted him, but he was too busy berating his intern. They made a U-turn and pulled away, and the sounds of his ranting faded into the night.

Harrigan, Ruth, and I got into Jackson's car, and he dropped us near the entrance where we had left the cruiser. A few neighbors were gathered by a fence, but they could have just been there to escape the heat. Like any area with poverty and high crime, the presence of police cars and sirens generated about as much interest as a fender bender.

The street was blocked off at both ends, but we were ushered right through. As we went down the hill, I looked out at the cracked sidewalks, overgrown lots, and sagging three-deckers. I thought back to when I roamed those lonely streets and felt like king of the world. Roxbury was the neighborhood of my youth, a place I had been running from all my life but never really left. I loved it as someone would love a wayward son, out of instinct and not always because it was deserved.

I looked back to see Ruth on her side, sleeping along the vinyl. She was as pretty as a picture, and anyone who saw her wouldn't have believed how feisty she was. Behind that angelic face was a woman that was as determined as she was quarrelsome, and I wouldn't have wanted it any other way. She may have been hard to handle, but she was easy to love, and that was what counted.

"What a beauty," I whispered.

Harrigan raised his eyes in agreement.

"Know what they'd say about you in St. Kitts, Detective?"

"Tell me."

"They'd say you've got life by the bullocks. That you're rolling in clover."

"I like you islanders. You always see the sun."

"Even when we don't, we know it's up there."

CHAPTER 30

IT WAS A WARM MONDAY MORNING—THE FIRST OF AUGUST—WHEN Harrigan and I followed a security official over the tarmac at Logan Airport. In the distance, a Boing 727 touched down on the runway and the ground shook. Parked near a commercial hangar was a silver Douglas C-47 with its props spinning and cargo bay open. And there on a freight dolly, ready to be loaded was the body of Travis Kemp. We were met by two ground crew members who escorted us to the casket and stepped away so I could be alone. When Harrigan turned to join them, I tapped his arm and asked him to stay.

I placed a hand on the coffin, dropped my head, and pretended to pray although my mind was blank. I reached into a paper bag I held under my arm and took out an American flag I had brought back from Korea. The brittle cotton was hard to unfold, and Harrigan helped as we draped it over the casket and secured it to the cargo straps with pins. I was never one for drama, but I owed Kemp a final tribute as a friend and as a soldier. I stood to attention, arched my back, and brought my hand to my forehead in a solemn salute that meant "thank you, farewell, and Godspeed" all in the same gesture.

The ground crew came over and turned the hand crank of the dolly to make it level with the cargo bay. As the four of us pushed, the casket slid along the metal rollers and into the cabin. When the turbines roared, the gust from the props blew hair into my face and made us all squint. The signal was nothing like the panic of the chopper pilots the night of the evacuation in Korea, but nevertheless, it told me it was time to go. Kemp was returning to Cleveland, to his own Roxbury, the place where he experienced most of his heartaches but also his joys. In the industrial shadows of that dying port town, he had tried to carve out a life of middle-class simplicity from the damaged substance of his past.

Like all soldiers, Kemp was haunted by the things he had seen and done and didn't do, and a cruel irony of war was that just because you survived didn't mean you could go on living. But if it was never too late to be a hero, it was never too late to be forgiven. Travis Kemp had stayed in the battle far longer than was expected of any soldier, and if he had earned anything for his sacrifices, it was the right to finally go home.

HARRIGAN and I drove through Dudley Square in the thick of the noontime rush. For once we were in no hurry. While we waited at a light, I looked out to society—to the automobiles, people, churches, and storefronts—with incredible wonder. In the garage of a corner gas station, I watched a mechanic unbolt the rims of a Buick. Across the street, two black women were inspecting corn outside a market. Sunny-faced kids skipped down the sidewalk, as excited as flies and giggling for no other reason than that life itself was pleasurable.

There was a glorious humility to it all. Countless wars had been fought, millions were dead, but humanity seemed to chug along to the inner rhythms of a new day. As cynical as I was, I always believed it was ignorance. But when I heard the laughter of the children, I realized it was innocence after all.

We continued down Washington Street along the bus route, and I could have pointed out every mailbox, street sign, and fire hydrant with my eyes closed. The people may have been different and the shops may have had new names, but the essence of Roxbury was still there. Like Whiskey Point, some things had survived the changes and gone unnoticed and probably would be there for generations. It was nice to know that not everything was temporary.

We drove up Valentine Street and parked along the curb. Harrigan turned off the ignition and said, "Take your time."

"You're coming too."

He hesitated and turned to me.

"Are you sure, Detective?"

"That's an order."

Without another word, he got out of the car. Together we walked up to the door and I knocked. When no one answered, I knocked a second time, then a third.

"It's a beautiful day," he said. "Maybe she's out for a walk?"

Harrigan may have been correct, but his words made me think of something. I went down the steps and looked along the narrow side of the house. I motioned for him to follow, and we walked into the backyard. Beside an old wooden shed, I saw Mrs. Russo kneeling down in a garden, her hair in a bun and a flowered apron around her waist. I remembered when Al's father used to sit on the roof and guard the vegetables during the Depression. The shed looked much bigger back then, but so did everything else.

As I approached her, I forced a cough so she wouldn't be startled. She turned around and her face brightened.

"Jody, I'm so glad to see you," she said, standing up.

"Mrs. Russo, this is Detective Harrigan."

She took off one of her potting gloves and shook his hand.

"Please, call me Natalie. Won't you two come inside?"

She picked up her basket of tomatoes, cucumbers, and summer squash, and we followed her to the back door. We crossed through a small mudroom and into the kitchen. A large pot was simmering on the stove, and all I could smell was bacon. She lifted the top and stirred it a few times.

"Ham and pea soup. Are you hungry?"

"We just ate but thank you."

She pulled out three chairs from the kitchen table, and we all sat.

"I read everything in the newspaper," she said. "I got a call Friday. From a Mr. Jackson. Nice man."

"The captain."

"He said they concluded it was that man who killed Al. That man who killed the other veterans. Is that true?"

"It is," I said.

"Why?"

Harrigan glanced over with a look of warning.

"What...Why is it true?" I asked, tripping over my words. "I mean, how do they know it's him? That what you mean?"

"No, why'd he do it? Why'd he kill them? What was the reason?"

It was the question I dreaded most but that I knew I couldn't avoid. How could I tell her that her only son had been involved in a massacre which killed two dozen peasant families? How could I say that he had known and didn't report it? As I reflected on the dilemma, I couldn't help but agonize over my part in it. Maybe I hadn't been present, but I was nearby; maybe I had forgotten, but amnesia was not always unintentional. If I wasn't prepared to deal with my own moral lapses, I had no right to expose Al's.

I faced her and said, "We'll both have to wait for the official report. At least for now, we know Al is in heaven, and a murderer is in hell."

She touched the gold crucifix around her neck, made a sad frown, tried to smile but couldn't.

"Well," she said. "What's done is done. It won't bring Al back."

I reached in my pocket and took out the divisional pin that was found on Russo the night of the accident. When I dropped it in her palm, she gazed at it like a gemstone. She may not have known what it was, but she understood what it meant.

"It's Al's pin," I said. "They found it on him."

She closed her fist around the piece and looked up tearfully.

"Thank you."

The pot bubbled over, and she went over to turn down the burner. When Harrigan and I stood, she knew it was time for us to go. She got a paper bag out of the cupboard and filled it with some of the vegetables from the garden.

"Here," she said. "These are for both of you."

I took the bag, and she gave me a big hug. Then she turned to Harrigan and hugged him too, and he was flustered. We walked down the hallway and into the living room, where the photograph of young Al rested on the mantel.

"Will you be seeing any of the men from the war? If so, I'd love to meet anyone who knew Al."

I stopped at the doorway, turned to her with a gentle smile.

"I'm sure I will. And when I do, you'll be the first to know."

End

The story continues in book 2,
City of Small Kingdoms. **Continue reading for a sneak peak, or follow the link below to purchase.**
https://links.liquidmindpublishing.com/9QtS

Sign up for Jonathan's newsletter for updates on deals and new releases!
https://liquidmind.media/j-cullen-newsletter-sign-up-2-jody/

CITY OF SMALL KINGDOMS

CHAPTER 1

OCTOBER 1945

WE BEAT UP A PRIEST, but we really had no choice. We didn't just beat him up—we kicked his skull, gouged his eyes, and ripped out his hair. By the time we were finished, he was lying on the ground in a pool of blood, groaning and half-dead.

It was the last thing Sweeney, Russo, and I expected when we went out that night. But it wasn't just any night—it was the first Halloween after the war. We had finally walloped the Japs, and after four years of rationing and blackouts, people wanted to live again. It was a wild and unpredictable time, filled with a restless energy that bordered on lunacy. Music blared from every front parlor; couples danced openly in the streets. The bars were busy every night of the week, and it was impossible to get a taxi.

By nine o'clock, most of the younger kids had gone home. Trick-or-treating was over, and it was time for mischief. Gangs of rowdy teens roamed the neighborhood looking for trouble. They broke bottles, smashed windows, and got into fights. Their hoots and cries echoed throughout the streets and, at times, turned Roxbury into a real-life horror show.

But Sweeney, Russo, and I stayed in the shadows and out of their way. Tired of walking and with our candy bags overflowing, we stopped at a corner and stood behind a giant oak tree.

"Hands up!" Russo said, pointing a cardboard laser gun.

With his clothes painted silver, I wasn't sure if he was a Martian or The Tin Man. I pushed the gun away, and he made an electric hum that sounded more like a foghorn.

I pulled out my plastic sword and put it under his chin.

"Where's me tribute, matey?" I said.

Dressed as a pirate, I made a pirate's sneer and pushed it harder.

"Stop," he whined. "That hurts."

I released the weapon with a hearty laugh and shoved it back in my belt. Then I turned to Chester, who was sitting on the curb, and said, "Who are you supposed to be again?"

"Thomas Aquine-*ass*," Russo blurted. "Aquine-*ass*, Aquine-*ass*!"

With his brown cowl and large hood, Sweeney looked like Friar Tuck without the tonsure. A thick wooden cross hung from his neck.

"Who the hell is Thomas Aquinas?" I said.

"He's the greatest Saint who ever lived."

I started to laugh but stopped when I saw that he was embarrassed.

"My ma made me wear it," he mumbled, looking down.

Chester "Chesty" Sweeney was that lovable but hapless friend everyone had. Short, fat, and clumsy, he stuttered when he spoke and stumbled when he walked. He was shy to a fault, and the mere sight of a girl would send him into convulsions of self-conscious angst. He was so chunky that he appeared to have breasts, and the kids in school taunted him with the nickname Chesty.

Like most of us, Sweeney was poor. He lived in a cold-water flat outside of Dudley Square with his mother, a religious fanatic who called herself an "Old Catholic" and believed demons were out to get her. His father died when he was eight after the trawler that he worked on was lost at sea in the Hurricane of '38. As the only children in school who didn't have siblings, Russo, Sweeney, and I hung out together as much for protection as for friendship.

"Thomas Aquinas?" I said. "I guess it can't hurt to have God on our side."

"Or this."

When we looked, Russo pulled out a pint of rum. Even in the darkness, I could see the brown liquid swishing side to side, and it gave me a nervous thrill. He twisted off the cap and handed it to me first.

"Go on, have your grog, matey."

"Cheers," I said, smelling inside.

I took a swig and instantly my throat burned, my eyes got teary. Nevertheless, I held the liquor down and had some more.

"Your turn, your holiness," I said, giving it to Sweeney.

His fingers trembled as he took it, and he gazed at the bottle like it was poison.

"C'mon fat boy!" Russo said.

When he tried to force Sweeney to drink, I shoved him away.

"No! He don't have to do anything he don't want to."

"Take it easy, Jody," Russo said, flaring his arms. "I ain't makin' him do nothin'."

It was then that we heard the low murmur of Sweeney's voice.

"I want to. I want to drink it," he said.

While Russo and I watched, he took a deep breath and raised the bottle. He closed his eyes with the solemnness of prayer and brought it to his lips. Then he began to guzzle.

Suddenly, we heard a noise. Sweeney let go of the bottle and it smashed.

"Aw, look what you—"

"Shhh!" I said.

I peered around the tree and saw a gang of older kids coming towards us. They were loud and drunk, swaggering down the middle of the road like a posse out for blood.

Russo looked over my shoulder.

"Who is it?" he whispered.

When they crossed under a streetlamp, I recognized the leader and gasped.

"Vigliotti!"

Anthony Vigliotti was a local thug who left school at fifteen and lived off the streets as a petty thief and swindler. Tall and thin, he had lanky arms that went almost to his knees. As an Italian with bright blonde hair, some people suspected he was adopted but no one ever dared to ask.

"Whadda we do?" Russo said nervously.

They were a half block away and moving with the slow yet all-consuming fury of a tornado. I watched as one of the boys tore a mirror off an automobile and threw it in an alley. Then another howled and pulled off a fence post. When some lingering trick-or-treaters fell into their path, they were pushed, jostled, and shoved to the ground. Even under the calming influence of the alcohol, I was frightened beyond words.

"We gotta go," I said.

The gang was now at the opposite corner of the intersection and moving fast. Together, we crept back from the tree and went in the other direction. We had only gone a few steps when Chesty stopped.

"My candy."

"Quick, quick," I said.

He scurried over, got the bag, and started walking back to us.

"Oh, what do we have here?" a voice said, and I cringed.

They spotted us.

"Run!" I shouted.

We spun around and sprinted for our lives. Russo tossed his card-board gun; Chesty dropped his bag, and the candy went everywhere. For some reason, I kept my plastic sword even though it was useless.

By the time we reached the next crossroads, Sweeney was lagging behind. With his fat legs, he was as slow as a bison in a stampede, and I worried they would get him.

"C'mon, man," I said, turning back to encourage him.

The gang was closing in—I could hear their voices behind us. We cut right and went down a small street. A long and rambling stone wall, eight feet high and hidden behind weeds, ran down one side, and by some miracle, I spotted a gate.

"This way," I said.

We ran over, but it was locked. Standing in the overgrowth, the three of us looked at each other and silently agreed that our only escape was over the wall.

"Chesty first," I said, and Russo nodded.

We took Sweeney under the shoulders and hoisted him up. He teetered for a moment then fell forward into the blackness, landing with a thud.

Vigliotti and his gang were only seconds away. Russo grabbed one of the iron slats, lifted himself up, and was quickly over. Alone and exposed, I was more afraid than ever, and my heart pounded. When someone threw a rock, it missed me by inches and bounced off the gate with a gong. I looked up and started to climb, expecting at any moment to be pulled down and beaten.

Just as I reached the top, blue lights flashed across the night. I glanced back, and a police car was speeding down the street. Instantly, the gang scattered, leaping through bushes, tumbling over trashcans, darting down driveways.

I thought the nightmare was over, but it had only just begun.

———

WHEN I OPENED MY EYES, I was lying on my back and staring at the stars. In those first few seconds, I didn't know where I was, but I was comfortable and not afraid. Out of the corner of my eye, I saw the sliver of a moon hovering over the tree line. Then somebody shook my shoulder.

"Jody? You okay?"

I turned my neck, and the back of my head was sore. In the pitch dark, I saw Russo's silver costume and then his face. He was standing over me, and I hadn't even noticed.

"What happened?" I asked.

"You slipped and fell. I think you hit your noggin."

I sat up on the damp grass and looked around dizzily, rubbing my crown and wondering where I was. When I saw the moss-covered wall beside me, I remembered what had happened.

"Where's Chesty?" I said.

"Don't know. He kept running."

I stood up and dusted off my clothes.

"Let's go find him."

We went up a short stretch of lawn and came to a courtyard with gravel walkways, hedgerows, and flower beds. All the vegetation was dead, but there was a cold lushness I couldn't explain.

"What is this place?" Russo wondered.

"Don't know."

We walked with a slow fascination, past benches, birdbaths, and statuettes of religious figures we knew but could not name. At the center of the courtyard was a large white sculpture of Jesus, seated on a rock and ministering to three boys. Two were on his lap, but the third was standing and facing away from the others.

Something fluttered above, maybe a bat, and we both jumped. I looked up and saw a bell tower rising above the buildings. With its open belfry and huge glass windows, I recognized it immediately. A chill went through me that was a blend of fear and awe.

"Kilda," I mumbled, staring hypnotically.

It was a structure I had only ever seen from a distance, and now it was right in front of me.

"Kill what?"

The old Christian abbey was only four miles from downtown Boston, but it might as well have been in the Himalayas. Built when the area was farmland, it was strangely out-of-place in the urban slums that surrounded it.

"It's an abbey," I said.

No one I met had ever been inside the property, and it was so isolated that even birds seemed to avoid it. As far back as I could remember, its name was never printed or published; it wasn't carved into an archway or marked somewhere by a plaque. Yet everyone knew it as St Kilda.

"Gives me the creeps," Russo said, stopping to look around.

"Let's keep moving."

Suddenly, we heard someone. We dove behind a hedge and got down on our stomachs. Peering through the branches, we saw a figure in the shadows of the portico. Whoever it was stepped out of the darkness and began to go across the grass. As he got closer, we realized it was not one person but two.

"He's got Sweeney!" Russo said in a quiet panic. "Who is he, Jody? Who is he?!"

I elbowed him and told him to shut up.

"A priest. Maybe a monk."

The man held Sweeney close, but I couldn't tell if it was a headlock or an arm restraint.

"Come out, boys."

When he called to us, Russo and I froze.

"Come out now," he repeated, this time louder. "I know you are there. Don't make me come get you, righto?"

Growing up in Roxbury, we had heard lots of foreign accents, but this one was unfamiliar. Russo looked at me for an explanation, and I just shrugged my shoulders.

When the man reached the middle of the courtyard, he stopped at the statue of Jesus with the children. Sweeney didn't seem to struggle; it looked like he couldn't move. We all respected, even feared the clergy, but for him, there must have been a deeper terror because his mother was so devout.

"Come out now boys," the priest continued, "or your friend is in mighty trouble. You don't want that, righto?"

In the moonlight, his silhouette cast an enormous shadow. He had on a long, black overcoat that should have reached his ankles but ended at his knees. Beneath it was a brown tunic which, ironically, was the same as Sweeney's costume.

"I count to ten then I take your friend away. Okay?"

With Sweeney firmly in his grip, he began to move in a circle, scanning the hedgerows and bushes, searching.

"Von, two—"

He spoke with a drawn-out emphasis that was probably meant to coax us but only made us more scared.

"He's crazy, Jody," Russo said, and he was right.

There was something sinister in the man's voice, and when he finally turned in our direction, I understood why. His eyes were wide, and his tongue was slack. He slurred and seethed like a rabid dog. He might have been drunk, but I had no doubt that he was insane too.

"He's got something, Jody!"

"Dree, vor," the priest said.

Squinting in the darkness, I looked closer and realized he was holding something to Sweeney's neck. My heart raced, and I began to feel sick.

"Whadda we do, Jody? Whadda we do?!"

"*Vive, seeeex...*"

When Sweeney whimpered, Russo began to panic, his legs shaking. I leaned in close, whispered in his ear.

"Go distract him," I said.

"Distract him?"

"I'll get him from behind."

"Get him?" Russo said, his hushed voice cracking. "We can't—"

I grabbed him by the back of the neck.

"He's gonna fuckin' kill him!"

"*Seven, Eeet...*"

The hideous enumeration continued.

Without another word, Russo got up and stepped out into the open, and the priest saw him immediately.

"Ah, come now," he said with a devious smile.

Russo went towards him, the man urging him with each wary step.

"Good boy. Closer now. Don't be afraid."

As he did, I darted behind the hedgerows and circled the courtyard, reaching down and loosening a white brick from the walkway. I stepped out onto the gravel and crept up behind the man when, suddenly, he lunged forward and grabbed Russo.

"Jody!"

Now he had them both.

What spell of courage or foolishness came over me, I didn't know. But I walked up and raised the brick as high as I could. Hesitating for a half-second, I thought about what I was doing and knew I had no choice. Then I swung the brick and smashed the back of his skull.

Instantly, everything went quiet. The man wobbled but didn't fall over. He let go of Sweeney and Russo and slowly turned around, looking at me with the dumb glare of an idiot who has been taunted. Even from ten feet away, I could smell alcohol on his breath, see the madness in his eyes. When a trickle of blood came down his ear, he wiped it and looked at his hand.

Then he snarled and charged straight at me.

"Get him!" I shouted, and all hell broke loose.

Russo jumped on his back and got him in a chokehold. I kneed him in the balls, and he was briefly stunned. When we finally wrestled him to the ground, Russo gouged his eyes while I battered him with kicks and punches. But the priest continued to resist.

"Stop!"

I looked back and Sweeney was standing in the distance, his tunic torn at the seams, tears streaming down his face. Even in all the chaos, I somehow noticed that his wooden cross was no longer around his neck.

"Help us!" I shrieked, but he wouldn't move.

The man grabbed me by the throat, and I bit his hand. Russo took one step back, wound up, and booted him in the jaw. The priest's head dropped to the ground, and he lay panting and snorting like a slain beast.

I ran over to Sweeney and said, "C'mon! We gotta go!"

"You killed him. You killed a priest."

"That's no holy man," Russo said, spitting blood. "Let's go fat boy. We just saved your life."

We ran towards the wall and were halfway there when the priest yelled out, "Boy, don't leave me here..."

Sweeney stopped so we stopped too.

"...You're a good boy, righto?"

He had the weak, quivering voice of someone in agony, but I had no pity.

"I gotta help him," Sweeney said. "I gotta—"

I stormed over and brought my face to within inches of his.

"You gotta do nothing. That guy is bats...bananas...nuts!"

But he wouldn't look at me. He just stood there shaking his head back and forth like a stubborn child.

"To hell with him," Russo said, hissing in disgust. "Let him go."

"Boy," the man cried. "My leg...it's broken. Help me."

Sweeney looked towards the courtyard, his cheeks flush and lips trembling.

"Jody," he said, "I have to—"

Without an explanation or even a goodbye, he turned and started across the grass. Russo and I watched as his plump figure lumbered towards the cloister and vanished in the shadows.

Tired, cold, and sore from the fight, we headed back to the gate. Once Russo was safely over, I climbed up and stood balancing at the top. I cupped my hands in front of my mouth and called out, "Chesty?"

Scanning the darkness, I looked for movement but saw none.

"C'mon, Jody," Russo said.

I tried one last time.

"Chesty?"

All I heard was the echo of my own voice.

CITY OF SMALL KINGDOMS

CHAPTER 2

JANUARY 1968

I HADN'T BEEN warm in two months. The winter chill seemed to dig into my bones and settle there like a deep and permanent ache. It hurt when I sneezed, and each time I coughed, I could taste bile. Half the department was out sick, and we were so short-staffed that Chief McNamara had to borrow officers from nearby Somerville. Even Captain Jackson, who hadn't missed a day since Truman was president, had been out for almost a week.

I looked up from my desk in a drowsy stupor. Through the foggy window, I could see only the outlines of buildings, the headlights of cars along Cambridge Street. I scribbled something on the document I was working on and put it in the drawer. I got my coat, turned off the lights, and locked the office door. Another workday was done.

The hallways of headquarters were desolate at night. The only sound was the muffled footsteps of the evening staff two floors above. I turned into a stairwell, went down three flights, and burst into the frigid night. It was the last week of January—the bowels of winter—and with the parking lot covered in black ice, I stepped carefully.

I had just got to my car when a voice called out, and I almost slipped.

"Mister!"

I turned around and saw someone coming out of the shadows. I put my hand on my .38 out of instinct, not because I felt threatened. When my eyes adjusted, I realized it was an Asian boy, perhaps fifteen years old, dressed only in a work shirt and white smock.

"Are you a police officer?" he said.

"Why? What's wrong?"

"We found something. Can you come?"

When I nodded yes, he turned around, and I followed him. We went down an alleyway that ran between the buildings, the underbelly of the city and a hidden world that most residents would never see. The pavement was rutted—there was litter and sludge everywhere. Rats scuttled in the darkness, and somewhere a tabby cat hissed.

We turned right, then left, then right again, and soon I was lost in the urban maze. Finally, we came to a dead-end, and in the distance, I saw a floodlight above a narrow door. A small wooden sign mounted above the lintel read: Lantern House Restaurant – Employees Only. A group of Asian workers was gathered by a dumpster, smoking obsessively, speaking in their native tongue.

"Please, just over here," the boy said, waving.

As I approached, the crowd parted, and a couple of men even bowed. They were all dressed the same, with rubber boots, soiled aprons, and white undershirts. Hours laboring in the hot kitchen must have made them resistant to the cold, I thought, because anyone else would have had hypothermia.

"What's this all about?" I said impatiently.

The boy looked at the men and then to me.

"They found something...inside."

I eyed them skeptically and walked over to the dumpster. Gripping the metal rim, I pulled myself up and looked in, but all I could see were dark piles of garbage.

"No," the boy said. "Under the hood, near the back."

I reached for my lighter, and it took three tries to start. I held out the flame and saw plastic bags, empty boxes, and canisters. Woven throughout was the organic muck of restaurant waste—fish heads, onion skins, pork rinds, rotten mushrooms. Even with a stuffy nose, the odor was enough to make me gag. A solitary seagull, as bold as he was hungry, landed in the heap and began to pick at a chicken bone.

I looked down at the boy.

"I don't see anything," I said.

He glanced over at the men, who were huddled together and watching.

"They were sure they saw it."

I shook my head.

"I don't see anything. Can they show me?"

"They won't."

I frowned and said, "Whaddya mean *they won't?*"

"It's a bad omen, Sir."

Suddenly, the bird flew away with a morsel in its mouth, and the workers all gasped.

My hand was getting numb from holding the cold metal. Just as I was ready to give up, a chunk of ice fell from a building ledge and went into the dumpster. Like a reflex, my eyes followed to where it landed, and I noticed something shiny in the corner. I held the lighter out again and, wedged between a plastic bag and an empty tin of canola oil, was a burgundy shoe—a woman's shoe.

I looked closer and shuddered when I saw the smooth skin of a human leg.

CITY OF SMALL KINGDOMS

CHAPTER 3

I TIPTOED INTO THE BEDROOM, AND SHE WAS ON HER SIDE, A DOWN comforter wrapped around her body. Her eyes were closed but that didn't mean she was sleeping. I took off my suit and hung it next to her nurse uniforms, which she had ironed and folded neatly. When I heard the bed creak, I turned around and whispered, "Ruth?"

"You're late."

"Something came up."

There was a dreamy pause.

"Funny thing about life. Something always comes up."

As I peeled the damp undershirt off my body, I realized I was sweating all over. I had witnessed hundreds of murders, but they never got any easier, and each one presented a new trauma.

"I made meatloaf," she said with a yawn. "You can reheat it."

"No appetite, but thanks."

"Since when?"

"There was a body in a dumpster near headquarters."

The moment her eyes popped open and she sat up, I regretted mentioning it.

"My gosh. How?" she asked.

"A porter found me in the parking lot. Took me to it."

"A murder?"

"I'd say so."

The light from the hallway broke across her face, and I could tell she had been crying.

"How was the appointment?" I said.

When she didn't answer, I thought she might not have heard me. But as I went to ask again, she blurted, "More drugs."

"More drugs?"

"More drugs."

I reached out to turn off the hallway lamp, and the whole apartment went dark. I climbed into bed and put my chest against her back, my arms around her stomach. Her purple negligee was absurdly unsuited for the weather, but she was never one to sacrifice femininity for comfort, and she was the only woman I ever met who wore perfume to bed. As I lay snugly against her warm skin, I was for a moment aroused, until I gave in to exhaustion and was out cold.

———

RUTH WAS STILL ASLEEP when I got up the next morning. I crept out to the kitchen and opened the cabinet above the stove. I reached for the empty Maxwell House tin that I kept hidden behind a row of soup cans. Inside was a small black box with the gold necklace I had purchased a week before for our first wedding anniversary. The actual date wasn't for two more days, but with the unpredictable schedules of a nurse and a cop, I had to improvise.

I sat at the table sipping tea, crunching on a raisin English muffin. The first rays of dawn came through the windows and filled the kitchen with light. When I looked out, I saw that it had snowed. On the side lawn, a cardinal was bathing in the flakes, a solitary left-behind from the hordes of birds that had long since fled.

Before I left, I put the box on the counter along with a small note I had asked a secretary at work to type for me. My penmanship had always been bad, and I knew that nothing would ruin a gift like a sentimental card whose sentiments were unreadable.

As I drove to work, I imagined the moment Ruth would awake to find it, knowing that the snowstorm would only add to her joy. She may have been from Southern California, but she had taken to New England like a Puritan. She loved the cold and hated the heat, which put her at odds with that large portion of the local populace that resented winter. She didn't always fit in, but she always knew where she stood, and although we grew up on different coasts, our hearts were on the same city block.

I loved her endlessly.

———

Enjoying *City of Small Kingdoms*?
Follow the link below to purchase now!
https://links.liquidmindpublishing.com/9QtS

ALSO BY JONATHAN CULLEN

The Days of War Series

The Last Happy Summer

Nighttime Passes, Morning Comes

Onward to Eden (Coming Soon!)

Shadows of Our Time

The Storm Beyond the Tides

Sunsets Never Wait

Bermuda Blue

Port of Boston Series

Whiskey Point

City of Small Kingdoms

The Polish Triangle

Love Ain't For Keeping

Sign up for Jonathan's newsletter for updates on deals and new releases!

https://liquidmind.media/j-cullen-newsletter-sign-up-2-jody/

BIOGRAPHY

Jonathan Cullen grew up in Boston and attended public schools. After a brief career as a bicycle messenger, he attended Boston College and graduated with a B.A. in English Literature (1995). During his twenties, he wrote two unpublished novels, taught high school in Ireland, lived in Mexico, worked as a prison librarian, and spent a month in Kenya, Africa before finally settling down three blocks from where he grew up.

He currently lives in Boston (West Roxbury) with his wife Heidi and daughter Maeve.

Made in United States
North Haven, CT
30 November 2023

44812039R00163